A BOSS FOR THE HOLIDAYS

Boss & Blessing

PATRICE BALARK

DEDRA B.

A Boss for The Holidays

Boss & Blessing

❀ Created with Vellum

MAILING LIST

ARE YOU ON THE LIST?

Click here https://bit.ly/2MO25jK
to join Twyla T. Presents' mailing list and receive new book release
alerts, exclusive giveaways, sneak peeks & more!

Receive instant new book release alerts by texting TwylaT to 22828

ACKNOWLEDGMENTS

First and foremost, thank God for giving us the talent to push through this book. We would like to thank everyone for reading our work. We appreciate our family and friends for the unlimited support. To our publisher thanks for all you do. Our TTP family, sky is the limit, let's continue to dominate the charts. Last but not least our readers, we are nothing without you.

Author Bae & Tha Pretty Pen Pusha

Melody squirmed in her sleep while trying to control her bladder with hopes of it going away before messing up her peaceful slumber. Rolling over to wrap her arms around her man, her eyes popped open when she felt nothing but an empty space.

What the fuck time is it? she asked herself before sitting up and grabbing her phone off the nightstand. It was 3:15 in the morning, and she hadn't seen or heard from Corey since ten p.m. the previous night.

Without hesitation, she dialed his number only for it to ring continuously until the voicemail picked up. Looking down at the phone with an attitude, she dialed the number right back and headed to the bathroom to relieve her overly full bladder. Pissed was an understatement; Corey hadn't pulled a stunt like this in months. She actually thought things between her and her man since their teenage years were starting to look up.

Getting comfortable on the toilet seat, Melody did what any female looking for her nigga would do, she logged into Facebook and headed straight to his page. With no luck or clues on his whereabouts, she headed over to the one bitch's page that put a damper in their relationship many years ago, Kim. Melody was never the type to come second to any female, but it seemed like no matter how many times Corey tried to do right, Kim always remained a factor.

As soon as her page loaded, Melody scrolled to the last status posted which was just two hours ago before reading aloud, *"Every night is a great night when I'm in his arms."* True enough, Melody knew that she could've been talking about any nigga, but her woman's intuition told her otherwise. Wasting no time, she got off the toilet, washed her hands, and rushed to her room. In the process of slipping into a pair of leggings and some sneakers, she got her best friend, Blessing, on the phone. She could've easily walked a few doors down to her condo and knocked on the door being that they stayed in the same high rise building not too far from the United Center on Chicago's west side.

"What, Mel?" Blessing answered the Facetime call in a tired, groggy voice.

Melody hated to drag her friend out of bed so early, but she needed a ride because Corey was in her car.

"Corey didn't come home last night, he at that bitch house in my car. I need a ride."

Before Melody could finish her sentence, Blessing's light was on, and she was up getting dressed. Thelma and Louise had nothing on Blessing and Melody when it came to being down for one another. It had been that way ever since they became next door neighbors at the tender age of eight; from children to adults, they were attached at the hip. From fist fights in the hood to retrieving their degrees from Alabama State University, they did it all together.

"Meet me at the elevator."

"Leaving out now," Melody replied, grabbing her mace and door keys.

Looking at Melody and Blessing, one would think they were the "too pretty" to fight type, but when it was time to fight, they were trained to go. Melody and Kim's beef had been ongoing for years and though Blessing would never tell her friend to leave Corey alone, she knew it was time. Melody was so much better than Corey and deserved so much more in a man. She was educated, beautiful, had a shape to die for and to top that off, she was a twenty-four-year-old schoolteacher. To be honest, any man would have been lucky to have her and keep her, in Corey's case. Melody was holding onto history; she felt like she worked too hard to let him go.

"I'm about to fuck both of them up!" Melody fumed as they power-walked over to Blessing's car.

"Corey got to be the dumbest nigga on earth."

"He ain't dumb, he just doesn't give a fuck, but it's cool. I got him."

"Fuck you about to do, kill him?" Blessing asked, weaving in and out around the few cars that was early morning traveling.

"Hell no, but he about to figure this out right here, right now!" Melody assured as Blessing turned up Kim's block and caught a park.

Just as Melody suspected, her car was parked across the street like it belonged there. Melody quickly pulled her phone out and shot Corey a text.

Melody: I'm in front of this bitch house, you have two minutes to come out or I'm coming in.

Blessing waited for Melody to make a move since this was her situation. Melody looked down at the phone awaiting a response from Corey. When she noticed the message never delivered, she knew he had either turned his phone off or it had gone completely dead. Melody blew some air out of her mouth in frustration before grabbing the door handle while Blessing followed suit.

"COREYYYYYYYY!" Melody started yelling at the top of her lungs, not giving a damn whose sleep she interrupted in the process.

Blessing stood off to the side and let her friend handle her business all while being ready for whatever the outcome may have been. When Melody didn't get a response, she marched up the five stairs that lead to Kim's front door and rang the bell. Mel knew once she saw a light come on, it was showtime. When the door opened, and Kim stood face to face with Melody, Blessing made her way up the porch standing right next to her best friend.

"Tell Corey to get the fuck out here now!" Melody spat as Kim covered her clearly naked body with the silk robe she was wearing.

"Look, whatever you and Corey have going on at home is not my problem, and I don't appreciate you disrespecting my home."

"Girl, fuck you and your home. COREYYYYY!" Melody yelled

out for a second time, purposely doing the opposite of what Kim asked her not to do.

"Get the fuck off my porch!" Kim spat, causing both Melody and Blessing to get in a fighting stance.

"It's gone either be him getting his ass beat or you getting dragged down this porch!" Melody threatened, causing Kim to take a step back. Kim knew from experience how Melody got down.

"Look, Blessing. I don't want any problems with you, you're like family to me. Please get your friend."

Blessing looked up at Kim with a stale face. "I'm not like shit to you, my loyalty resides with her. The fact that you are swallowing my cousin's dick means nothing to me."

As soon as those words left Blessing's mouth, Corey pushed Kim to the side and came out. Corey was a handsome man, and no one could take that away from him, but he wasn't shit to women. He loved Melody without a doubt, but he couldn't leave the bitches alone. He had a certain charm about himself that would drive any woman crazy. Corey would easily put one in the mind of the rapper Dave East, everything was a replica, from the height to the tattoos that covered eighty percent of his body.

As soon as Corey was in arm's reach, Melody tried to smack him, but her small frame was no match for him. He grabbed her hands while laughing it off, only pissing Melody off further. When Kim saw Corey grab Melody from behind and walk her down the stairs, she slammed her door closed.

"LET ME THE FUCK GO, COREY!" Melody yelled while trying to break loose from the bear hug he had her in.

"Blessing, why the fuck you bring her over here? I swear to God, you stay breaking the code, bro, wait until I tell Uncle Walt this shit," Corey threatened to tell Blessing's father.

"I don't give a damn what you tell. I'll pull up again and help her whoop you and that bitch. You gone be sick when she finds a nigga that's gone treat her right."

"Nah, you gone be sick when you have to bury yo best friend, play with me."

"Whatever, nigga. Mel, you good?" Blessing asked while walking toward her car.

"Yeah, she good. Take yo bald head ass home, opp," Corey joked as he and Melody climbed into Melody's car.

Blessing flipped Corey her middle finger before hopping in her car and speeding off. Melody got comfortable in the passenger seat before folding her arms across her chest. Tired of talking about the same shit over, she decided to remain silent.

"So, you about act like a baby?"

"I'm good, Corey. I'm good on talking, and I'm definitely good on you."

Corey knew Melody like the back of his hand. He knew that if he flipped the script and gave her the silent treatment, she would be the first to break the ice, so that's exactly what he did. Corey turned the radio up and rapped along to the music. Like clockwork, Melody couldn't take it.

"Why me, Corey? What have I done so bad for you to keep fucking me over like this?"

She sat there with tears rolling down her face, but she quickly wiped them away. Corey's face softened because he hated to see Melody cry. He knew she was the best thing that had ever happened to him. His mother, uncle, and of course Blessing had told him many times over. At one-point, Corey and Melody were inseparable, but all of that changed when she went away to school. He started fucking with Kim a month after missing her, not expecting things to get as serious as it did. In the beginning, Kim was cool with being the side bitch. She knew her place whenever Melody was in town. Shit started to get messy when Melody graduated and moved back home for good. Kim was his sex slave, down for any and everything while Melody was his backbone. In a perfect world, he would have had them both.

"You right, I have no real reason behind the shit that I've done to you, and I'll probably die if you did half the shit to me. I'll change my number and whatever else you want me to do to fix this shit."

Melody rolled her eyes and smacked her lips because this would be the second time Corey had changed his number and not his actions. Not believing a word that was coming out of his mouth, Melody decided to do him one better.

"Nah, don't change shit. I'm gone do the changing this go around."

"And what the fuck is that supposed to mean, Mel?" Corey asked, finally pulling into the parking garage of their building and killing the engine.

"Exactly what I said, let's go in. I'm sleepy," she replied in a calm yet threatening voice that left Corey drowning in his own thoughts.

❦   2   ❦

"Ouuuu friend, look. There go a park right there," Blessing heard Melody say just as she spotted an empty spot in the first row near the door.

"This motherfucker packed," Blessing spat before pulling inside the space and killing the engine.

"Well, what you expect? It's Labor Day, and we ain't the only ones last-minute shopping," Mel replied, grabbing her bag out the backseat and jumping out.

Walmart in Forest Park on a normal day was horrific, so you could only imagine how it looked on the holidays. With a billion shoppers and only three lines open, Blessing prayed she wouldn't be in there all day. Thankful that they only needed to grab a few things, she snatched up the first cart she saw and headed inside. With her best friend on the side of her, the two made their way to the grocery section where they got two cases of water and a case of Pepsi. With only chips left on their list, Blessing and Melody made a right on the next aisle. Picking up whatever she laid her eyes on, Blessing tossed it in the cart before heading to checkout.

"Look at these lines. This shit don't make no sense," Melody cursed while looking around for a manager to complain to.

"Don't even worry about it, Mel, all this shit finna be two dollars. Let's go to self-checkout," Blessing joked as the two headed in that direction with the cart.

Moving quicker than they anticipated, the friends were out the door and loaded in the car ten minutes later. Hitting 290, Blessing rolled down the windows to her BMW 5 Series and cruised to the westside of Chicago. Making her exit at Independence, she drove a few more blocks before finally pulling up to her dad's house. Noticing how packed the block was, Blessing knew that more than half the vehicles out there belonged to her family. It was the Taylor family's annual Labor Day, end of summer barbeque and this year, her father was the host. Growing up the only child, raised by a single man, Blessing's upbringing was slightly different from an average girl.

Walter "The Bully" Taylor, an infamous boxer from back in the day, took on the responsibility as sole parent when Blessing's mother died giving birth to her. With help from her favorite auntie, Vera, Blessing had turned out pretty well. With a Bachelor of Arts in Theatre, and her own dance studio, she was living out all her dreams, except one.

"Friend look, yo ugly ass boyfriend here," Blessing noted, pointing to Corey's black Charger that was parked in her father's driveway.

First cousins, Blessing and Corey grew up more like brother and sister. Blessing and her dad lived on the first floor while her Aunt Vera and Corey occupied the second unit inside her grandparents' building. She loved him dearly, however, he was not the man for her best friend. Never was. Never would be.

"He said he was picking up his car and coming straight here. I guess he wasn't lying... THIS TIME!"

Electing on remaining quiet, Blessing pulled out her phone and placed a call to her dad. There was no way they were carrying all that heavy shit in when there were a backyard full of men. After ending the call with him, she grabbed the bags of chips in the back and headed to the two-flat apartment building. The sound of Earth, Wind, and Fire could be heard from down the street, while the smell of meat on the grill blessed the noses of everyone in the neighborhood. Blessing loved spending time with her family, although they were dysfunctional as fuck.

"Why yo ass always in some mess? I told you that whatever Corey and Mel got going on don't involve you," Walter fussed as he made his way down the sidewalk.

"What is you talking about?" Blessing screwed up her face and asked while walking into her father's open arms.

"You know what the hell I'm talking about. Corey called me right after yo ass left and..."

"THE NIGGA TOLD ON ME!" Blessing yelled just as Corey came emerging from the backyard.

"I sure in the fuck did. Mind yo business." He walked past her and replied, before pulling Melody in for a hug.

Smacking her lips, Blessing turned around and stuck up her middle finger before joining the rest of her family in the backyard. Just as she expected, the yard was full of different generations and although she was her parents' only child, she never grew up alone. Making her rounds to different tables, Blessing mingled and engaged with everyone present. Not a big fan of holidays, she always enjoyed the time she spent with her love ones. Spotting Melody near the tent, Blessing made her way towards her just as Corey walked up with a plate.

"Ugh, I thought you was alone," she snarled, taking a seat next to her while Corey smiled at her awkwardly.

"What the fuck you looking at?" she snapped, sitting up straight and crossing her legs.

"Nun. I can't look at my beautiful, smart, intelligent cousin?" Corey replied with a devilish grin, a grin that Blessing knew too well.

"Nah, I ain't trying to hear that. You a sneaky, dirty, dog and I don't trust...."

Blessing's mouth dropped ,and her words froze at the sight of her ex-husband, Kevin McCall, walking inside her father's backyard. Together since eighteen, the two got married in 2018 after Blessing graduated college. After being wed only a year, Blessing filed for a divorce six months after their first anniversary. Legally separated for a year now, it had been months since the last time she seen Mr. McCall. Cutting her eyes at Corey, who was practically rolling on the floor laughing, Blessing tried her best to remain cool.

"The fuck he doing here?" she turned to her cousin and asked through clenched teeth.

"I invited him. You know like how you always inviting yo self in my business and shit," he replied before standing to his feet and greeting Kevin.

"Wad up, my nigga. Long time no see," Corey said as the two men embraced with a manly hug.

"Mannnn, I know. I be trying to be around more, but yo cousin act like she hate me," Kevin glanced down at Blessing and stated.

"That's cause she do... NIGGA!" Melody turned up her nose and snapped, causing Blessing to giggle.

"Man shut up, and let's go. Leave them to talk in private," Corey pulled Melody up from her seat and replied as she hesitantly walked away.

"Blessing, I miss you. I love you, and I'm sorry. It's been a year. We can go to counseling and fix this but..."

"Fix what? Ain't shit fixable about our situation, Kevin."

"Yes, the fuck it is. We been together for six years. I let you have yo moment and shit, but it's time to stop playing games."

"GAMES? You mean the game where you cheated and..."

"I can admit, I fucked up, but you want to divorce a nigga after cheating one time!" Kevin barked, before quickly adjusting the bass in his voice.

"Nah nigga, it's the results from you cheating is why I filed for a divorce. You can keep on trying to drag this shit out if you want to, but there will be absolutely no reconciliation. That shit dead, nigga," Blessing slowly rose to her feet and explained while staring him deep in the eyes.

She loved Kevin with everything in her, but she was not made out to be a fool. It was true, they had history and although her world once revolved around him, that shit stopped the second she found out he had a baby on the way. At the tender age of only twenty-four, Blessing had been through more shit than women half her age. Instead of enjoying her twenties and living life, she was dealing with bullshit from lames, but little did she know, all that was about to change.

$\mathscr{H}$ 3 $\mathscr{H}$

"**G**ood morning everyone, welcome," Melody greeted her new students as they walked in, talking loudly.

It was Melody's first day teaching eighth grade at Dvorak Elementary school, and it was hard to hide the excitement on her face. She had always been passionate about teaching children. Though she enjoyed a much younger age group, she was prepared to take on the task of educating preteens. Knocking the invisible wrinkles from the fitted, black pencil skirt she was wearing, she also made sure the buttons on the red silk blouse were secured. Slightly nervous, she stood tall on the five-inch red bottom stilettos and started to speak to her class.

"Quiet down guys. Sit anywhere you like but choose wisely because that will be your assigned seat for the rest of the year."

Turning her back to the class to write her name on the dry erase board, she instantly knew who her class clown was going to be when he made an outburst.

"Damn, Ms. Caston," he said, causing some to laugh and others to grasp for air before covering their mouths.

His remark caused Melody to spin on her heels. "Excuse me? What did you just say?"

Taken back by the boy's choice of words, she placed the marker down and walked over to where he was seated. He folded his arms across his chest and looked at her with a slick grin on his face. Melody was appalled by his actions.

"I was just saying you look really nice in that skirt, Ms. Caston," he had the nerve to lick his lips and smile in Melody's face.

"No, you were just saying you apologize for the remark you made, and it will never happen again unless you want to be expelled. That is no way to speak to a female and if it ever happens again in my class, you'll be sorry."

The entire class gave Melody their undivided attention as if she was talking to each of them individually. She could tell the boy was slightly embarrassed and felt bad about his remark.

"I apologize, Ms. Caston, it will never happen again."

Melody nodded her head before holding her closed fist toward him for a fist pump to relieve the tension and let him know she was a cool teacher. He didn't have to go the extra mile to get laughs. Walking back to the front of the class, she asked each student to introduce themselves and tell her one thing that they admire. Moving around the room, Melody smiled at the cool group of kids she had the pleasure of getting to know, but one student in particular stood out to her.

"Nice to meet you all, I'm Arianna Bryant. Ms. Caston, I know you said name one thing we admire, but I have two," she boasted with a charming smile to follow.

She was a beautiful girl with a huge curly ponytail pulled neatly to the top of her head.

"Nice to meet you, Arianna, and if you admire two things that's perfectly fine, please continue."

Arianna smiled at Melody and continued to share her admirations with the class.

"First thing I admire is dancing, and secondly, I admire my dad. He's nice to me and teaches me a lot."

Melody couldn't help but smile as Arianna spoke so highly of her father, but it only made her wonder about her other parent. She knew it wasn't her place to pry, so she pushed the thought to the back of her mind and turned her attention back to her new favorite student.

"Sounds like you are a lucky girl, your dad seems like an awesome father and you have to show me some of those dance moves one day!"

"Anytime, Ms. Caston."

"Alright, I guess I should share what I admire with you all, huh?"

Melody leaned back on her desk and folded her arms across her chest before continuing.

"I admire life and those who I choose to share my life with, meaning family, friends, and of course you all. I look forward to us having a wonderful year together."

The rest of the morning was smooth sailing for Melody and her class. Lunchtime had snuck up on her quickly, and she was glad because she was starving. After taking her class down to the cafeteria, she headed straight to the teacher's lounge to retrieve the leftover meatloaf and mashed potatoes that she packed from last night's dinner. Entering the lounge, she had to look around and make sure she hadn't entered the wrong room; the teachers were just as loud as the students. Some were older while a couple of younger teachers that looked to be in their early thirties sat over in the corner. After warming her food, she headed over to the younger teachers table and took a seat. Melody could tell just off the gossiping they were doing when she walked up, they were going to give her an earful.

"Hello, I'm Ms. Caston, I teach the eighth-grade class," Melody introduced herself before taking a seat at the round table.

"Ohhh we know exactly who you are. Mr. Johnson, the gym teacher, has already told everyone about the new pretty teacher aboard, but welcome. I'm Ms. Brown and this is Ms. Williams," she introduced before extending her hand toward Melody.

Shaking her hand and smiling; she instantly knew this was going to be an informative lunchbreak. Before the other teachers could even start a conversation with her, her cellphone started to ring. When she saw it was her mother, she silently thanked her for the incoming call.

"Hey, Mama," Melody answered through the Air Pods in her ear while digging into her lunch.

"Hey, my baby. So how's your first day going at the new school?"

Melody's mother, Martha, was the one person she held near and dear to her heart. Growing up it was always her, her mother, and grandmother; Martha being her mother's only child and Melody being her one and only. The trio was tragically broken apart last year, the day before Thanksgiving when Melody's grandmother lost her battle to kidney failure. Growing up, holidays were a big thing in the Caston's household, but Melody couldn't bring herself to even think about celebrating without the matriarch of their family. She never had the pleasure of knowing her father, but she didn't miss out on any love, plus Blessing's dad always treated her like his own daughter, and her mother did the same with Blessing.

"So far so good. I absolutely love my class, but I can say I already have a favorite student named Arianna. She's such a sweetheart, Ma."

Melody was really intrigued by Arianna, she had so much personality, yet she was polite and respectful.

"That's wonderful, I'm glad you're having a good day. Mama would be so proud of you!"

Mel knew that if she stayed on the phone with her mother any longer, both of them would be in tears from reminiscing, so she wrapped up the call.

"I know she would. I have to go so I can finish up my lunch before it's time to go back."

"Ok baby, I love you. Talk to you later."

"Ok, I love you too."

It seemed like the teachers were waiting patiently for her to end the call because they wasted no time sparking up a conversation.

"How's the eighth graders treating you so far?" Ms. Williams pried.

Melody chewed her food and wiped her mouth with a napkin before responding.

"It's actually great, I have a bright group of kids," she boasted about her new class, meaning every word.

"I had a few of them last year. I overheard you speaking on Arianna, she's a great kid and comes from a good family."

"You mean a *FINE* family, those Bryant men baaaaabbbyyyy!" Ms. Brown corrected her while using her hand to fan herself.

Melody didn't know how to respond, not knowing if it would be appropriate. She just sat there and listened instead.

"Honey. Fine is an understatement, and let's not speak on how they fund everything. Seriously though, the Bryants are very active when it comes to Arianna," Ms. Williams finished.

"That's good to know, thanks for the information and nice meeting you ladies."

Mel gathered her things before heading back to class. The rest of the school day the conversation with the other teachers plagued her mind. Melody was glad to learn that she had active and supportive parents on board because between eighth grade activities and graduation, she was going to need all hands-on deck.

The bell rang just as she assigned homework for the night. After gathering her belongings, she walked outside with her class. Securing her paperwork inside of her Tory Burch tote bag, she stood off to the side and watched her kids go their separate ways. Ms. Caston smiled at the completion of her very first day as she made her way to her car. Just as she grabbed her door handle, a black Maserati pulled up to the school, grasping all of her attention. When Arianna ran to the car, Melody instantly replayed the words that her colleagues spoke on earlier.

"*Well damn, Mr. Bryant...*" she said, with her eyes glued to the foreign whip as it pulled away.

❧ 4 ❧

"Coach B, do you need me to get the pompoms out of the backroom for practice today?" Kali, the captain of Blessing's Angels, peeked her head inside of her office and asked.

"Yeah go ahead, I'm on my way out right now," Blessing looked up from her MacBook Pro and replied before finalizing their next competition and shutting the laptop closed.

Blessing's Dance Studio was Blessing's heart and soul. It was a wedding gift from Kevin, the small five-thousand square foot building housed her and her angels for the past year and a half. It was an all-female dance squad with girls ages ranging from eight to sixteen, Blessing's Angels were growing more and more by the months. With a total of twenty young black girls under her wings, Blessing and her angels were making a name for themselves inside the world of dance. Specializing in hip hop, jazz, ballet and majorette, they were a force to be reckoned with.

"AIGHT ANGELS.... LET'S GO!" Blessing exited out her office and yelled onto the dance floor as her girls scattered about like chickens with their heads cut off.

"Five...four...three...two...one," she counted down and smiled while everyone took their places and stood at attention.

"Good evening, my angels," she cheerfully spoke, making brief eye contact with each and every girl.

"Good evening, Coach B," they spoke back in unison, giving her their full, undivided attention.

"As I discussed Friday, next week we will be having tryouts. However, there are only two slots available, which means, only two special girls will be joining us. The end of the year dance off is approaching, and although we've been practicing since the beginning of the year, now is the time to really get shit cracking. Each competition until then is practice for us as well, it's going to prepare us for the final dance. School; now, I know it just started, but... if them grades not up to par, ya lil asses will be cheering from the stands.... understand?"

"Yes, Coach B," all twenty said in unison, mixed with a few different attitudes and body gestures.

"Aight, bet. Since we all on the same page. Let's get to stretching. Kali, count off." Blessing instructed before walking off to the side and pulling her phone from her pocket.

"Heaven, I know you can bend down lower than that. Don't play with me!" Coach B warned before unlocking the iPhone and reading over her messages.

312-562-9990: Can you please talk to me, Blessing? Just give me 5 minutes, and I promise I won't bother you anymore.

Smacking her lips and rolling her eyes to the back of her head, Blessing deleted the text message from Kevin before shooting her best friend a text.

Blessing: Hey bestie! Haven't talked to you all day. Them 8th graders beat yo ass, didn't they?

Hitting the send button, Blessing checked on her girls who was almost done warming up. Going back to her phone, she hit up Facebook and liked a few statuses and pictures before it vibrated in her hand.

Melody: Bitch FUCK THEM KIDS!

Laughing out loud at her response, Blessing decided to reply later and tend to her girls now. Practice was two hours and although that may have seemed long, it really wasn't. From yelling about the same thing over and over to damn near breaking up fights, those one-hundred and twenty minutes flew by.

"Okay so listen up, Angels. We gon start off today with the hip hop routine. That's one of our strong points, and I know we gon kill it, so I want y'all to run that from the top so we can use the rest of the day on some of our not so strong suits."

Going to the music app on her phone, Blessing selected the appropriate playlist before ensuring she was connected to the Bluetooth speakers inside the studio. Once that was done, the loud sounds of FLY's, *Swag Surfin* came blasting through the speakers and just like clockwork, Blessing's Angels kilt that shit.

I'm on Hypnotic, exotic
This Polo on my body
Got a bad girl beside me
And her friend right behind me
And I'm swagging, I'm surfing
I'm swagging, I'm surfing
I'm swagging, I'm surfing

"1,2,3,4,5,6,7,8 AND 1,2,3,4,5,6,7,8." CLAPPING ALONG TO EACH BEAT, Coach B's eyes danced amongst her girls while her head bobbed up and down.

She was happy with what she seen, and she knew that with the two new girls, her full-size squad would be bringing home that trophy in no time. Going over the routine with them one more time, Blessing switched over to stand battle. With a team full of beasts, Coach B was feeling pretty confident with her Angels. After taking a brief water and restroom break, Blessing had them back up and sweating for the last forty-five minutes of the class. As always, she found herself tired from the day and released the girls ten minutes early.

"Same time. Same place. Tomorrow!" she shouted out as they all chucked her the deuces on their way out the door.

Straightening up a little around her place, Blessing retreated to her office where she packed up her things, shut off the lights, and locked up. Hitting the alarm on her car, she checked her phone, ignoring a call from Kevin before getting inside and driving off. The ride from the studio to her condo was ten minutes. During that time, she drove in silence, thinking about her next moves. Pulling inside her building's parking garage, Blessing grabbed her bags before jumping out and securing her vehicle. Noticing Melody's car a few spaces down, she thought about knocking on her door but decided not to when her knees started to ache. Walking through the lobby, she spoke to the front desk attendant as he held the elevator open for her.

"Goodnight, Mrs. McCall," the middle-aged white man greeted her with a smile before pressing the button for the fifth floor.

"Ms. Taylor, Joseph," she politely corrected him with a grin just as the elevator closed.

Exiting at her floor, Blessing secured her Nike bookbag and Gucci purse on her shoulders before making sure her Nike's were tied tight. Picking up the pace a little, a devilish grin invaded her face seconds before knocking on Melody's door and running. Fumbling with her keys, Blessing glanced back to see if she was coming before finding the right key. With one swift move, Blessing was inside her condo before Mel was able to answer her front door.

Flickering on the lights, she dropped her bag on the floor and purse on the couch before noticing a bouquet of roses and a Louie Vuitton giftbox on her table. Easing her way over towards it, Blessing's eyes surveilled the spacious layout before making her way past the flowers, cautiously checking each room in the place. Once the coast was clear and she finally confirmed she was home alone, she dialed in the pin code to the security system before taking a deep breath. Heading over to the table where the mysterious gifts were, Blessing snatched the card off the red roses and read the message aloud.

I've loved you since the day I laid eyes on you freshman year. I know I've said sorry a billion times, but Blessing, I really mean it. I'm lost without you and rather die.... HOPE U FEEL THE SAME

❄ 5 ❄

Melody had officially completed her first week of teaching at Dvorak, and the glass of wine she was sharing over girl talk with Blessing was well needed and earned. She had a lot going on between preparing for the upcoming family and friends open house at the school and constantly thinking about her relationship with Corey, she was all over the place.

"Sooooo, how was your first week? You haven't heard anymore gossip from the messy teachers?"

Melody had told Blessing about the teachers and their remarks about the Bryants, and she was just as messy as them.

"No, nothing new, but I'm sure they'll have a story to tell next week. But bitch!"

"What?" Blessing sat straight up in her seat, prepared to sip from the tea that she knew Melody was brewing.

"Ever since they bragged about these Bryant men, I've been dying to see exactly what the hype is about. I know they have some real money judging by the different foreign cars that picks Arianna up from school every day."

"Hmmm, Corey better watch out. Sounds like you trying to bounce on some new dick," Blessing teased while Melody threw a pillow at her head.

"Girl bye, how about we focus on finding you a new man?"

"No, thank you. I'm good. I gotta get rid of one nigga before I could think about another one." Blessing leaned forward and pulled a card from her back pocket and handed it to Melody.

Mel's eyes almost popped out of her head as she read the words that Kevin wrote on the card.

"Blessing, fuck him! Don't let Kevin get you upset. You been doing good without him, and he can't take it. That lame ass nigga thinks he can buy you and your love."

"I know, but it's like this man won't stop bothering me like he's not the one who cheated."

"That's the thing, he thinks he owns you. Kevin has always been an arrogant asshole."

"Tell me about it."

"I wish you'll accept one of those dinner dates thrown your way. You still young, enjoy yourself. Live life."

Melody just wanted to see her best friend as happy as she used to be. After Kevin hurt her, she turned cold, not giving any man the time of day.

"I don't have time for no nigga or the bullshit that follows. Besides, none of the men that I have crossed paths with has held my attention, I'm good."

"Really? What about the guy, Aaron, that we met at the mall? He was really nice."

"No, I hate how close together his eyes were." Blessing waved Melody off before shifting in her seat.

"Kendall from the…"

"Hell no! He buttons his shirt all the way up to the damn neck, I will not!" Blessing cut Melody off before she could finish her sentence.

Melody fell back in her seat laughing at her friend's last remark. Though Melody knew it would take a special kind of man to make Blessing love and trust again, it was worth a try. Kevin had really turned Blessing's heart cold.

"Ok, I give up!" Melody threw her hands in the air.

Mel stood up from her couch just as Corey walked through the front door with groceries. She had been giving him one-word answers since the day she caught him up. As much as she loved him, right now she didn't want to be in his presence. She could give Blessing the best advice in the world, but she never applied it to her own relationship. Corey had been trying his best to make up with Melody by staying in the house after work and watching movies that she liked. These were all of the things that made her fall in love with him many years ago, but her feelings for him were slowly changing.

"What's up, big head?" Blessing spoke to her cousin before standing to leave.

"Shit, what's good, bald head?" Corey shot back, removing the items from the bag.

Blessing stuck her middle finger up as she always did before heading out the door. Melody still hadn't acknowledged Corey, instead she grabbed her purse and keys and headed to the door.

"So, Mel, we just gone keep doing this childish ass shit? When I walk in, you walk out?" Corey said, looking over at Melody as she folded her arms across her chest.

"I already told you, Corey. I'm on what you on. You see how this shit feel? It doesn't feel good."

"I thought we were moving forward, we were just cool last week at the barbeque."

"*You* were cool, I played along because I didn't want to ruin the mood, but understand, I'm done sweeping shit under the rug, Corey. If you want Kim, go. I'm not about to keep fighting for this relationship alone."

Melody was speaking directly from the heart, meaning every single word she spoke. Corey tilted his head to the side because he wasn't used to hearing Melody speak the way she was speaking.

"Mel you don't have to fight at all, fuck Kim. I love you."

"Actions, Corey, actions. You know how many times we've had this same conversation?"

Melody was honestly growing tired of hearing the same damn song. Corey had stopped doing all of the things that made her fall in love with him.

"How am I supposed to show you when you won't even stay in the same room with me?"

Melody finally placed her purse and keys back down on the table and looked back over at Corey.

"You want to know why, Corey?" she asked, folding her arms across her chest.

Corey stopped what he was doing and walked over to her, standing directly in front of her. He looked Mel directly in the eyes, he was losing his forever girl, and he was the only one to blame. He had to fix what he had fucked up.

"Yeah Mel, I do want to know why. I want to know everything that you feel, everything that I fucked up, so I can fix it!"

Melody's mind and feelings were all over the place as she listened to Corey lay his feelings out on the table. Not sure if believed a word he was saying, she still listened to what he had to say. Corey's eyes became glossy, and it did something to Melody's heart because Corey had never spoke to her with such emotion.

"This is the last time, Corey. The last time I let you hurt me; the last time I trust you with my heart. Don't make a fool out of me, I already feel stupid."

"I promise baby, I love you."

"I love you too, Corey."

Though Melody was still uncertain of her feelings, she spent the rest of the night with Corey. They ate a meal that he prepared before running her a hot bubble bath. This was the man that she fell in love with, but how long would he keep it up was the real question.

❧

LAST NIGHT WAS EVERYTHING, IT ALMOST FELT LIKE THE OLD DAYS, but him cheating on her was still weighing heavily on Melody's mind. She found herself checking Kim's Facebook page more than her own because she just knew Corey would end up back tracking. Needing to clear her head, she headed to her mother's house. Melody always kept her relationship problems away from her family because she knew her and Corey would always end up back together. This time around, she wasn't sure; something felt different, so she had to get her mother's input.

Using her key to enter her mother's home, she walked in and called out her name.

"Maaaaa!"

"I'm in the kitchen!" her mother yelled from the back of the house.

Melody made her way through the house, stopping along the hallway to glance at the pictures hanging on the wall that held so many memories. She could feel herself falling deeper into a slump the closer it got to the holidays and her grandmother's death anniversary.

"Hey baby, I wasn't expecting you. Are you hungry?" Martha asked as she moved about the kitchen.

"No, I'm ok. I just stopped by to kill some time and check on you," Mel replied, flopping down in the chair.

"What's going on with you, baby girl?" Martha questioned, knowing her child like the back of her hand.

"Nothing much, Ma," she lied, glancing down at her phone to avoid eye contact.

Melody contemplated on telling her mother what was really going on inside her relationship. She knew lying to her would be useless, so she played dumb to stall time.

"Why you figure something wrong? I said I was cool."

"Well for one, you're about to bite a plug in your bottom lip and you only do that when something is bothering you, so let's talk about it."

Not being able to dodge her mother's words, she had no choice but to start talking. "It's Corey, Ma, I caught him cheating on me."

"With that same little loose heffer that you have been feuding with all these years?"

Surprised by her mother's response, she shook her head up and down as tears welled in her eyes. For some reason, hearing it aloud from her mother made her feel stupider.

"Yes, I'm ashamed for still loving this man."

"Ashamed? No, baby. Love is something that we can't control, the heart wants what the heart wants, but staying with someone that consistently hurts you is a problem."

Melody took her mother's words to heart because she knew they were genuine.

"Yeah, a problem that I don't know how to fix. I've been with this man for years, he's all I know. How do you walk away from your comfort zone?"

"Baby, let me tell you something about a woman. When we are gone mentally, there is nothing and nobody that can change our minds. Once Corey loses you mentally, your physical will follow, meaning his touch won't affect you anymore, his kisses won't make you weak, and his presence will soon go unnoticed."

Mel was now sitting there with a face full of tears because she was feeling everything her mother was saying. As bad as she didn't want to admit it, Corey was definitely losing her mentally.

6

Blessing woke up five minutes before her alarm Saturday morning and instantly regretted having drinks with Melody the previous night. As bad as she wanted to lay in the bed, she knew that missing a Saturday morning at the gym would throw off her whole week. On top of eating and drinking over the holiday weekend like she didn't have any home training, she was naturally thick, which meant all the extra weight went to her thighs and butt. Dancing before she could walk, Blessing stayed in shape over the years, however, there was nothing she could do about her thick frame.

Finally rolling out of the bed, Blessing grabbed her phone to pause the alarm and headed straight to the bathroom. Handling her hygiene and then placing her waist-length box braids in a high ponytail and bun, Blessing was ready and out the door in twenty minutes. Dressed in a pair of Nike training leggings, she threw on a hoodie over the matching sports bra. Taking the elevator to the lobby, Blessing cut her eyes at Joseph before heading through the revolving doors. Since the incident with Kevin and the flowers, the entire condo building was afraid of her.

The morning after the incident, she stormed into management's office and went off. They had absolutely no business allowing him access to her place and thankfully for them, Blessing didn't pursue legal action, and everyone was able to keep their job. Hitting the locks on her car, she double checked her surroundings before getting inside. Cranking up the engine, Blessing pulled out and into the busy Chicago traffic. Staying near the United Center had its pros and cons and the tourist making traffic worse, was definitely a con.

"You dirty bitch! That's why yo shit look like that now!" Blessing yelled out the window while laying it heavy on the horn at a woman who was driving like a bat out of hell.

Making a right on Roosevelt, Blessing pulled in front of B&B's Boxing Gym and killed the engine. Grabbing her gym bag from the backseat, Blessing walked around to the curb and hit the alarm. Entering the gym, breathing in the atmosphere, instantly put a huge smile on her face. Outside of dancing, boxing had the other half of her heart. Growing up in the ring, Blessing's hands was deadly, which was a reason why bitches didn't try her in the hood. Quicker than the blink of an eye, Blessing had a left hook that would knock the biggest nigga out. About fifteen years ago, her father opened the gym and welcomed trainers from across the city to come and train their boxers there. A landmark in the hood, B&B's Boxing Gym had become Blessings second home.

"Boss Lady, who ass you kicking today?" Leroy, one of her father's childhood friends and manager, asked the moment she walked through the door.

"Nahhhh, I'm sparing these bitches this beautiful Saturday morning, Roy, I'm here to work out." Blessing laughed, dropping her gym bag on the bench and removing her pink boxing gloves.

Stretching for an extra five minutes, Blessing placed her Air Pods in her ear and went to her workout playlist. Hitting the shuffle button, her head immediately began to bounce to the song selection. Quickly getting in mode, she then headed over to an available punching bag and went to work. Doing six sets, Blessing barely broke a sweat, sending her to the other side where she grabbed a rope. Double tapping the earpiece, she changed the song before getting back in a zone. Jumping rope was her favorite pastime, and it was a sure way for her to burn the calories she needed to burn. Completely tuning everyone and everything out, Blessing spent the next fifteen minutes jumping. After a few dozen squats and weight lifts, she was heading to the showers to clean up. Changing into a pair of sweatpants and tee-shirt, Blessing made a stop by her father's office where she noticed the light on. Softly knocking three times, her father's deep voice finally could be heard from the other side, inviting her in.

"Hey, Daddy!" Blessing beamed before closing the door behind her and stepping further inside.

"Hey, baby girl. Where you come from? I ain't see you out there when I walked in," he quizzed, standing to his feet and giving his daughter a hug.

"I was showering. I been here almost two hours. You the one late," she replied, looking over his shoulder at the paperwork he was working on.

B&B's Boxing Gym may have been owned by her father, but Blessing ran that place just like she did her dance studio. Her father was getting up in age, and she wanted to ensure that she would be able to continue his legacy once he was gone. Going over a few things with her dad, Blessing found herself spending an extra hour in there with him. Their bond was like no other and although she wished she had gotten the chance to meet her mother, she couldn't imagine what her life would be like. She was used to it always being just them two. Glancing down at her Apple Watch, Blessing noticed that time had gotten the best of her, and it was time to leave. After saying goodbye to her dad, Blessing spoke to everyone else on her way out and jumped in the car.

Tossing her bag on the seat, she placed her phone on the charger for the quick ride to her aunt's house. Auntie Vera was the closest thing she had to a mother, which was why she held her dear to her heart. Like a true best friend, Blessing told Vera everything, which was why she was headed over to talk about Kevin. Parking across the street from her father and Vera's place, Blessing killed the engine and hopped out. Crossing the busy two-way street, she fumbled through her keys before finding the one to her aunt's house. Ringing the doorbell as a warning, Blessing entered the building and headed up the stairs to the second floor. Knocking once before twisting the knob, Blessing called out her aunt's name before finding her sitting on the couch, watching Law & Order.

"You heard me calling you," Blessing fussed, closing the door behind her and joining her out on the couch.

"Yeah, stop coming in my shit hollering," Vera cursed before placing a gentle kiss on her niece's cheek.

"Ain't you tired of watching reruns of this shi—" she paused, catching herself, just as Vera threatened her with her eyes.

"No, I am not tired of watching this SHIT... If you must know, and what you doing over so late in the day, you usually dun been by here already on a Saturday," Vera notated, pausing her show and giving Blessing her full attention.

"I stayed at the gym longer than expected talking to yo brother," Blessing replied before pulling out her phone and ignoring a call from Kevin.

"Why yo face all frowned up like that?" Aunt Vera quizzed, noticing the displeased look on Blessing's face.

"It's Kevin and..."

"Chileeeeee, that man still bothering you?" she interrupted her and questioned, pulling a Virginia Slim Menthol cigarette out and placing it in her mouth.

"He had been M.I.A until yo dirty ass son invited him to the barbeque, now the man won't leave me alone. I blame Corey and—"

"Blame Corey for what?" he emerged from the back of the house and asked out of nowhere.

"Boy, I ain't even know yo ass was back there. You better let me know when you in my house. Yo ass don't live here!" Vera snapped her neck in the direction of her son and said.

"Nah, what about me? What I do?" Corey ignored his mother's comment and asked.

Blessing went over the story with them both, explaining how Kevin broke into her place with bags and flowers, begging for her apology. Pulling out her phone, she went to a picture she took of the items and showed them.

"Wait... this nigga threatening you? Cause that shit seems like a threat to me," Corey barked, handing the phone to his mom for her to take a look.

"Oh naw, that nigga crazy. You might need to get a restraining order," Vera suggested.

"Nah, that nigga ain't no killer, but I'm damn sure gon put a bug in his ear about this shit. Aye, Blessing... my bad from inviting that clown, I thought it would be funny and plus, I was pissed at you for bringing Melody over to shorty's crib," Corey admitted.

"And yo ass just as dumb as Kevin. I can't understand for the life of me why Melody puts up with yo shit. I can't wait for that girl to wake up and leave yo ass," Aunt Vera ranted.

"Man, Ma, here you go with that shit. You sound just like her bald-head ass," Corey replied, pointing across the living room at Blessing.

"Boy, FUCK YOU!..... Sorry, Auntie," she apologized, cutting her eyes at Corey and giving him the middle finger as a substitution.

Talking with her aunt and cousin for another hour or so, Blessing lost track of time for the second time that day. It was almost three in the afternoon, and she still had practice with her Angels at six. Racing home to take a nap, Blessing felt a sense of relief after telling her family about Kevin. She just prayed that they were right, and he wasn't as crazy as he seemed.

❧ 7 ❧

The week had flown past so fast, and the day of the open house had caught up with Mel quickly. Melody sat in her car and touched up her makeup as the families made their way inside the school. Once she was pleased with her look, she finally got out and made her way inside. Looking like a student herself; she opted on a pair of black distressed jeans, a number twenty-three authentic Bulls jersey with a pair of black and red number eleven Jordan's that came out that day. Her twenty-two inches of Brazilian hair was straightened to perfection, stopping right above the red Hermes belt that held her pants in place. Though Mel was a teacher, she came dressed and ready to participate in the sport's themed event.

"Hello, how are you?" Melody greeted some of the parents and teachers in passing.

Making her way to her class, she put a slight pep in her step when she noticed some of her students arriving. The open house was being held in the large gym room, so Melody locked her personal things inside of her class before making her way down to the gym.

"That's my teacher, Ms. Caston!" Melody stopped in her tracks when a student called out her name.

When she turned around, she saw Arianna and her family walking towards her like royalty. *Damn, those teachers told not one lie about the Bryant men.* There were two men along with an older woman walking closely behind Arianna as they approached her. The closer they got, the better they looked, it was hard for Melody to keep a straight face. The fact that both men were dressed in black jeans with red Jordan t-shirts that was identical to Arianna's, made Melody's heart smile. The closer they got that, Melody couldn't help but to zoom in on the diamonds each of them were dripped in including the woman. That alone let her know that they were of importance. Melody noticed they all, except for the older woman, had on the same shoes she had on her feet.

"Heyyyy, Arianna!" Melody pulled her in for a big hug.

"I see you, Ms. Caston with the drip," Arianna complimented Melody while comparing their shoes.

"I mean, I try," Melody joked as Arianna proudly introduced her family.

"This is my dad, Darrius, but everyone calls him Boss; my Uncle Black, and my granny, Sandy."

"Pleased to meet each of you, Arianna speaks highly of you all."

"She speaks highly of you also. In fact, she wouldn't let us come here to meet you without getting you a gift," Sandy replied, extending a small giftbag in Melody's direction that caused Arianna's face to light up.

Melody flashed a huge smile before accepting the gift and hugging Arianna for a second time. Deciding to save the gift for later, she held the bag tightly.

"Pleased to meet you, Ms. Caston," Boss chimed in.

He extended his hand to Melody, and she quickly shook it before moving over to Black. When Black held her hand slightly longer than normal, Arianna peeped his game and busted him out, sending them all into laughter.

"Uncle Black, can she have her hand back? Leave my teacher alone!"

Black playfully punched Arianna as they all finally made their way to the gym. Melody placed her gift bag under the table that was setup for her class. For the most part, she had some cool parents on her team, but there were some that were a little rough around the edges.

When Melody looked up and saw the messy teachers headed her way, she shook her head and placed her hands on her hips before laughing. She and the messy teachers had become quite cool over the past week.

"How about those damn Bryants," Ms. Williams greeted her first and stated, causing Mel to giggle.

"Chile, I thought y'all were exaggerating! They look like trouble," she replied, briefly scanning the gymnasium.

"No, they look like good dick and domestic problems, but I'm down for it," Ms. Brown leaned in and whispered, sending them all in an uproar.

Literally in tears, Mel quickly gained her composure when she noticed Uncle Black heading their way.

"Oh shit, let's go. One of the good dick brothers is coming," Ms. Brown announced, grabbing Ms. Williams and pulling her away.

They all left Melody standing there alone as Black made his way over to her. She ran her hands through her hair; it was something about that man that made her nervous. He had a dangerous yet, calming aura about himself that could be a gift and a curse.

"Why everybody leave when I walk up?" he asked as his cologne filled her nostrils, standing there at six feet, dark chocolate skin that had not one single flaw, and a full beard covered his face giving her actor Lance Gross vibes. When he stood there rubbing his hands together awaiting an answer, Melody quickly replied.

"Oh, they had to get back to their tables. By the way, you all are doing a great job with Arianna, she's a great student."

"Appreciate that, but Mrs. Caston fuck all that..." When he flashed a smile displaying a smile almost perfect as hers, she had to look away.

"*Ms.* Caston, I'm not married," Melody quickly corrected him.

"My bad, *Ms.* Caston, correct me when I'm wrong. I like that."

If Melody didn't know any better, she would've thought Black was flirting with her, and she might've liked it. Trying hard not to blush, she once again looked away. She scanned the gym and spotted Arianna and the rest of her family speaking with the art teacher. Not wanting to give off the wrong impression, Mel took a few steps back. It was bad enough the messy teachers had their eyes glued to them, and she knew they were going to have a million questions.

"Why you look away every time I say something to you? I make you nervous?" he asked, this time looking Melody dead in the eyes.

His stare sent a chill down her spine, it was tantalizing. Melody wanted to look away so bad, but he had her captivated.

"Um no." She flashed a smile, displaying the deep dimples embedded in her cheeks.

"You gone let me take you out tonight after this shit over?" Black asked, causing Melody to tilt her head to the side.

"This shit?" she retorted, throwing her hand on her hip.

"My bad, I meant after this..."

"Open house," Melody helped him out.

"Right, so yeah about tonight," he got right back to the conversation at hand.

Melody knew her accepting a date from Black would be considered cheating, so she quickly declined.

"I can't make it tonight."

"Ok, tomorrow night?"

Melody could see that Black was very persistent, and she thought it was cute. Not able to resist his charm for a second time, she agreed to spend her Saturday night with Mr. Bryant.

"Sure, you can pick me up here in front of the school at seven, next Saturday."

"Bet. You must have a lil boyfriend," he chuckled before running his hands over his face.

"And if I did?" Melody quizzed with a smirk before folding her arms across her chest.

"Shit, fuck that nigga."

Melody's mouth dropped at his response; she didn't know if she was offended or turned on.

"Uncle Black!" Arianna yelled from across the room and motioned for him to come and meet another one of her teachers.

Black nodded his head at his niece before making his way over to her.

Melody shook her head at his charm, she couldn't believe she let him trick her into a date. Furthermore, what the hell was she going to tell Corey?

❧ 8 ☙

"**G**irl, fuck Corey! And I mean that from the bottom of my heart. You know I love that nigga like a brother, but when was the last time he asked you on a date? Like for real?" Blessing rambled on in Melody's ear as she listened to her vent about open house.

"You ain't shit, B. That's yo whole blood cou—"

"I wouldn't give a fuck if it was my daddy. When a nigga don't deserve you, he don't deserve you. PERIOD!" Blessing cut her off and stated before opening an email from Kevin and rolling her eyes.

"Speaking of don't deserve you. Why this nigga Mr. McCall just email me—"

"Emailed you saying what!" Melody blurted out, causing Blessing to laugh.

"Yeah, I blocked him and now he been spamming my shit. I don't know when this nigga gon get it through his head. I might fuck around and get a restraining order like Aunt Vera suggested."

"Restraining order? Blessing, you'll beat the dog shit outta Kevin, and he knows that too." Mel chuckled, however, Blessing didn't find anything funny.

"Nah, it's deeper than that. That man might try to hurt me for real for real and.... Hold on friend. Come in!" Blessing called out to the person on the other side of the door.

"Coach B, all the girls are here, and we're ready when you are," Ty, her assistant peeked his head inside and stated.

"Thanks boo. I'll be out in five minutes. Make sure they've stretched. Tryouts starting immediately," she replied with a smile before placing her phone back to her ear.

"Bye, bitch. Gone head and handle yo business. I'mma come down the hall later with some wine. I gotta tell you about my student's family," Melody told her.

"Nah, I got time. Tell me more now. You said they be in Maseratis and shit. You think they part of the mob?" Blessing quizzed with a raised eyebrow while Melody laughed loudly in her ear.

"Them damn people ain't part of no mob. You be reading too many urban fiction books."

"Nah for real, you laughing but I remember one book by Twyla T. when—"

"BYEEEE, BLESSING! I'll see you later!" Melody screamed into the phone before hanging up in her face.

Laughing aloud, Blessing closed her laptop before grabbing a bottle of water and the clipboard off her desk. Instead of having a regular day of practice, Blessing and a few of her head Angels were scouting two new girls for their team. They would teach them three mini-routines that they'd later perform. Blessing would then select her two new Angels based on that. In addition to the routines, each girl would have to do a minute solo performance. Only in business for a year, Blessing expected a decent turnout, however, she was not prepared for what was behind her office doors.

"Damn!" she mumbled to herself before walking over to Ty and grabbing the microphone.

"How many we got?" Blessing asked while he looked over the clipboard in his hands.

"It's twenty-eight girls and only two slots. Good luck, Coach B." Ty smirked.

Making her way to the middle of the floor, Blessing cut the mic on and softly cleared her throat, getting everyone's attention. Shocked at the turnout but proud nonetheless, Blessing's eyes scanned each girl and smiled as they looked on eagerly. She couldn't believe all the young faces amongst her; they all wanted to be an Angel but unfortunately, she couldn't choose them all. Glancing down at her clipboard one final time, Blessing spoke, finally kicking things off.

"First and foremost, I want to say thanks to each and every one of you for being here today. As you know, we are looking for two new Angels to join us this mid-year. I want ALLLLL of you to know how much I appreciate you and regardless of tonight's outcome, NEVER GIVE UP!" she paused, giving them a hopeful grin before continuing.

"Now, what I'mma do is, divide you all up into five small groups. Inside these groups, you will learn three routines, in which you'll have to perform in front of me. My team and myself will keep notes and take points, the girls with the most points at the end will win a spot. In addition, you will also have one minute to do a solo dance of your choice. I know this may seem like a lot or even overwhelming but trust me, if you do your best, it will show," Blessing assured them.

"Now, when I call ya name, I want you to go over and stand by your Angel captain," Coach B instructed before dividing all twenty-eight girls up.

Once everything and everyone was situated, tryouts officially began, sending Blessing back to her office to finish up more paperwork. She knew her Angels and Ty had things under control, therefore, she used the freed-up time to get more things done. Trying her hardest to focus, Blessing couldn't help but be distracted by her ringing phone. Rolling her eyes to the back of her head, she cursed underneath her breath as Kevin called back to back, private. Letting out a long sigh, she put her phone on do not disturb and contemplated on getting a new number. She had a second phone strictly for business and although Kevin had that number, she was happy that he hadn't started calling that phone yet. A part of her was confused as to why he was reaching out so much when the last she heard, he had moved his baby mother and kid into the home they once shared. Tossing him and all his bullshit to the back of her head, Blessing focused on the task at hand. Glancing up at the clock on her laptop, she noted the time before finishing up the last things and joining everyone back on the floor.

"Okay! Okay! Okay! Let me see what y'all got. We gon start with Heaven's team," Coach B said as she made her way over to the speakers.

As planned, each team put on their best performance, and Blessing was pleasantly surprised. The girls danced their heart out, leaving everything on the floor and making her decision an even tougher one. With the solo performances being the determining factor, Blessing was able to see each girl's personality as it shined through their routine. Giving the girls a break, Coach B and her team retreated to her office where they totaled the points.

"Okay, so tell me what y'all think. Wait... First, tell me which girl is your favorite," Blessing asked her team as they snuggled inside her small office.

"Number seventeen," Kali, the captain, yelled out first.

"Yep, it's number seventeen for me too, sis," Kiera, the co-captain, followed.

"I enjoyed a few of them but I gotta say, number seventeen was the best. She's well-rounded in hip hop, jazz, and I even think the baby done took some ballet lessons or sumn," Ty added in while Blessing listened on attentively.

"Well, that was easy because she was my top pick as well. I also like number five, how y'all feel about her?"

Blessing and her crew's huddle lasted about ten minutes as they went around in a circle and picked the final girl. Finishing up things in there, they all then headed back in the room where all the girls waited impatiently.

"I wanna say thank you again to you all. What you did today was not easy, and I want y'all to give yourselves a round of applause for all your hard work," Coach B stated as everyone in the studio gave themselves a pat on the back.

"Now, as y'all know, I only have two spots, which means that twenty-six of you will not make it today, BUT I welcome you all back in January for the new year enrollment. I've seen so much talent this evening that it made my head spin, in fact, I know about ten girls now who I want on the team for sure, but unfortunately, I can only give two girls that chance tonight. The two numbers I'm going to call will be Blessing's newest Angels. I want you two to come up here with me while the others grab your things and exit."

Taking a deep breath, Blessing double checked her clipboard before looking amongst all the girls. As much as she loved her job, she hated this part the most. She hated crushing dreams and making young black girls feel like they all weren't good enough and although that wasn't the case, they still felt that way. If it was up to her, they all would be Angels but unfortunately, it didn't work like that.

"Number five, Madison Moore," she announced first while everyone cheered her on.

"And last but definitely not least, number seventeen, Arianna Bryant," Coach B spoke as the vibrant, talented new Angel made her way upfront.

❧ 9 ❧

"Your honor, we the jury find the defendant, Darrius Bryant, not guilty, on both charges of first-degree murder."

A cocky smile crept across Boss's face as the jury read the verdict to the case that could have changed his life, for the worst. Glancing over at his lawyer, he winked his eye before standing to his feet and adjusting the custom Tom Ford navy blue pinstripe suit he wore. As the court erupted with mixed emotions, Boss couldn't help but feel like the man. He had yet again, dodged another bullet.

"Order in the court! Order in the court!" Judge Gary yelled as she banged her gavel, demanding everyone's attention.

"Mr. Bryant, I don't know what you did or how you did it but, this better be the last time I see you in my courtroom," she threatened with promising eyes, however, her evil glare still wasn't enough to put fear in his heart.

Shooting her a smile, Boss thanked his lawyer one final time while everyone else exited the courtroom. Following close behind, he joined his family in the hall. His mother, Sandy, was the first to greet him.

"My babbbyyyy," she sang, pulling him in a hug and rocking back and forth.

"I told you I was good, Ma," Boss assured, slipping away from her and over to his father.

"My boy," Dino, his dad spoke, pulling his oldest son into a manly hug.

"This lil shit really had y'all worried, huh?" Boss asked, looking back and forth between both parents.

"Not me.... JIGGA.... KELLY... NOT GUILTY!" Black sang as they made their way out the courthouse doors and down the steps to the two awaiting Rolls Royces.

"This nigga stupid!" Boss chuckled before hugging his mother and father again.

"We gon meet y'all at the house," he told them as they parted ways and jumped in their cars.

With Black behind the wheel, he drove the foreign like it was a Chevy through Chicago's street like they weren't two of the most wanted men in the city. As the sons of Dino Bryant, Boss and Black were born into a life of crime. Their father not only was the plug, but one of the most feared yet respected men of his time. Passing that torch down to his boys, Boss and Black were ten times worse than their dad. They practically ran the Cartel themselves, and they knew it was only a matter of time before Dino handed everything over to them, officially.

"Judge Gary got it out for yo ass," Black spoke, breaking the silence amongst them.

"Man fuck that old bitch. She got it out for every black motherfucker. She can suck my dick," Boss replied, loosening the tie around his neck and getting comfortable in the seat.

"Fuck ha! But you know Pops ain't trying to hear that." Black looked over at him and shrugged before merging onto Dan Ryan, heading towards Olympia Fields where their estate was located.

"Don't you gotta pick up Ari?" Boss heard his little brother ask, changing the subject and forcing him to glance down at the gold Rolex on his wrist.

"Nah, Arica said she was picking her up today. Matter fact, she supposed to be dropping her off at the crib right now," he replied, noticing the time and shooting the mother of his child a text message.

"Oh word, she in town? I saw on Instagram she in L.A.... that shit must've been old."

"Man that bitch flew in yesterday morning, in such a rush to get Ari like she missed her. I let her pick her up from school yesterday, and she stayed at her crib overnight, but I don't know how long she plan on sitting still," Boss explained just as Arica replied to his text.

Arica: On Wednesdays, Thursdays and Fridays, I will start picking Ari up from school and dropping her off about 9pm.

Reading the message twice in his head, Boss read it aloud to his brother, hoping that it at least made sense to him. Arica, along with everyone else on the planet, knew how Boss was when it came to his one and only baby girl. Practically a single father, Boss was raising Arianna alone with little to no help from her mother. A stripper turned Instagram model, Arica Anez partied and traveled like she didn't have a care in the world. Taking on the role of full-time dad when Ari was eight, it had only been the two of them for the past five years, which was why Boss was so protective of his baby girl. Peeking her head in every other week or so, Arica tried her hardest to make up for lost time, however, it was already too late.

"What you think she on? Think she on some sneaky shit?" Black quizzed, pulling in behind his parents and killing the engine.

"I don't know what she on, but she bet not have her dancing on those teams or no shit like dat," he barked, slamming the door and joining his parents on the grass.

"What you over there fussing about now? You sound just like yo damn daddy," Sandy told her son from the porch steps.

"It's Arica, Ma. She in town and trying to negotiate a schedule with me like she got an input."

"She *does* have one, Darrius, that's that girl's mother."

"Mother? She ain't seen my baby since the Fourth of July. She ain't got input on shit. She lucky I allow her the time, I allow with Ari. That bitch bet not have her dancing or ..."

"What's wrong with dancing? You know Ari love music and dance, why would you penalize her for her mother's mistake? Just cuz Arica chose the path of stripping, does not mean Arianna will too."

"Yeah, aight. I'll kill that bitch," Boss warned, walking past his mother and into the house.

"Yeah son, we are well aware that you make good on your threats, which is why yo ass always in trouble with the law. I don't know how many times I gotta tell you and yo brother, you niggas are not invisible," Dino preached, his words going in one ear and out the other.

"Pops, we keep telling yo ass, this not the eighties, these lil niggas nowadays don't give a fuck about nothing or nobody," Black chimed in.

"I keep trying to tell his ass the same shit, that's why I be on whatever with whoever. These niggas bleed just like me and until you make a name for yourself, niggas gon keep trying you but on my daughter's head, I bet niggas think twice before they come at me crazy," Boss flopped down on his parents' cream couch and explained.

Times were different and although their parents didn't understand, it was clear as day to Boss and Black. Making a name for himself and leaving a legacy to Arianna and any other future children was his main priority. Boss didn't want to be a ruthless nigga; it was in the cards he was dealt. He didn't have a soft spot for nothing or no one in the world but his daughter, or so that was the case until a new blessing came along.

"**B**ro, these niggas really partying," Boss said to Black as they sat behind the dark tints watching one of their many trap houses while people walked in and out freely.

The music coming from the first floor of the two-flat building could be heard from across the street where they were sitting. Pissed off would've been an understatement, the Bryant men took their family business very serious, and the sight in front of them was unacceptable. Everyone on their payroll from pack workers to the Chicago Police Department knew they were not to be fucked with in any way, shape, form or fashion. They had made many examples out of people in the past with hopes of it keeping the others on a straight and narrow path, but that shit was short lived.

"Come on, let's get to the bottom of it," Black replied, reaching for his door handle.

"Nah, chill."

Black released the handle and remained in his seat while Boss screwed the silencer on his pistol. Though the first floor was a lucrative trap house, the second floor housed an older tenant that was also on their payroll. They thought having her around would keep heat away from the building, not knowing that their own workers were drawing the attention.

"I'm surprised Ms. Sarah hasn't called one of us yet about the noise," Black said as he grabbed one of the many Kush filled Backwoods from the cupholder, lighting it.

"Nigga, how you think I knew what was going on?" Boss replied while laughing along with Black.

"Ms. Sarah's ass don't waste no time," Black retorted while coughing from the smoke before passing it.

"Hell naw, she living rent free to keep an eye on those niggas, she better call. Come on," Boss replied, grabbing the blunt and inhaling a huge cloud of smoke before hopping out of the driver seat as Black climbed out the passenger side.

The crowd in front of the house was thick, and the fact that they thought shit was this sweet, pissed Black off all over again. For one, they were fucking up his plans and secondly, these niggas knew better. He screwed his silencer on his pistol as they made their way across the street, walking ahead of Boss, he walked up and grabbed the first worker he saw and slammed him to the ground.

"You bitch ass niggas think it's sweet, huh?" Black spat as Boss made his way up the stairs.

"Black, bro I told that nigga Lil Kenny not to do this shit!" The worker explained as Black followed Boss inside.

As soon as they walked through the door, everyone paused like a deer caught in headlights. Both Boss and Black scanned the room for Lil Kenny, but he was nowhere in sight. Boss shot the nigga who was playing DJ a look that instantly made him stop the music. The room became so quiet, you could hear a pin drop until the sound of a female moaning came from one of the rooms in the back of the house. Black looked over at his brother as anger covered both of their faces. Boss walked over to the same worker that Black had slammed just moments ago and gave him an order to clear the entire house inside and out; shit was about to get real.

Both Black and Boss followed the female's voice until they reached the bedroom right off the kitchen. Without warning, Boss stepped back and kicked the door open, causing both parties to jump and take cover. The female quickly used a sheet to cover her naked body while Lil Kenny tried to explain the situation to his bosses.

"Boss, Black hold up. I can explain this!"

With Lil Kenny being their blood cousin, the son of their father's sister, they gave him a few moments to gather his thoughts before taking action. Both brothers stood there silent with guns in hand. The female took off running out the room and they let her; their problem was with Lil Kenny only.

"It ain't shit to explain, you niggas took it upon yourselves to put our entire operation at risk. So, it was basically fuck us, huh?" Black spat through clenched teeth as his cousin sat there looking dumb.

"Lock this muthafucka down and meet me in the basement!" Boss roared, his voice echoing throughout the entire house.

Their workers footsteps were all that could be heard as they followed Boss's order. Black followed his brother down to the sound-proof basement they used specifically for violation. The smell of flesh was the first thing that hit Black's nostrils, but to him, it was the smell of roses. The entire basement, except the drains in the floor, were covered in plastic for the jobs that sometimes got gruesome.

Both Black and Boss stood in the middle of the floor as all eight of their workers made their way down the stairs. Faint whispers could be heard as they all pointed the finger at one another.

"Whose idea was it to throw a fucking party?" Boss spoke, causing the grown ass men to look at the floor like children.

"It was Lil Kenny's party," one of the guys finally spoke up, causing Kenny to ball his face up in anger.

"It wasn't a party. I invited a few people over to chill and drink, that's it."

"Muthafucka, that's a party!" Black growled, walking up to his cousin, connecting a blow to the right side of his face.

"Black, what the fuck!" Kenny yelled before walking up, only to be met by both Black and Boss's pistols.

"Black what, nigga!?" Black spat as Kenny balled his face up while looking at both of his cousins.

Fear covered the other guys faces as they watched on; the Bryants never wanted to be feared, but respect was mandatory.

"I'm real disappointed in you niggas, we make sure you and your families are fed and this is the thanks we get? I'm taking an extra ten percent from your pay for the next month, and you can thank this nigga. Get the fuck out my face before I kill all you muthauckas!" Boss enraged, dismissing the team.

Kenny tried to walk out with the rest of the guys, but Boss stopped him dead in his tracks.

"Kenny stay."

Black took a step back and let Boss handle Kenny because if it was left up to him, Kenny wouldn't be getting shit but a bullet, family or not.

"Y'all doing all this over a party? I know it was that old bitch upstairs that called y'all," Kenny said, digging a deeper hole for himself.

"Shut the fuck up!" Boss ordered, but Kenny was the type that needed to have the last word.

"You niggas act like y'all was never down. Do what y'all gone do, so I can slide."

Boss and Black looked at one another in disbelief before they both began delivering blows to Kenny, instantly breaking his slim body down. Showing no mercy, they beat their cousin like he was a nigga off the streets. This was light punishment only because he was family, and they didn't want to explain his death to their father.

"Kenny, take this as a warning. You out of line, and I suggest you fall back in place quickly. I haven't been to a funeral this year, but I don't mind sitting in the family section consoling my auntie," Boss warned while kneeling next to Kenny as blood covered his face.

Black was a man of few words; he liked to let his gun talk, so he let Boss handle Kenny. Pulling his iPhone out to check the time he cursed at himself. It was a thirty minutes to seven, and he had told Melody he would meet her at 7:00 on the dot.

"Come on Boss, let's ride," he said to his brother before stepping over his cousin's body as he laid there in pain.

Boss grabbed a towel and wiped Kenny's blood from his hands before following Black up the stairs. Everyone looked away as they made their way out the same door they came in; no further words were needed, they had made themselves very clear. Walking out into the dark, the mid- September chill smacked them dead in the face. Black walked on the side of Boss as they watched one another's back out of habit and hopped in the car.

"That's your fifth time looking at your phone and you've been in a rush since we got here, what's up?" Boss asked, pulling away from the curb into the light traffic.

Black put his phone down and lit another blunt to regain the high he had prior to getting out of the car before responding to Boss.

"I got a date," Black replied before filling his lungs with smoke.

"With who? Boy, Cresha gone fuck you up," Boss laughed while referring to Black's girl of the last two years.

Cresha was the last person on Black's brain, in fact, she hadn't crossed his mind since he crossed paths with Melody. He was taken back by her beauty before he even noticed how fat her ass was and that alone was big in Black's book. Though he had love for Cresha, she was starting to annoy him to the point he barely went to the condo he got for her and ignoring her calls had become his norm. He knew he would have to eventually end things with her, but that was neither here nor there. Cresha was crazy for Black, so she took whatever he dished out.

"Fuck Cresha, she's getting on my nerves. Bitch keeps talking about taking shit to the next level when we can't even get along long enough to fuck. I ain't been to the condo in months, bro," Black vented to his brother, leaving nothing out.

"I always thought she was ghetto as hell with that blonde ass hair she be rocking, good luck returning her to the hood. You got her accustomed to a life she can't maintain on her own, that's gone be a problem."

"I don't give a fuck, she better get unaccustomed," Black replied, causing Boss to laugh as he pulled in front of Black's home.

Black shook his brother's hand before grabbing the door handle.

"Aye, nigga," Boss rolled down the window, stopping Black before he made it too far up the porch.

"What up?"

"You never told me who you were going on a date with."

A smile spread across Black's face as Boss awaited an answer.

"Ari's teacher."

"You lying, you a slick ass nigga." The same smile spread across Boss's face.

"I swear to God."

"That's a grown ass woman, my boy," Boss informed his brother, slowly raising his window.

Black knew he would have to take a different approach with Melody; he was used to ghetto hoes whose idea of a romantic date was riding down Lakeshore Drive with a blunt and a bottle. Melody definitely gave him grown woman vibes, and he was cool with that.

"And I'm a grown ass man…" he shot back before disappearing into the house.

❧ 11 ❧

"**S**mall fucking world!" Blessing and Melody yelled in unison as they compared notes, making the discovery that her new Angel, Arianna Bryant, was in fact Mel's favorite pupil.

It was crazy how big Chicago was, yet it was so small. What were the chances? And then on top of that, Melody had a date that night with Arianna's uncle. It had been a week since the young girl joined the team, however, she had only attended one practice session. Impressed more than she was at tryouts, Blessing seen something special in Arianna. She just couldn't put her finger on it.

"So girl... who be picking her up? Her fine ass daddy or uncle? Matter fact, where that child's mother at? Ari don't speak much of her. I wonder if she's dead." Melody paused, twisting her head to the side, staring off into the empty air.

"Oh shit! I'm sorry, B, I ain't mean to say it like that," Mel shot Blessing an empathetic look and apologized.

"Girlllll, you good. My mamma been dead almost twenty-five years and..."

"Annnnndddddddd what you wanna do special this year for yo big twenty-five. You know it's less than three months away, and this yo golden year baby! We gotta show out!" Melody screamed, jumping to her feet and twerking in front of her.

"Bitch movvveeeee and go hommmmeee!" Blessing whined, pushing her away and standing to her feet.

"You know I don't do birthdays and–"

"A lie, you do everybody's birthday but your own, and I understand why but friend."

"But these nuts! Don't you got a date you need to be getting ready for because. I sholl got practice, and it's starting in thirty-minutes." Blessing cut the tv off before moving about and gathering her belongings.

"Bitch! You putting me out?" Melody stood in the middle of the floor and quizzed with a raised eyebrow.

"Baby, you ain't gotta go home but you gotta get the hell outta here." Blessing laughed while her best friend's mouth dropped to the floor.

"I'm appalled. I've been kicked out of better places," Mel sassed, grabbing her keys and charger off the coffee table.

"You ain't appalled. You a nigga that steals," Blessing said, reciting a line from their favorite movie, "Friday After Next."

Sharing a laugh, Blessing straightened up her condo a little before locking up and heading out the front door with her bestie in tow.

"Hey Blessing. Hey Melody," Cresha, their neighbor, spoke as she made her way to the pool which was located on their floor.

"Hey girl!" the two spoke back in unison, waving at her daughter, Maya, who walked along side of her.

"Blessing, don't forget to tell me when you have tryouts again. You know my baby wanna be on yo squad," Cresha stated.

"I got you. I know it'll be January, but when I set the exact date, I'll let you know," she replied before parting ways with both her and Melody.

Taking the elevator to the lobby, Blessing took the same route to the parking garage where she hopped in her car and took off. Her dance studio was only ten minutes away, however, it was Kali's birthday, and her and Ty were throwing her a surprise party. Setting up and decorating the night before, Blessing made sure everything was perfect for her captain's fifteenth birthday. Purple and gold balloons and streamers hung throughout the studio, putting the final touches on everything. Only letting Ty in on the secret, Blessing wanted it to be a surprise to them all. With the end of the year competition coming up, Coach B planned on working they asses like dogs, and Kali's party was the last fun ride they'd have for a while.

"She's going to love this," Ty beamed, admiring the final touches Blessing added after he had left.

"I hope so. You know I go hard for my babies," she replied, just as the sound of the door opening, caused them both to turn around.

"Oh my God! Coach B!!!" Kali walked in and wailed, covering her mouth and kneeling down as tears filled her eyes.

"Happy Birthday, Sweetie!" Blessing walked over to her and exclaimed, pulling her up and into a bear hug.

Blessing's Angels filed in one by one until everyone was shocked and present. She loved seeing her girls excited and happy, it made all her hard work worth it. With no children of her own and no siblings, nieces or nephews, her Angels were her world, and she'd go to war for those brats. Blessing planned a day of fun with them, however, there was still a few pieces of business they needed to straighten out first.

"Okay, Angels, listen up!" her soft voice sounded, getting their attention almost immediately.

"We got all night to party, but we gotta take care of some things first, such as those consent forms. Where they at?" Coach B held her hand out and asked while the girls rambled through their bags and turned in their paperwork.

"Ouuuu, Coach B, I left mine on the backseat. I'mma call my mamma, so she can bring it back," Arianna approached her with big bright brown eyes and stated.

"Okay, no problem." Blessing looked at her and smiled before turning up the music, allowing the girls to socialize.

Coach B ran a tight ship, which meant no talking or bullshitting in her studio, unless it was dance related. Most of her Angels either went to school together or grew up in the same neighborhood, therefore, they were already familiar with each other. She didn't mind them socializing amongst one another; however, they sometimes took things overboard. Taking a seat in the corner, Blessing scoped out everyone, giggling at the many personalities in the room.

Her childhood dream was to run a dance studio, specifically for colored girls from the hood. Glancing down at her phone, Blessing sent Melody a text, requesting her date's vehicle information before heading over to UberEats and placing an order. Deciding on pizza, wings, and fries, she made sure they had enough to drink before finalizing everything. Surfing the apps on her phone, Blessing hit the Snapchat icon just as all the girls erupted in cheer. Quickly looking up, she slowly stood to her feet and walked over to the circle that was formed around Arianna. Instantly smiling, Coach B watched on as her newest Angel put on a show. Dancing to Meghan's Thee Stallion's *Savage*, the spunky young girl hit every move like she created the dance herself. Knowing damn well that the dance went viral less than twelve hours ago, Blessing was amazed at how fast she learned the routine.

Joining in on the fun, Coach B took that time to show her grasshoppers how shit was really done. Securing her box braids on the top of her head, Blessing took it back to her college days and showed her Angels why she was captain of the Alabama State Stingettes. The *oohs and ahhs* from her girls let her know she was doing something right, but it was when Ty joined in that the entire studio went crazy. Everyone, including Blessing, loved to see Ty's skinny frame twist and turn like he was gracing the runway. Dancing until her phone rang, Coach B paused the show before heading to the door to grab the food. After placing everything down and making sure everyone had a plate, she tried escaping to her office but was stopped by Arianna.

"Coach B. My mother is outside, can I go grab the consent form from her?" she asked.

"Nah baby, go eat. I'll grab it," she replied, walking to the door while Ari skipped away.

Peeking out into the darkness, Blessing unlocked the door and stepped out once she noticed the headlights from a double-parked Range Rover. Looking up and down the sidewalk, she shivered from the cool September breeze just as the driver's door open and out walked one of the most beautiful women she had ever laid eyes on. Without a doubt, Blessing knew from the woman's identical face that she was Arianna's mother. Dressed in a tight red mini dress, she had the body of a Fashion Nova model, making Blessing question if that's where she knew her from. Tossing her assumptions to the back of her head, she put on a fake smile as the woman approached her.

"You must be Arianna's mom. Hi, I'm Blessing, her coach," she extended her arm and spoke.

"Hey, I'm Arica. That silly ass girl always leaving shit," she replied, taking in her warm hand and shaking it before handing over the forms.

"Girl that's kids period!" Blessing replied as the two shared a brief laugh.

"Well girl, let me get back in here with my babies. It was nice meeting you." Coach B smiled before turning away and pulling out her phone.

Blessing: Well the bitch ain't dead

Melody: WHO?

Blessing: Arianna's mom, she just came up to the studio to drop off some paperwork

Melody: Word? What she look like?

Blessing: A BAD BITCH lol..... but I seen her somewhere before and imma wreck my brain until I figure it out (thinking emoji)

❧ 1 2 ❧

Mel sat in front of her vanity, trying to get ready for her date with Black. She applied a light beat to her already perfect skin and topped it off with a coat of nude lip gloss. Though the weather was changing to fall, she still opted on a black knee length bodycon dress that would display every curve on her body. She was excited about tonight, but her nerves were getting the best of her. Corey hadn't left out the house not one time that day, it was like he knew she was up to something.

"Come on, baby let's watch a movie, I ordered dinner," Corey said to her before climbing into the bed, getting comfortable.

Melody had always been the type to crack under pressure, and Corey was laying it on thick. Out of all the things Corey had done to her, she still felt like shit for even accepting a date with another man. He had been trying so hard to make things right and that's all she wanted.

"Yeah baby, we can definitely have a movie night," she replied, putting the makeup brush down and joining her man in the bed.

She didn't have a number on Black, but he would get the picture when she didn't show up at the school. Mel and Corey laid in bed playing and laughing just like old times.

"I love you, Mel," Corey pulled her close so that they were face to face.

"I love you too, big head," she leaned in and kissed him on the lips.

Mel sat up and slid her feet into her slippers before pulling her robe closed.

"I'm about to get me a glass of wine, you want something?" she asked, making her way out of the room.

"Nah, I'm waiting on the food," he replied, grabbing his phone from the nightstand.

Melody walked into the kitchen and grabbed a wine glass from the cabinet before pulling her sangria from the fridge. She looked up when Corey's watch vibrated on the island that sat in the middle of their kitchen. Mel paid it no mind and continued to pour her drink, but when it went off a second time, she grabbed it. Putting his mother's birthday in to unlock it, she shook her head at how dumb men were.

She leaned over the counter resting on her elbows as her eyes widen when Kim's name popped up. Mel scrolled up and began to read the messages that were sent just moments ago.

Kim: Come see me.

Corey: I told you that shit is over.

Kim: Really Corey?

Corey: Really.

Mel smiled while reading Corey's response. She moved around the kitchen to make Corey think she was busy while she read along.

Kim: So, you don't want this threesome? We're waiting on you.

Corey: Fuck, you just got my dick hard.

Kim: Get here.

Corey: This the last time Kim.

Kim: Whatever, that's my dick.

Her heart dropped, but not a single tear followed. She placed the watched down and caught a glimpse of the time. It was six thirty which meant she had about thirty minutes to get to the school to meet Black. Mel downed her glass of wine before walking back to the room. Corey's phone started ringing as soon as she walked in, Mel found it comical when he tried to act like something was wrong.

"What? Bro, where you at? Calm down, Kev, I'm on my way."

Mel sat back down on the bed and scrolled through her phone.

"Baby, I gotta go get Kevin. He fighting with ole girl."

"You want me to come with you?" Mel asked, looking up into his lying ass face.

"Hell naw, I'm gone go to jail if a mufucka fuck up and hit you. I'll be back in a lil bit, the food almost here."

"Ok, be careful."

"Ok." Corey grabbed his keys and was out the door.

No sooner than the front door closed, Mel was getting dressed and facetiming Blessing at the same time.

"You cancelled, didn't you?" was the first thing Blessing said when she picked up the phone. She knew Mel so well.

"I was about to cancel until I picked up Corey's watch and saw him texting the bitch, Kim, in real time."

"You lying!"

"Bitch, she offered the nigga a threesome and he went. Lied and said Kevin got into it with his bitch and left."

"What you wanna do?"

"Shit, I'm about to meet Black that nigga better hope I come home."

"Yasssss, bitch! Share your location and have sex, I mean, fun!"

They shared a laugh before ending the call, and Mel was out the door in record time. She took the ten-minute drive and caught a park at the school just as a white Maserati identical to the black one that picked Arianna up from school pulled up. Mel was nervous; she hadn't been on a date in years, though she had asked Corey multiple times to take her on one, it had yet to happen.

Black stepped out of the car and left the engine running as he made his way over to Melody as she got out. Mel sized him up as he got closer to her. He rocked a black jean jacket and pants with a white tee that had Balmain written in black across the chest. She couldn't help but notice the black diamonds that shined even in the dark. He walked up and gave her a hug as she inhaled the scent of weed and cologne.

"Wassup, beautiful?"

"Nothing much, handsome," Mel replied, causing him to lick his lips and flash the sexiest smile ever.

"Lock your car up and hop in with me," Black said, waiting for her. They walked over to his car and to her surprise, he opened her door.

She tried her best not to create a habit of comparing his actions to Corey's, but Corey had never opened her door. As soon as she stepped foot in his car, the weed smell hit her in full force bringing back memories of her and Blessing's teenage years when they engaged. The first thing Black did when he got in was grab a blunt and lit it, but not before letting the sunroof completely back. Mel appreciated the gesture and got comfortable in the plush white leather seat.

Black turned the radio up and the sounds of Tori Lanez came through the speakers. Mel was enjoying the ride, and the view of the Chicago skyline lit up in front of her as they made their way downtown. She had no idea where this man was taking her, and at this point, she really didn't care. He was taking her mind off the bullshit for the night.

"You want a drink?" Black asked, reaching in the back seat, pulling a bottle of Remy to the front.

Mel thought about it for a second before accepting his offer as he opened the glove compartment and grabbed a sleeve of plastic cups. She helped him out and removed a cup before placing them back inside and shutting it closed. Black was already drinking from a red solo cup, so she grabbed the bottle and poured herself a drink. Not being much of a drinker, she knew this cup would last her all night. She took a nice long sip before clearing her burning throat.

"Take it easy, baby, that's a grown folks drink," Black joked without taking his eyes off the road.

"Whatever," Mel finally responded before taking another sip to show him she was a big girl.

The liquor mixed with the music and the cool wind was a vibe, and it didn't help that he was sitting next to her looking sexy as hell. Mel always thought Corey was the finest man walking the earth, but Black was dancing circles around that nigga.

Mel was relieved to see that they were turning into the parking garage of the AMC Theater because her bladder was getting the best of her. Black killed his cup before killing the engine and though she had to relieve herself bad, she took another gulp, killing half of her cup as Black came around and opened the door. When Black grabbed her hand, electricity shot straight through her body, and it made her feel good. This was the first time Corey's actions didn't bother her, hell, she hoped he was having a great night because she definitely was.

"I'm about to use the restroom."

"Aight, you like scary movies or that soft shit?" he asked, causing Mel to laugh at his choice of words.

"Nah, I'm cool on that soft shit," she mocked him before disappearing to the back where the restrooms were.

Mel relieved her bladder and checked in with Blessing to tell her she was enjoying her night thus far. Corey hadn't texted nor called, and she was glad. After washing her hands and giving herself a once over in the mirror, she made her way back to the front. Black stood near the bar waiting on her. She threw her hips a little harder with each step as she made her way over to him.

"We have a few minutes to kill before the movie starts, I ordered you a shot of Remy," he said, handing her the glass.

"Thank you."

Mel took a sip of the drink as her phone started to vibrate. She looked at Corey's name flashing across the screen and cleared his call. He called back to back, and she declined every single call.

"That's your lil boyfriend?" Black asked before drinking from his glass.

"Ex-boyfriend," Mel corrected him. She was done playing with Corey.

"Tell him, you occupied with yo new nigga," Black stated, causing her to look at him and slightly blush.

"My new nigga, huh? What about your lil girlfriend, I'm sure you got one."

"I had a lil situation, but that shit dead."

"Lil situation? Is that what y'all call em now?" Mel joked before killing her shot.

"Nah, I just used situation in the place of bitch to be respectful."

"I appreciate that."

Mel was seeing double from the liquor, but she was really enjoying her time with Black. He had great conversation and come to find out they had a lot in common. Mr. Bryant had her attention—her undivided attention. They watched their movie and to Mel's surprise, she stayed awake during the entire show. They walked to the car hand-in-hand discussing the gruesome movie they had just watched. Being that they were headed into October, Mel thought about what she wanted to do with her class for Halloween.

"You have any kids?" Mel asked while her students were on her mind.

"No, but I am Ari's godfather."

Hearing Arianna's name made Mel remember that she had just joined Blessing's dance class.

"Speaking of Arianna..."

"What she do?" he asked before Mel could complete her sentence, automatically thinking Arianna was in trouble at school.

"Nothing, nothing at all. I was going to say how small the world is. My best friend owns a dance studio, and she was bragging about this new dancer. Come to find out it was Arianna."

"Dance class?" he questioned briefly looking over at her with a raised eyebrow.

"Yeah, she's on the team."

"Hmph," he chuckled but didn't say another word as he stroked the perfectly trimmed beard on his face.

Something told Mel that she had said too much, but it was too late to turn back, and she knew she had messed up...*Fuck*...

$$\text{❧} \quad 1\, 3 \quad \text{❧}$$

"What's up, Joseph?" Black spoke to the doorman as he entered the building of the condo that Cresha stayed in.

"Hey Black. Long time no see, you been alright?"

"I'm good, man," Black replied before stepping on to the elevator, taking it up to the eighth floor.

Black got the condo for Cresha a year after they became jammed, finally moving her out the hood, and though he rarely stayed there, he made sure all of the bills were paid. At one point, he thought she would be the one to make him settle down. She was all he wanted until the nagging and shit started. Black felt like he owed her after she did a one-year bid for him, and he would forever have love for her. They formed a dope ass bond over the last couple of years, but their fire was burning out, at least on Black's end.

Black used his key to unlock the door, walking in like he had been living there. Cresha was so busy gossiping on the phone, she didn't even notice his presence. He stood there watching her as she stood over the stove in a pair of boy shorts and a tank top. The sight of her slim-thick body made his dick rise. Cresha finally turned around and jumped, dropping her phone on the floor.

"Shit Black, you scared me! What are you doing here?" she asked, placing her hand over her chest.

"I was in the area."

"Oh, ok cool, you hungry?"

"Nah, I'm cool," he replied, taking a seat on the couch and grabbing the remote to her tv.

Cresha wasn't talking like she normally would; to Black's surprise, she was cool. She sat on the side of him and ate her food while watching tv. His whole purpose of stopping by was to address the crazy shit that she had been texting.

"You wanna talk about these messages?" he asked, pointing at his phone.

"Nope, I don't. I was tripping, and I'm sorry," she replied, pulling his legs onto of her lap as she removed his shoes and massaged his feet.

This was the shit he liked; if only she could stay this way, but he knew that facade wouldn't last long. Cresha would do almost anything to get Black to label her as his woman, another thing that turned him off from her was the fact that she had no goals. Black ran business opportunities pass her on several different occasion, and he even agreed to fund whatever she decided on, but she never acted on it.

"I hear you, where lil mama at?" he asked, referring to her daughter.

"She's with my momma. Why? You want your dick sucked?" she asked, grabbing his belt buckle as he looked down at her.

"Nah, I gotta meet Boss," he replied, leaving a salty look on Cresha's face because he had never turned her down.

"You probably going to meet a bitch." She rolled her eyes and snatched her plate from earlier off the coffee table.

Black knew she was about to start talking that crazy shit, so he got up and walked to the bathroom. Cresha was talking to herself because he wasn't trying to hear none of the shit she was saying. He handled his business and washed his hands before making his way back to the front.

"I'm gone," Black said as he made his way to the front door.

"Bye."

He shook his head as he made his way out, and as soon as he got in his car Melody called. She had perfect timing.

"Yo," he answered, pulling out of the parking garage.

"Hey you."

"Wassup, baby?"

"Nothing much, I'm starving."

"Where you at?" he asked, putting his turning signal on as he headed to him and Boss's favorite taco spot.

"I'm leaving the school, I just got off."

"I'm on my way to this taco spot that me and my brother come to all the time, come up here."

"Where? I love tacos!" she said overly excited.

"I'm about to drop the location, it's not too far from your job," he replied, doing exactly what he said.

"Ok, got it! See you in a minute."

Ever since their date, they talked and texted every day, all day, and he fucked with her. He sat there behind his tints watching his surroundings as waited on either Mel or Boss to pull up. When he saw Melody turn the corner, he killed the engine and got out. He adjusted his jacket while watching her walk across the busy street in her stilettos. He thought it was the sexist shit ever; she was beautiful to him. He held his arms open to greet her with a hug before walking her inside the semi-crowded restaurant. They took a seat at an empty table as a waiter immediately approached them.

"Black, hola my friend. Hola," the older Mexican guy spoke to both him and Melody.

"What up? Give us a minute, my friend," Black replied, giving Mel time to look over the menu because he already knew what he wanted. Black leaned back in his seat as she looked over the menu.

"How was work, Ms. Caston?" he asked, causing her to look up and smirk.

"It was good, how was work for you, Mr. Bryant?" she retorted, causing Black to chuckle.

"It was alright."

Mel laid the menu down and looked into his eyes. "What exactly do you do?"

He knew this question would eventually come up, but just as he was about to answer, the door swung open, and Boss walked in. Black stood up as he approached the table and shook his hand, pulling him in for a hug. Every Wednesday was their day to meet for lunch, no matter what they had going on they never broke their self-made weekly tradition.

"Ms. Caston," Boss greeted Melody while extending his hand.

"Please, call me Mel," she replied as Boss nodded his head and shook her hand.

"Bro, you didn't order?" Boss asked as Black shook his no.

"Nah, Mel was looking over the menu."

Boss walked past an entire line of people and over to the door that read "employees only" before walking in the kitchen to put his order in. Melody's mouth dropped at Boss's actions as Black laughed at her reaction. She was going to be dropping her mouth a lot when she was in their presence.

"He can just walk back there like that?" she asked, pointing at the same door Boss walked through.

"You can do what you want to do when you're a Bryant. You ready to order?"

"I'll just take two steak tacos with everything," Mel said, pushing the menu aside.

"Aye Boss!" Black called out to his brother who was in the kitchen, giving orders like he owned the place.

"What's up?" Boss asked from behind the counter.

"Put an order in for two steaks with everything."

"Aight, would you like a drink, nigga?" Boss joked with his brother before laughing.

"Please," Black responded, using his hands to make a praying gesture.

"I love you all's bond, I wish I had a sibling," Mel admitted as she admired the connection between the two men.

"You're an only child? You probably spoiled as hell."

"Growing up I was, but not so much anymore."

"Awwww, my baby ain't got nobody to spoil her? I got you."

Black meant what he said. He was crushing on Mel hard, and the crazy part was he wasn't even thinking about hitting her yet. He was drawn into her beauty and personality. He looked at her as she tilted her head to the side and stared at him.

"You know you say all the right things? I bet you have all the ladies going crazy."

"Nah, them hoes, I mean ladies drive themselves crazy," Black chuckled before folding his arms across his chest.

He didn't mean any disrespect to Mel, but he was very blunt. Of course, she wasn't the only female he fucked with, but she was the only one holding his attention. Mel didn't bother responding to his last statement, and he hoped he didn't leave a bad taste in her mouth. He made room as Boss finally joined them at the table.

Both Boss and Black looked at Mel as she bit into the best taco in town, and she unknowingly closed her eyes.

"That shit a hit, ain't it," Boss asked, dressing his tacos up with all the works.

Mel's eyes popped open at the sound of his voice. She quickly grabbed a napkin and wiped her mouth before responding to him.

"I swear to God, I want to go back there and hug the cook," Mel joked, placing the napkin down.

"Go ahead," Boss replied, giving her permission as if she was serious.

Black was sure she had so many unanswered questions about him and even Boss, like who fuck they really were and what they did. He was also sure she noticed the way people in the restaurant dared to look in their direction for too long. She had no idea the caliber of niggas she was surrounded by.

"Damn, what the fuck a nigga gotta do to get a table in this bitch!"

Black briefly looked up as Mel's eyes darted to the tall, loud guy who was causing the disturbance. He stood with two other men that found his irate behavior comical. Neither Boss nor Black paid the man any mind while everyone else in the restaurant, including Mel, had their eyes glued to him.

"Niggas over there chilling, niggas in the corner holding up the table, this shit is bad for business," the same guy continued to rant.

Boss wiped his mouth and tossed the napkin on the table, and Black look over his shoulder. Mel watched as they looked at one another. Black decided to leave before he had to show his ass in front of Mel. He hoped that the nigga would've left once he realized there was no available tables but that would've been too much like right. Nigga's loved putting on shows.

"You done, baby?" Black asked Mel, leaning back in his seat as the man went on, now focusing in on the table they were occupying.

"Yes," Mel assured him, gathering her things.

She followed both Boss and Black's actions, so she stood when they got up and prepared to leave. She walked between the two men as Boss led the way. She grabbed Black's hand as they maneuvered through the crowd.

"About muthafuckin time. Damn, she got a fat ass," the loud guy said, referring to Mel.

Mel ignored him, but Black stopped walking. Of course, when Black stopped, Boss did the same. When the other two guys looked up into the Bryants' faces, it was like they had seen a ghost.

"Dawg, chill," one of the guy's homeboys tried to calm the situation.

"Listen to ya mans," Boss warned the guy in a calm tone.

"Chill? Fuck these nigg.." was all the guy could say before Black grabbed him by the back of the neck, slamming his head into a nearby table and instantly causing his nose to leak and dishes to shatter on the floor.

Black hated Mel had to see that side of him, but disrespect was to be handled the moment it was dished out.

"Fuck what niggas!?" Black spat, slamming him for a second time as everyone grasped for air.

Black stood him up as he staggered while holding his nose; he didn't even try to fight back.

"Apologize to her," Black demanded, turning him toward Melody.

"I'm sorry," the guy did as he was told before Black released him to his friends.

Boss shook his head and chuckled at the sight of the bloody man before turning to the workers behind the register that looked on.

"Should've listened to ya mans. Aye, put the damage on our tab," Boss said before they led Mel out the door.

❦   14   ❧

Tossing his head back, Boss bit down on his bottom lip as he tried to control the nut that was reaching the tip of his dick. Grabbing the back of Trina's head, he tightened his grip seconds before exploding in her warm mouth. The "Throat Goat" as he liked to call her, always came through in the clutch when Boss was having a fucked-up day. In his line of business, things seemed to get stressful a lot, but he was born for the shit. Gaining the nickname as a one-year-old, Sandy, his mother, claimed he came out the womb running things. Never changing his ways, the name stuck with him, however, his bossiness grew ten times worse. Without a care in the world, Boss was more afraid of living than dying, that's why he walked the earth like the cocky nigga he was.

"Damn, shorty," he sat up straight and growled while she wiped her mouth and smiled.

"Hold on, I'm not done," Trina replied with a seductive grin before going inside her shorts pocket and pulling out a Magnum.

Never taking his eyes off of her, Boss glanced at the clock on her wall before focusing back on the strip tease show she was putting on in front of him. Trina had a nice body and although her head was immaculate, her pussy wasn't enough to make him stay. Feeling his phone vibrate in his pocket, Boss stood his feet, pulling the black Amiri jeans over his ass. Digging for his phone, Boss read over a message from Black before stuffing it back in the pocket of his hoodie.

"You really finna leave without giving me some dick?" Trina snapped, placing her hands on her hips and rolling her neck.

"I'll be back through later. I gotta go handle some business right now," he calmly replied, grabbing his pistol off the table and placing it on his waist.

"Later? I ain't no put to the back-burner ass bitch. I'm tired of you thinking you can come through here whenever you want to. Boss, I deserve more and…"

Boss was out the door and walking down the stairs before Trina could finish her sentence. Never being the type to explain himself nor repeat himself more than once, he avoided a great deal of things by being that way. Being big on time, Boss knew it was one of the most precious things on earth, which was why he used his wisely. He tried his best directing his energy to the right places and staying clear of nagging bitches was one of the ways he did that. Bringing his Maserati to life, Boss chuckled aloud as he rolled down the passenger's side window.

"I hate you, boss. I swear, I won't ever call you again!" Trina yelled from the porch, jumping up and down while wearing nothing but a bra and panties.

Shaking his head from side to side, he threw up two fingers before turning up the music loudly and speeding off.

I'm the biggest boss that you seen thus far (Ross!)
Got the biggest cars, Spanish broads, no bra
Call that other lame for the walks in the parks
I ain't come to play games, I just wanna play my part
Tell ya girlfriend come talk with me, dog

STOPPING AT A RED LIGHT TWO BLOCKS FROM TRINA'S CRIB; OUT OF habit, Boss checked his surroundings, noticing a group of young boys beating buckets on the curb. Rolling down his window, Boss hit the horn three times before motioning them over to him. Throwing the gear into park, he let off the break slightly, going into his pocket and pulling out a wad of cash. Peeling off eight hundred-dollar bills, Boss handed two hundred to each of them.

"Good looking, Boss," all three said in unison just before the light changed.

Peeling off into the flow of traffic, he turned the music back up and cruised the streets until he made it to his destination. Pulling in front of Affiliated Clothing, Boss killed the engine and jumped out. Waving at the bypassers who called out his name. He hit the alarm on his car before disappearing inside the store.

"Boss! Boss! Boss!... Heyyyyy, Boss!" the customers along with his all-female staff spoke as he made his way through his establishment.

Affiliated Clothing, Boss's and Black's clothing store was located on 16th and Pulaski, in the heart of their hood. Taking their sense of fashion to another level, the brothers opened up the spot six years ago when Boss turned twenty-one. Only a year apart in age, the Bryant boys were businessmen before they were officially adults. Successful and still thriving, Affiliated Clothing cleaned most of their dirty money. After speaking to everyone individually, Boss pulled the store manager, Nisha, into his office to speak in private.

"WANT ME TO CLOSE IT?" SHE WALKED IN BEHIND HIM AND ASKED, pointing back to the door.

"Never mind, I know that look on yo face. I'll close it," she continued with a seductive grin, shutting and locking it.

Boss took a seat in the black leather chair behind the oakwood desk and watched Nisha not only secure the door but undress herself as she made her way towards him. Watching her lick those full set of lips he loved, Boss felt his dick rising in his pants. Signaling with his fingers, he then instructed her to turn around. Pulling up her skirt, Boss forced her onto the desk, where he began playing with her wet pussy.

"Damn, you was ready for a nigga, huh?" he whispered in her ear before going inside the drawer and pulling out a condom.

"My pussy started dripping the moment you pulled up," she replied in a sexy tone.

Saying all the things he liked to hear only made his dick harder. No longer wanting to waste any more time, Boss slid the condom on before ramming his nine inches inside her sweet pussy. Going to work, Nisha gripped the ends of the desk with hopes of keeping up. Picking up the speed, Boss sent her to pound town, hitting all the spots she loved.

"You—I'm—Oh my God, Boss. I'm about to cum," she moaned out, her juices covered his dick, making him bust as well.

Cleaning up inside the bathroom in his office, Boss went over a few things regarding the store before sending her on her way. Noticing the time, he finished up around there before heading to his next destination. Going to the messages in his phone, Boss double checked the address before pulling in the parking lot of a strip mall. Grabbing a spot a few doors down, he checked for his pistol and proceeded down the street. Stopping in front of the door, Boss glanced up at a neon sign that read, "Blessing's Dance Studio" before twisting the knob and walking in.

"HOLD ON! HOLD ON! TY, CUT THE MUSIC. CAN I HELP YOU!" a woman about five-six with a mocha complexion stood in the middle of the floor and yelled.

"Ari, let's go!" Boss ordered, never taking his eyes off the woman standing in front of him.

"Ari, stay! Who the fuck are you, sir?" she twisted her head to the side and asked, challenging him.

"I'm her father, and I ain't sign her up for this shit, so you need to shut the ...."

"Watch yo mouth!" she warned with her top lip curled up, before continuing.

"Cause between the hours of six and eight, Ari belongs to me!" Coach B snapped, pointing to herself.

Instead of being annoyed or agitated, Boss was turned on. Ari's dance instructor was by far the *most* beautiful woman he had ever seen in his life. Without a spec of makeup and her hair tied in a scarf, not even the sweat dripping from her forehead could turn him off.

"This my dad, Coach B. I am so sorry," Ari stepped in between the two and apologized.

"No need to be sorry baby, especially not for a grown man's actions," she replied with a smirk before rolling her eyes at Boss.

"Angels, take five while I get rid of this unwanted guest," she continued as her girls obeyed.

"Man look baby girl. I ain't trying to hear none of that shit you talking. I ain't agree to this, so let me get my daughter, and I'll be up out of here," Boss finally stated, looking down at Ari who had tears in her eyes.

"Like I saaaaaid, Mr. Bryant, she ain't going nowhere until class over. You might be the boss in the streets, but I'm the boss in this bitch," she stepped forward and cursed, causing Boss's dick to get hard for the third time that day.

Usually that tone from a woman would turn him off, but it was something about her words that intrigued him. He liked her feistiness, and had they met under different circumstances, she'd probably be his bitch. Not one for many words, Boss left things at that.

"You got two minutes to get yo shit and get in the car," he looked over at his daughter and barked before directing his attention back to Blessing.

"I'll see you around.," he promised before turning on his Timbs and walking out.

"Nah, nigga! I doubt that!" he heard her yell, her words causing him to chuckle and think…. *Maybe dancing wasn't so bad after all……*

15

"So, wait...he walked straight through your practice?" Mel asked as Blessing explained how rude Boss was.

"Yes, walked in that bitch like he owned he it!"

"Poor Arianna. I know you went off!"

"Girl, I stepped straight to his ass. He had me sooooo fucked up!" Blessing laughed while hitting her hand with a closed fist.

Mel paused for a second and looked at Blessing before pointing at her. "You like him, don't you? "Melody teased, causing Blessing to roll her eyes to the back of her head.

"No, I do not, I'll leave the Bryants to you."

A smile spread across Mel's face as she tossed her phone onto Blessing's coffee table. "That's cool, I think I might really like that nigga."

"I can tell, I held a whole conversation with you earlier, and all you did was briefly look up from your phone and smile."

"I'm sorry, his conversation is on point, and he says all the right things. Nigga like a breath of fresh air."

"A breath of fresh air? Damn, that's deep. I see new dick in your near futureeee," Blessing sang with her arms in the air while sticking her tongue out.

"I hope so because Corey can't touch me."

Corey had no clue Mel knew that he went to Kim's house that night, and he was still running with the whole Kevin situation. She showed no emotion, and just like her mother told her that his presence would soon go unnoticed, she couldn't have been more accurate. Mel had finally had enough, and Black was making the transition very easy.

"I don't blame you, he wanna keep going back to that nasty bitch."

No sooner than those words left her mouth, there was a knock on her door.

"Who is it?" Blessing yelled, walking over to the door.

"Me man," Corey said from the hallway as Blessing let him in.

Mel rolled her eyes and looked at the tv as he walked in and joked with Blessing. When her phone chimed, alerting her of a text message, she grabbed it. Looking down at the beautiful message her mother had just sent her, she smiled while replying.

"Who the fuck got you smiling?" Corey asked looking over at Mel, causing her to briefly look up.

She ignored his question and continued to respond to her mother. It wasn't his business who was making her smile. It damn sure wasn't him.

"Oh, so you don't hear me talking to you?" he spat, turning red in the face.

"Corey, please stop talking to me. You came to visit Blessing, right?"

When Corey walked over to Mel and snatched her phone, all hell broke loose. She jumped up and charged him as he turned his back and tried to see who she was texting.

"Give me my fucking phone!"

"I'm not giving you shit!" he shot back, trying to keep Mel off of him.

Blessing managed to snatch the phone back and hand it to Mel before getting in the middle of them. Corey tried to walk up on Mel like he wanted to hit her, but he knew better.

"Corey, chill the fuck out! You doing too much, and you not about to come down here with that bullshit."

"Get out my business bro, you always running to her defense!"

"Running to her defense!? Didn't you just jump yo ass up and run out the house the other day to defend Kevin?" Blessing snapped, pointing her finger at Corey.

"Kevin? I ain't talked that nigga in weeks, since I checked him about yo ass, but you can't ride for me!"

That was all Mel needed to hear, Corey had just confirmed what she already knew.

"Oh so, you haven't talked to Kevin in weeks, huh? So where you go Corey?"

"Let's go home and talk!"

"We ain't got shit to talk about, you ran out the crib to see yo bitch!"

Mel had never stepped to Corey without breaking down crying, but she stood there with not a single tear. Though she wanted to cry bad, it wasn't going to happen in front of him. She grabbed her keys and quickly walked out the door. She knew Corey wasn't too far behind, so she slowly jogged while her heart was beating out of her chest.

"Corey, let her calm down!"

"Fuck that!" Mel could hear him yelling.

He came in the house right behind her, but she ran and locked herself in the bathroom. She could hear Blessing trying to calm him down, that's when the tears started to flow heavily. Though Blessing knew everything that went on in their relationship, she was still slightly embarrassed by Corey's actions. She didn't deserve to be treated the way he had been treating her and this time around, she was choosing herself.

"Mel please just talk to me baby. I swear to God I didn't do shit. We can call her on the phone."

"Leave me alone Corey. You can take all your shit to her house, I told you last time was the last time!"

"Melody please open door, we can move out of town and start over! I can't lose you, Mel."

"Corey, please. You should be worrying about which one of us is moving out of here because one of us has to go."

She sat on the toilet biting her lip while her leg shook uncontrollably, she had to calm herself down. She had to get the hell out of the house even if it only for a few hours. With her world crumbling right before her eyes, all she could think about was Black.

Mel: I need to see you!
Black: When?
Mel: ASAP.
Black: One of the guys having a fight party tonight, pull up.
Mel: Ok, send the location.
Black: Aight! Bet

❧ 16 ❧

"I cannot believe I let you talk me into going to a fucking fight party," Blessing fussed as she struggled to get the Fashion Nova jeans over her plump ass.

"Girl, shut up. As many times as you've dragged me out the bed. You need to be quiet," Melody shot back, flopping down on B's king size bed.

"Lies..... Bitch, the lies you tell. You know damn well I don't like people," Blessing joked, adjusting the Gucci belt around her small waist.

"You need to be getting out as much as possible. Always talking bout I need some new dick. Hoe you need some dick, period!" Melody mumbled loud enough for Blessing to hear.

"Bitch bye. I take pride on having sex with only one nigga. You want my shit loose like yours," B whipped her weave around and said, causing Mel's mouth to drop to the floor.

"Blessing, you think you can fight. I'll pick up something and knock yo strong ass out!" she jumped off the bed and threatened, reaching for the huge vase inside of Blessing's room.

"I don't want no smoke Lord. I don't wont noooo smoke," Blessing surrendered, holding both hands in the air and laughing.

Pouring them both a glass of Stella Rosa Black mixed with a double shot of Henny, the friends talked shit until they both were ready and out the door. It had been awhile since the last time Blessing went out. Falling into deep depression after filing for divorce, she found it hard to have a good time when dealing with a broken heart. Finally over her ex-husband and his pain, Blessing wasn't quite ready to date yet, however, she was at least open to meeting new people.

"Look at all these foreign cars," Mel admired as she drove down the block in Naperville where the party was located.

"Girl, where the hell you bringing me? This look like a Chris Brown video shoot," Blessing noted, noticing the half-naked fake bodies floating around.

Circling the block two more times, Melody and Blessing finally lucked up on a park a few houses down from the mansion where the fight party was being held. Stepping out the car in a pair of six-inch Giuseppe boots, Blessing grabbed her bag before adjusting the crop top and stepping onto the curb. It was early October, however, the temp was in the low seventies and everyone was enjoying it. Locking arms with her best friend of over twenty years, the pair headed down the street, ignoring the stares and grunts sent their way.

"Let me text Black and tell him we outside," Melody pulled away and stated, grabbing her phone, doing as she said.

Continuing their strut, Blessing and Mel hit the porch, and like clockwork, a man resembling Ari's father stepped out and greeted them.

"What's up beautiful?" he pulled Melody in for a hug and said before addressing Blessing.

"And you must be Coach B," Black guessed, extending his arm for a handshake.

"Nice to meet you." Blessing smiled, accepting his gesture before sliding pass him into the house.

Stunned by its beauty, the two-level mansion was one straight out of a fairytale. It resembled Uncle Phil's crib on The Fresh Prince of Bel-Air. With a pool table in the middle of the marble floor and the fight playing on a projector on the wall, Blessing didn't know what to focus on first. Pretty women in all colors and sizes glided around the place like they lived there.

"Aye. We gon go watch the fight downstairs. Come on," Black said, interrupting her thoughts and leading them down a set of stairs.

"I gotta use the bathroom," Blessing announced just as they hit the landing.

"It's a bathroom right there. Gone in. It ain't occupied." Black chuckled, causing both B and Mel to eye him suspiciously.

Slowly walking away towards the direction he pointed her to, Blessing knocked on the door twice before twisting the knob and walking in. Grasping for air, her mouth dropped at the sight before her. Her heels were glued to the floor, and as bad as she wanted to move or look away, she just couldn't do it.

"What? You ain't never seen an anaconda before Coach B?" Boss asked while holding his dick as piss flew into the toilet.

"I – I'm – I didn't think anyone was in here. I'm so, so sorry," she apologized, her eyes never leaving his dick.

Boss undoubtably had the prettiest penis she had ever seen in life. Grant you, she hadn't seen many, but there was no doubt in her mind that they ain't have anything on him. Thick and long, it shared the same chocolate color with his skin and for some odd reason, looking at it made her mouth water. Embarrassed was an understatement, but, she wasn't too ashamed, she still hadn't looked away.

"You wanna shake it for me?" Boss twisted his head and asked, and those words finally snapped her out of her trance.

"Ugh! Boy, fuck you!" she snapped, turning away and slamming the door.

Blessing could hear Boss laughing loudly as she walked away, but she didn't dare look back. She no longer had to pee and all of a sudden, was ready to go home. She knew the chances of him being present was high, however, she didn't expect to run into him like that. After pulling Arianna out of the class a few days ago, Blessing was sure that she wouldn't see him again, but she was wrong. Spotting Melody and Black sitting on a couch off in the corner, Blessing headed in their direction with a mug on her face.

"Damn, that was fast. What's wrong with you? Why you looking like that?" Mel sat up and asked while Black listened on.

"Ummm, I'm ready to go. I mean, I think we should go."

"Go? For what? We just got here? Why you wanna go?" Melody quizzed with a puzzled looked on her face.

Just as Blessing opened her mouth to speak, her soft voice was drowned out by Boss's deep baritone.

"Cause she seen my dick and now she ain't never gon be able to get it off her mind," he appeared behind her and answered.

Boss was so close to Blessing that his words caused goosebumps to form on the back of her neck. She had been around a few men in her day but none of them were like Mr. Bryant. He was cocky as fuck, which usually was a turn off since her ex-husband was the same way. Kevin thought he was the man, and that money could buy him anything, even love. The youngest realtor tycoon in the Midwest, Kevin came from a wealthy family who also thought the same. Swearing on her life that she'd never deal with a man like that again had her wondering why Boss's presence alone made her pussy wet.

"I didn't know someone was in there, and I opened the door, and this nigga was pissing," Blessing spun around and snapped, her reaction causing Boss to smile.

"Soooo, that's why you laughed? You knew yo brother was in the bathroom. You a petty ass nigga," Melody roared, playfully punching Black in the arm.

The rest of the night and rest of the fight consisted of Blessing sitting in a recliner alone, texting Melody who kept Black company. Trying her hardest to ignore Boss, Blessing was relieved when he got a phone call, forcing him to get up and leave. Able to relax a little more, she downed a cup of Patron with hopes of forgetting all about the night.

"You ready best friend?" Blessing heard Mel say while she stood to her feet, knocking the wrinkles out of her blouse.

"Yup. Let's go."

Standing alongside her, Black led the way through the mansion, taking the same route out as they did in. Looking at the time on her phone, Blessing was shocked to see how many people was arriving as they were leaving. It was one a.m. and although at their age the night was still considered young, Blessing and Melody had old souls and needed their rest. Stepping onto the porch, she immediately noticed the drop in the weather and regretted not bringing a jacket. Still leading the way, the girls followed Black as he weaved in and out of traffic.

"Wait. You leaving already?"

Turning around, Blessing locked eyes with Boss who grabbed her by the tail of her shirt. Neither of them spoke any words, instead, they simply stared into each other eyes as if they both were afraid to look away. So many responses skated through her head. Should she be rude? Should she be smart? Or should she ignore him? The man had her lost and although she'd never admit it aloud, she liked it.

"Why does it matter? You been ghost all night," she blurted out, kicking herself in the ass for the statement the second it left her lips.

"Awwww Coach B, you was looking for me?" Boss replied, tossing his arm around her shoulder and walking down the street.

"No. No. No the fuck I wasn't. Move!" She shrugged, knocking his arm away and powerwalking ahead.

He had her messed up, and she refused to fall victim to a Bryant like Melody. Everything about Boss screamed run away and never look back, and that's exactly what she planned on doing. With Melody and Black boo'd up already at the car, Blessing regretted coming and knew she should have went with her first mind. A few feet from Mel's ride, she attempted to keep walking, but Boss's deep voice calling out her name slowed her down.

"Coach B! Coach B!"

"What!" she snapped her neck around and shouted while he stood in front of her with a smirk.

"Let me take you out," he said with a straight face, reaching forward and grabbing her hands.

"Nah, you ain't shit but trouble. I'm good," she sassed, looking him up and down.

"I can see that you good. I'm trying to make you better," Boss stepped in closer and replied, biting down on his bottom lip.

"Make me better, huh? You can do that by letting Ari back on the team." Blessing took a step forward and challenged, so close she could smell the Henny and double mint on his breath.

"Nah man, I can't cuz..."

"Exactly, we ain't got shit to talk about. Bye Mr. Bryant," Blessing snarled before yanking away.

❧ 17 ☙

Black jogged up the steps that led to the huge double doors connected to his parents' house. Though him and Boss had their own separate mansions on the Bryant's estate, they enjoyed spending time at their parents' home. The Bryants had always been a very close-knit family, especially around birthdays and holidays.

"Is that my faaaavorite uncle in the world?" he was greeted by Arianna who was holding his mother's Yorkie, Chanel.

"Favorite, huh?" Black asked, stepping out of the wheat Timberland boots he wore on his feet.

"Yeah, you know you my favorite uncle."

"Ari, I'm your only uncle."

Black knew his niece had something up her sleeve. The little girl had everything, yet she was always coming up with something else to add to her want list.

"Oh yeahhhh right. Uncle Black, I need a favor."

He walked right pass Ari and headed to the theater room with her on his heels.

"Family don't do favors, whatever you do for family is done and never spoken of again, now rephase your question."

"*Rephase*? Yeahhh, Ms. Caston is definitely rubbing off on you," she laughed as Black threw a pillow at her.

"Hey, hey, hey, that's a thousand-dollar pillow y'all tossing around!" Sandy sassed, appearing in the doorway as Ari threw the pillow back.

Ari was right, Black had found himself trying to use correct grammar when he was in Mel's presence. Though that thug shit was embedded in him, he had plenty room for improvement.

"Get yo granddaughter," Black said to his mother while laughing at his niece as she stood in a fighting stance.

"I quit, for real. Uncle Black, can you get me the new Yeezy's, pleaseeeeeee!" Ari begged with her hands in a praying gesture

"Ari, I told you I would get those shoes for your birthday," Sandy said, fluffing her pillows.

"But Granny I need em noooow, my birthday is all the way on the thirty-first," Ari whined, throwing a fake tantrum.

Black made a mental note to grab the shoes for Ari first thing in morning.

"For your birthday," Sandy replied, standing on her word.

"It's cool, Paw Pawwww!" she stormed off, yelling for her grandfather who was next on her list.

Black shook his head while trying to find a movie to watch.

"You alright favorite son?" Sandy asked.

He looked at his mother and nodded his head before speaking. "I'm straight, Ma. Y'all good, life is good, everything all good. You aight?"

"I have not a single complaint besides your father and that damn snoring. I have to sleep on the other side of the house," she joked as her husband and Ari walked in and caught the end of the statement.

"How that saying go granddaughter? It be ya own folks."

"People, Paw Paw, it be your own people," Ari helped him out, sending the entire room up in laughter.

"Let's go little girl, you're going with one of your parents!" Sandy pulled Ari out the room.

Dino walked in and took a seat next to his youngest son as the movie *New Jack City* came on the projector. This was always his and

Boss's favorite movie growing up; it taught them what not to do in the drug game. Black knew his father had something to talk about since he never really watched tv. He briefly looked at the screen before speaking.

"Son, you know I don't like to hear my sister cry."

Black already knew this conversation was about the beating they put on their cousin last week. He really wasn't trying to hear shit about Lil Kenny; he had brought that violation upon himself.

"Luckily, she ain't grieving," Black replied, never taking his eyes off the screen.

"And she better not have to anytime soon. Moving forward I will handle Kenny."

He sat there listening to his father; it fucked with him how soft he was on his nephew but kept his foot on both him and Boss's neck growing up.

"Aight," was all Black said. He knew any other response would lead to a disagreement that he didn't have time for.

"Alright, I love you son," Dino said, standing to his feet.

"Love you too, Pop."

Turning his attention back to his movie, he pushed that shit his father was talking to the back of his mind. If it came down to it, Black would still kill Kenny with no hesitation, especially to protect his immediate family. He had finally started to enjoy his movie when an unsaved number flashed across his screen.

"Yo," he picked up, placing the phone up to his ear.

"Hey Black, it's um, Iesha."

Iesha...Iesha...Iesha, he repeated the name in his head, trying to put a face or body with the name.

"I'm sorry sweetheart, I don't know an Iesha," he said, still not knowing who he was talking to.

The girl popped her lips loudly on the other end of the phone. "Sparkle from Ocean's," she replied, using her stage name and instantly jogging Black's memory.

Black knew exactly who she was. He took the bitch to the hotel one night on some drunk shit. He was surprised to even be getting a call from her; they both fucked and went their separate ways. Though they exchanged numbers neither of them used the seven digits.

"What's up stranger?" Black asked, reclining his chair and getting comfortable.

"Um nothing much. You know that night we had sex, I think the condom may have broken or something because I'm pregnant."

Black removed the phone and looked at it with a stale face as if she could see him.

"So, let me guess, it's mine?" he asked sarcastically.

"Yes, you were the only person I was with around that time. I have nothing to lie about."

"So, I'm supposed to believe that I was the only nigga you fucked that entire month? See, I find that hard to believe because you left the club with me for free, so I could imagine what you would do for some bread. Find you somebody safe to play with sweetheart."

"I'm not that kind of bitch. I left with you because I liked you! Look, I didn't call you to cause any problems. If you could just give me the money for an abortion, you'll never hear from me again."

"Aight bet, drop your location."

"Ok thanks Black."

"No problem."

As soon as his phone chimed and she dropped an address, he got up and walked to the front door. He put his shoes on as his mother moved around the kitchen.

"You not staying for dinner?" she asked, taking something out of the oven and placing it on the counter.

"I'll be back in little bit."

"Ok baby."

Black stepped out into brisk fall weather and walked to his car, but not before making sure his pistol was secured on his waist. He hopped in and called Boss.

"What up?" He answered on the first ring.

"Shit, about to slide to this bitch crib and see what's to this baby situation she just dropped on me."

"Who Cresha?"

"Hell naw, you remember that bitch Sparkle from the party at Oceans a while back?"

Boss let out a chuckled before speaking. "Is it yours?"

"Nigga, it's a possibility. I'm gone get to the bottom of it."

"You and these bitches," Boss joked on the other end of the phone.

Black laughed at the audacity of his brother before responding. "Says the nigga that got Nisha thinking she's part owner of the store because she's fucking her boss."

"Man, that bitch crazy."

He talked shit with his brother the entire thirty-minute drive, it consisted of small talk and a replay of him and their father's brief conversation. Ending the call with Boss, he pulled up to the address provided and killed the engine. Making his way up the porch of the bi-level townhouse, he checked his surroundings before ringing the bell. She came to the door wearing little to nothing, instantly making Black remember why he left the club with the bitch, she was bad.

"You can come in." She stepped aside and allowed him to walk past.

Looking around her place, he was surprised at how clean it was. Black finally turned and looked at her before speaking.

"So how much is the abortion?"

"Honestly Black, I want to keep my baby."

He looked at her with a stale face because that wasn't part of the discussion they had prior to him coming there. He looked down at her stomach which was semi flat. Doing the math in his head, he realized something wasn't adding up.

"How far along are you?" he asked, folding his arms across his chest while awaiting answer.

"Three and a half months," she quickly replied.

"Aight, you got an ultrasound or something?"

"I took multiple tests," she replied, holding three piss sticks in his direction.

This bitch was acting like she had been rehearsing that role all night, and he wasn't buying it. Black tilted his head to the side and looked at her.

"Bro I'm not touching that shit. Take a new one while I'm here. I want to see you open it."

Sparkle blew some air from her mouth and rolled her eyes before walking off. Just like any other nigga, he watched her ass bounce with every step. He had to control his dick because he was seconds away from bending her ass over one of those couches. When she returned with a new box of pregnancy test, he watched her as she tore the plastic with her teeth.

"Are you happy now?" she asked, pulling a new stick out and walking off to a nearby bathroom.

As soon as she shut the door, Black walked over and stood close. He could hear uttering on the other side of the door. When he realized it was two females whispering, he grabbed the knob and tried to enter.

"Unlock the door, I want to see you piss on the stick."

"I'm, I'm almost done!" she yelled back.

Growing impatient, he took a step back and kicked the door damn near off the hinges. He locked eyes with Sparkle and a very pregnant female that stood in the tub.

"Wait, I can explain," she threw her hands in the air, trying to clarify.

Grabbing Sparkle by the hair, he pulled her out of the bathroom and threw her body to the floor. Black was no woman beater, but he had no problem slapping the shit out of her of few times for playing in his face.

"Why the fuck you playing with me!" Black pulled his gun out just to scare her because he had no intentions on shooting her.

"I am so sorry!" she yelled as her friend stood back, crying for her.

"You definitely a sorry bitch and a dead one too!"

Black found the entire situation funny; bitches was really out here on some grimy shit with niggas. The joke was now over; he was now curious as to why she thought it was cool to gamble with her life.

"One of you bitches better tell me what's up, or I'm killing both of y'all!"

Wasting no time, the pregnant bitch started singing like a bird.

"We are close to getting evicted, we were desperate. I am so sorry!" she explained while shaking in fear and holding her stomach.

Black shook his head in disbelief before placing his gun back on his hip. Something about the pregnant woman softened him, but this bitch Sparkle made him want to fuck her up. He looked back and forth between both women. Unknowingly, that baby in that woman's stomach had saved both of their lives. Reaching into his pocket, he pulled out a stack of hundred-dollar bills, peeling off twenty bills, he threw it at the her.

"Bitch if you needed some money, all you had to do was ask," he said before walking out.

❧ 18 ☙

Boss pulled up to Arica's house and blew the horn before throwing the car in park and grabbing his phone out of the cupholder. Placing a call to Ari, he let her know that he was outside, and she needed to hurry before the rain started. Checking the rearview mirror as well as the sides, he placed the iPhone on the charger before hitting the horn. Checking the flip phone inside his pocket, Boss prepared to return a call when Arianna came flying down the stairs. Smiling at sight of his only child, Boss's emotions quickly changed when Arica came storming out behind her. As teenage lovers, he was once crazy about the feisty Puerto Rican mami. She had given birth to Ari when they were only fifteen years old, but the two grew older and grew apart. Boss lost all respect for his baby mama five years ago when she decided to move to Atlanta to strip. Strictly by choice, he financially took care of Arica although they weren't together. Therefore, degrading herself was something she wanted to do.

"Hey baby!" Boss rolled down the window and greeted Ari as she tossed her overnight bag in the backseat.

"Hello father," she replied with an attitude, yanking the seatbelt across her and securing it.

Laughing aloud, Boss thought Ari's stubbornness was the funniest shit in the world. It had almost been a week, and she still was upset with him about pulling her out of dance class. Giving him short answers and the silent treatment, he tried his best to ignore her, but her act was starting to get a little old.

"Man yo ass better chill out. Fuck wrong with you?" He chuckled, looking over at her as she folded her arms across her chest.

"Nigga you know what the fuck wrong with her. You ain't letting her dance!" Arica stood in front of the car and shouted with her hands on her hips.

"Where yo laptop at?" Boss turned to Ari and asked, completely ignoring his baby mother.

"I forgot it. It's at the door though. I'll go get it," she mumbled, reaching for the door handle, but he stopped her.

"Nah, I got it," he told her, jumping out and walking past Arica like she was invisible.

Walking up her stairs, Boss opened Arica's front door in search of his daughter's bookbag. Spotting it on the couch, he headed over to where it was and snatched it up before turning around and heading back out.

"Boss, don't be walking in my shit like it's yours!" Arica blocked the doorway and yelled.

"Man move," he looked her in the eyes and sternly stated, causing her to move immediately.

"How the fuck are we supposed to co-parent and you won't even talk to me?"

Boss kept his eyes forward on the way to his car. He hadn't said more than two words to Arica since finding out she had put Ari in that dance class behind his back. She knew more than anybody how he felt about his daughter being on a dance team, and she still did it anyway. Boss knew a conversation with Arica wouldn't end well, therefore, he tried his best to stay clear of her. If it wasn't for Ari's love for her mother, he would have ended her life a long time ago.

"I swear to God Boss, you act like...."

"Listen bitch," he turned around and barked.

"The only reason you alive is because of her," he paused, pointing to his Black Maserati at Ari whose face was buried in her phone.

"You a goofass bitch and no matter how much I try to respect you, you fucks it up every time," he growled, stepping in closer.

"Darrius, I – I am a good mother and—"

"Mannnnnn, shut the fuck up." He laughed, turning to walk away but quickly doubling back.

"What's Ari's favorite movie? What's her favorite food? Better yet, what soaps is she allergic to?' he stood in front of her and calmly asked, looking her dead in the eyes.

"Exactly." He smirked, after a few seconds of silence.

Jumping in the car, Boss peeled off and headed to Pappadeaux's, Ari's favorite restaurant. For the past three years, every Tuesday, him and his baby girl went on a date. Movies, bowling and dinner, just to name a few, were some of things they engaged in. As a busy man, Boss wanted Arianna to know that no matter what, he always had time for her and that nothing and no one came before her.

"Ari, wake up," he shook her and said after finding a park and killing the engine.

"Where are we Daddy?" she rubbed her eyes and quizzed.

"We at yo spot. Get out," he told her before the two headed inside and grabbed a table.

Picking up a menu out of habit, Boss knew exactly what he wanted and although Ari did too, she looked over one as well. After placing their orders and buttering himself a slice of bread, Boss addressed his daughter.

"How was school today?"

"It was cool," she glanced up from her phone and replied.

"Cool, huh?" he repeated, while the waitress placed the drinks in front of them.

"Yup," she mumbled, causing him to chuckle lightly.

"Arianna, how long you gon be fake mad at me about this dancing shit?" Boss asked, taking a sip from the Pepsi.

"Forever Daddy. You don't understand. I love dancing. I love being a Blessing's Angel," she popped her head up and replied, practically with tears in her eyes.

"You love being a what?" he questioned, trying not to allow the tears to soften him up.

"I love being on Blessing's team. She teaches us so much Daddy. She makes dancing fun, and on top of all that, she's soooo raw Daddy," Ari beamed from across the table.

"Raw, huh?" Boss repeated.

"Yeahhhhhh..... She showed us some videos of her when she was in college. She was killing it, and she still got it. I didn't think old people could dance like that."

Laughing aloud, Boss listened as Ari rambled on and on about her dance teacher. Most of things she said didn't surprise him, especially since he had already done his research. Boss knew everything about Blessing, from her ex-husband down to her full social security number. Intrigued from the first encounter, Boss had to make sure everything checked out before diving in. He had never encountered a woman like her, and if she planned on being in him and his daughter's life, he needed to know what was really to her.

"Oh word, so she brings everyone in the class milkshakes at the end of the week?"

"Yup. Coach B loves milkshakes," Ari confirmed, stuffing a fried shrimp in her mouth.

"Cool. Cool. What's her favorite kind?" Boss tossed his napkin on the plate and quizzed.

"Daddy. You been asking *a lot* of questions about Coach B. Why is that?" Ari twisted her head to side and asked.

"Man, mind yo business. I ain't asking a lot of questions. Come on, let's go. You gotta get ready for school tomorrow," Boss said, dismissing her and tossing a hundred-dollar bill on the table.

The entire ride back to the estate, Boss couldn't get his mind off of the things Ari said about Blessing. Outside of being attractive, he was pleased to learn that she was well-rounded as well. Thankful for her strip-free background, which he was afraid of most, he wanted to get to know her better, and he knew exactly how.

$$\text{\#} \quad 19 \quad \text{\#}$$

"You alright baby? You need anything before I head to church?" Martha asked as Mel snuggled under multiple blankets, trying to keep warm.

"No, I'm fine Momma."

Mel was coming down with a serious cold, and she wanted nothing more than to be at home in her own bed, but she had been occupying her mother's couch since her fight with Corey. He had been blowing her phone up non-stop and the fact that his mother stayed next door to her mother wasn't helping.

"You know you have to go home and face that man soon or later. Whose name is that place in anyway?"

"Mine," she replied dryly, not really in the mood to talk about the situation.

"Well, he should be the one sleeping on his mother's couch!" Martha snapped as she gathered her things and prepared to finally walk out the door.

Melody didn't bother responding, instead she grabbed her phone and strolled through Facebook. Trying hard to stay away from both Corey and Kim's pages, she still ended up reading a status that Corey had uploaded just minutes ago.

"I'm just trying to fix what I fucked up!"

Rolling her eyes up in her head, Mel closed the app and tossed her phone on the coffee table. She felt nothing and had no sympathy for Corey. He had officially lost her.

"Ok I'm gone, here's some tea and medicine. Get yourself together, so you can go get your house in order."

"Dang Ma. If you want me out, say that," Mel joked as she forced herself to sit up and sip the hot tea.

"Don't play with me little girl. I'm going straight to work after service, so I'll see you in the morning. I love you," she kissed her daughter's forehead before walking out the door.

Mel had to get it together; not only for herself, but for her students. She promised that they would start decorating the classroom for Halloween, so calling off the next day wasn't an option. She had gone out and spent over two-hundred dollars of her own money on everything from giant spiders to electronic witches that would fly back and forth across the classroom. Mel was just as excited as the kids were; she always loved Halloween.

Melody hated being sick because she felt so helpless; all she could do was curl back up in her spot and watch reruns of Martin. The medicine kicked in and caused her to doze off, but the vibrating of her phone instantly disturbed the sleep that she was finally getting. Reaching over to grab the phone, she slid the bar over and answered a facetime call from Black. The first thing she did was turned her camera off, there was no way he was seeing her looking like shit.

"Hey you," Mel spoke while sniffling, trying to stop her nose from running.

"What's up baby? Why you sound like a nigga, and why your camera off?"

Mel couldn't help but laugh at his little joke. She was losing her voice due to the cold she was coming down with.

"Because I'm a little under the weather and ugly," she replied before sneezing multiple times.

"You got soup and shit?"

Mel shook her head while turning on the camera, he never seemed to amaze her with his choice of words. She was slowly starting to love everything about that man, even his hood slang.

"I have some tea and Dayquil, that's it."

"Drop your location, I'm gone slide on you."

As bad as she wanted to see him, there was no way she was going to let him see her sick. She felt like shit, so she knew she looked like shit.

"I appreciate that, but I'm actually staying at my mom's house for a minute."

"Aw ok, you can't have company?" he joked.

"Yes, I can," Mel retorted, laughing at his remark that made her feel like it was back in day when she really couldn't have company.

Mel thought back on how she and Corey used to sneak in one another's house when they first started dating. Not wanting to reminisce on the past, she quickly pushed the thoughts to the far back of her mind and decided to let Black come over. Her mother wouldn't be back until tomorrow anyway, so what the hell?

"Bet, I'll grab something to eat and get you some shit from Walgreens because I'on like this Barry White shit you keep doing with your voice," Black laughed at his own words.

"I'm gone kick yo ass when you get here, you been heavy on the jokes since we got on the phone."

"You think you can whoop me?"

"I got hands Black, you lucky I'm sick," Mel warned him, finally flipping the covers back.

She had no clue where she got the strength to move from, but there was no way she was going to be looking like shit in Black's presence.

"Righttttt, I hear you Mayweather. Text the address."

"Whatever, I'm sending it now."

She did as she said and sent the address to his phone, but for some reason even at twenty-four years old, she was nervous about having male company in her mother's house. After gathering all of the tissue pieces she had scattered all over the couch, she sprayed everything down with Lysol. The last thing she wanted to do was pass her cold off to him. Pulling her hair into high ponytail, she made her way to the bathroom to take a quick shower. After letting the hot water massage her body, she washed herself and stepped out. Dressing down in full body onesie, she sprayed herself with a couple squirts of Beautiful Day body mist before returning to the couch. As soon as she got comfortable under the covers, Black was texting saying he was outside.

Mel got up and walked to the door, praying Corey wasn't sitting on his mother's porch. She peeked her head out and saw that the coast was clear as Black got out of his car. The sight of him made her pussy wet, he was perfect. He was effortlessly fly, rocking a simple grey jogging suit with the word "Affiliated" written across the chest in black. It looked he had gone out and brought the whole store back. Mel looked at all the bags with a confused look as he stepped inside. She noticed the first thing he did was remove his shoes, and that said a lot to her about his upbringing. Her grandmother and mother didn't play about wearing outside shoes in the house.

"How you know my momma was gone kill you if you stepped on her carpet with those shoes on?" Mel joked, walking over to the couch as he followed behind her.

"Shid because my OG the same way," he replied, taking a seat on the other end of the couch from where her pillows were. Mel grabbed the bags and began removing the items; he literally had everything from orange juice to Vick's Vapor Rub.

"You weren't playing, you got everything. I appreciate this, I'm gone have to cook you dinner or something one day."

"You ain't about to kill me," he replied, leaning back on the couch as Mel's mouth dropped.

"Boy what? I can really cook!"

"Bro, tacos and chicken alfredo don't count."

"Ouuuu, you tried it," Mel shot back while pointing her index finger at him.

They both shared a laugh before tuning in to a movie Mel heard everyone talking about on Facebook. They couldn't enjoy the movie due to Melody's phone ringing back to back. She knew it was Corey because he had been calling and texting nonstop since that morning. Ignoring the call and shutting the phone completely off, Mel decided to join Black at the other end of the couch. Laying on his chest gave her a sense of comfort. Between the meds kicking in and Black rubbing her head, she unknowingly drifted off to sleep, and he did the same.

Black's phone vibrated under her, waking her up while he didn't budge. She could tell he was a deep sleeper. Grabbing her phone and powering it back on, time had flown past and it was a little after one in morning. Text messages from Corey flooded her screen. He had officially lost his damn mind sending threats about if she didn't call or text him back, and Mel was disgusted. When Black's phone rang for a second time, her mind instantly told her it was a female, and she was lowkey jealous. She tapped him to wake him up with no luck, so she shook him.

"Your phone is ringing. Might be an emergency," Mel said with a slight attitude.

Knowing she had no room to even be mad, she still didn't like the thought of another female having his attention. He opened his eyes and pulled his phone from his pocket as it rang for a third time. He looked at the screen and ignored the call, confirming the conclusion Mel had already jumped to.

"It's late, I'm gone head out and let you get some rest for work," he said, standing to his feet walking over to the door to put his shoes on.

Mel tried her best not to show her attitude, but she couldn't stop thinking about him leaving and going to lay up with the next.

"Ok, see you," she replied dryly.

Black turned and looked at her. "What's wrong?"

"Nothing."

"So, why yo face and shit all screwed up? Talk to me."

His tone was so calm, yet so demanding. Mel knew she had no room to mad at him for anything being that he wasn't her man, and that she had her own thing going on with Corey. Rolling her eyes into her head, she was honest with him.

"I got myself in my feelings thinking that was a female calling your phone."

"It was, but that shit shouldn't make you mad. I'm here ain't I?"

"Yes, but."

"But what Mel?"

"Is she your girlfriend?"

Maybe it was too late because she was starting to form feelings for Black, but she was never in the business of breaking up happy or unhappy homes. She knew firsthand how it felt to get cheated on, and she didn't want to put that type of hurt on the next woman.

"Nah, I don't have a girlfriend, a wife, or none of that shit," he confirmed.

"So, what am I?"

Mel wanted to kick herself in the ass when she let those words escape her mouth. She didn't know if she was prepared for him to even answer that.

"Right now, you're my homie, and I fuck with you. You clearly got shit going on that you got to handle," he replied, looking down at her ringing phone as Corey's name once again flashed across her screen.

Though his words were true, it wasn't what she wanted to hear. At that moment, she knew she wanted more of Black and less of Corey. Black showed qualities of a man, from the way he talked to the actions that followed.

"That's cool."

"Ball is in your court baby."

Mel nodded her head and walked him out to the porch. He pulled her in and wrapped his arms around her body. She closed her eyes and took it all in; she didn't want to let him go. Finally opening her eyes, she quickly jumped back. For one, Black's dick was poking her in the stomach and secondly, she had locked eyes with Corey's mother.

"Call me when you make it to wherever you going," Mel said. taking a step back. She couldn't believe her luck.

"Home Mel, I'm going home."

"Ok," she replied as he walked to his car.

Ms. Vera stood on her porch in her nurse scrubs, smiling as she watched Black leave. Mel had forgotten she got off work from the hospital around that time.

"He's handsome," she said, sending a nervous feeling through Mel's body.

Ms. Vera had always been real with Mel, and believe it or not, she was the first to tell her to move on from her son. She always said, "I'm a woman before anything."

"He's just a friend," Mel started to explain.

"Aht, you are a grown woman and don't have explain anything to me. Goodnight, baby."

"Goodnight Ms. Vera."

❧ 20 ❧

"Did both of the parties read this?" Judge Rhodes asked, glancing up from the documents in her hands.

"Yes," both Blessing and Kevin answered in unison.

"Do both parties understand and did you sign it willingly and voluntarily?"

"Yes," Blessing spoke up first, followed by a dry response from Kevin.

"This contains a permanent waiver of alimony. Do you understand that it would be very difficult, if not impossible, for either of you to seek alimony from the other in the future?"

"Yes, Your Honor!" she eagerly stated again, this time glancing over at her lawyer who wore the same smile on her face.

"Then I will find the marriage is irretrievably broken and grant you a divorce."

Standing to her feet, Blessing wanted to hug the Judge and her lawyer. She hadn't been that happy in a long time. After being separated for a year, she was beginning to feel like it would never end. On top of Kevin holding things off with hopes she'd change her mind, he was starting to give her stalker vibes. However, as of lately, he'd been quiet. Knocking the wrinkles of out of Dolce and Gabbana blouse,

Blessing picked up her Louie Vuitton briefcase and exited the court-room doors. Meeting her lawyer in the hallway, the two black women embraced with a hug before walking towards the elevators.

"Thank you, Mrs. Dowdy. I can't believe it's finally over," Blessing beamed, hitting the arrow down button.

"Finally over, and I couldn't be happier. You deserve this independence and so much more," Attorney Dowdy replied, displaying a perfect set of teeth.

"I couldn't have done this without you."

"Thank you for taking a chance with me as well as my firm. I gotta go talk to my paralegal, but I'll give you a call later."

Hugging one last time, the two departed ways, sending Blessing to the lobby where she walked to the parking garage. She searched for her keys inside her briefcase and grabbed them along with her phone then proceeded forward. Letting out a long sigh, Blessing rolled her eyes to the back of her head when she noticed a man standing by her car. Flicking the blade attached to her keychain, she was prepared to slice Kevin up, if need be.

"You got five seconds to get the fuck away from me and my car," Blessing threatened, hitting the locks and skating around him.

"So you really doing this, huh?" Kevin stood still and questioned, his eyes following her every move.

"Mr. McCall, I am officially a single woman. We have absolutely nothing to talk about and if you don't leave me alone, I will file a restraining order," she calmly replied, opening the door and getting inside.

Bringing the engine to life, she rolled down the window before hitting the horn twice. Kevin had less than thirty seconds to move or he'd be underneath those BMW tires. Still standing in the same spot, Blessing shook her head before shifting gears. Just as she let off the brakes, Kevin quickly jumped out the way.

"You gone regret this bitch!" he screamed, smashing the top of her car with a closed fist just as she sped away.

Aggravated, but refusing to allow Kevin to ruin her day, Blessing placed the Gucci shades over her brown eyes and cruised the sunny downtown streets. Turning up the sounds of Cardi B and Megan Thee

Stallion, *WAP*, she rapped along like she was a member of their entourage. Not missing a lyric, Blessing twerked in her seat just as her phone chimed with a text message.

Arianna Bryant: Hey Coach B. I miss you. Wanna meet up for lunch?

Eyeing the text message suspiciously, Blessing's fingers hesitantly started moving on the keyboard as she replied back. She had a close relationship with all of her Angels and since the night her father pulled her out of class, her and Ari had been texting back and forth religiously.

Blessing: Sure honey, time and place!

After learning that Ari was in the area, she agreed to meet up with her and whom she assumed was her mother. Receiving the location to her phone, Blessing plugged it into her GPS and headed that way. In less than ten minutes, Blessing pulled inside the parking lot of JoJo's Milkshake Bar and killed the engine. She had heard about the restaurant but never made time to check it out. Grabbing her wallet and phone, Blessing shot Ari a text letting her know she arrived before jumping out and making her way inside.

"Coach B! We over here!" Ari sprung from a table in the back and screamed over the loud music and conversations.

Smiling at the sight of her Angel, Blessing slowly strutted through the establishment, admiring the photos and memorabilia on the walls. Finally making her way to the booth, she instantly regretted accepting the invitation when she noticed her father occupying the other side of the bench.

"Why you ain't tell me yo Daddy was here with you," Blessing whispered, pulling Ari in for a hug.

"Cuz you wouldn't have come. I'm sorry Coach B, but he pays good in allowance," Ari mumbled back, causing Blessing to laugh at her honesty.

Pulling away from their embrace, Blessing's eyes landed on Boss, who looked at her like she was his favorite meal on a plate. She couldn't deny the attraction, especially when a blind woman could see how fine Boss was. Judging from eyesight, he stood about six-four, with a muscular build, a clean bald head made for licking, and a long full beard with a string or two of grays hiding within. He was the type of nigga that made your eyes water, he was just that fine.

"What up Coach B," he spoke with a smirk, snapping her out of the wet dream she was falling into.

"Mr. Bryant." She nodded her head before sliding in the booth next to Ari.

"Call me Boss," he suggested with a smile that almost made her cum.

"Ok, Mr. Bryant." She grinned, causing both him and Arianna to chuckle.

An awkward silence captivated the table once they were done, sending everyone's eyes in the other's direction. The last thing Blessing wanted to feel was uncomfortable and although she was in an uncomfortable situation, she still didn't feel out of place. As intimidating as Boss was, she wasn't afraid of him. In fact, it was actually the opposite, she felt secure. Grabbing the menu with hopes of erasing those thoughts out of her head, the waitress arrived with three milkshakes on the tray.

"A strawberry shortcake for you Princess. We have a mint chocolate float for you Sir, annnddddd an Oreo with extra extra chocolate fudge for you Queen." She placed the final glass in front of Blessing and smiled.

Returning the gesture, she waited until she was gone before addressing the table.

"You a slick nigga," she pointed at Boss and stated before turning to Ari.

"And I'mma beat yo ass," she threatened, pulling Arianna into a headlock.

"He made me! He made me snitch!" she shouted, waving her arms wildly in the air.

Feeling like she had enough, Blessing released her before fixing the curly ponytail on top of her head.

"So what else you know about me?" she locked eyes with Boss and asked in a serious tone.

"Enough to make me wanna know more," he replied with challenging eyes, his words sending chills down her spine.

Thoroughly impressed by the physical and mental, but as bad as Blessing wanted to, she just couldn't see herself taking Boss seriously. That same blind woman who could see how fine he was, could also see that the nigga had hoes. On top of being divorced for only an hour, she didn't want the problems that came with him. She tried to think of ways to let him down nicely in her head, and just as Blessing thought of a way, Ari opened her mouth and spoke, throwing a curve ball in her game.

"Coach B. One date. Just one date, and he promised to let me back on the team. Pleaaasssseeeee!" Ari begged, poking out her bottom lip.

Blessing's eyes traveled from her over to Boss who held both hands in the air and shrugged.

"You a dirty nigga," she picked her straw up and stated, tossing it at him from across the table.

"Why you using this baby as bait?" she continued, twisting her head to the side before agreeing to what she thought was right.

"One date! And she's back on the team whether you like the outcome or not," Blessing specified, pointing her long red stiletto nails in his direction.

"All I need is one date," he arrogantly replied, sitting up straight and staring deep into her eyes.

❧ 21 ❧

"**A**rianna hand me the tape please," Melody called out from the top of the chair she was standing on, hanging up a fake spider. Like she promised, her class worked a half day and spent the other half decorating their class. Turns out Ms. Caston lucked up on the perfect group of kids; her class was full of smart, lit students that she adored.

"Here you go Ms. Caston."

"Ok, you all can start getting your things together before the bell rings, and I'll finish up here. Remember to bring a family size snack to the party next Friday and let me know if you need money."

Her class talked amongst each other as they gathered their things before the bell rang. Like she promised, Mel stayed behind and finished hanging the decorations. She stood in the middle of her class and admired all of their hard work before gathering her things to head out. Grabbing her phone, she was relieved to see that Corey hadn't called nor texted her since yesterday. Maybe, he had finally gotten the picture.

Mel was starting to feel a little better, and she was having a great day. She decided to stop by her house and grab a few more things since she knew today was Corey's late day at work. Pulling into her parking garage, she blew out some air when she realized he wasn't at work. She wanted to leave, but she didn't drive all the way to the house for nothing, so she climbed out and headed inside.

"Hey Mel!"

"Hey there Joseph, how are you?"

"I'm alright, good to see you," Joseph the doorman small talked as she made her way to the elevator.

"Same, see you later," she replied, stepping on as the doors slid open.

Mel gave herself a pep talk before inserting her key and walking in. She could hear things being tossed around, and there were bags and boxes all over the living room. She dropped her keys in her purse and sat it on the couch before walking to the bedroom. The sight of Corey snatching shit out of the closet like a crazy person had her puzzled. He looked up and locked eyes with her, and it was like she was staring into the eyes of the devil himself.

"Aw look, the hoe finally made her way home."

Taken back by his words, Mel looked around to see who the fuck he was talking to. Corey had never, in all of her years of knowing him, called her out of her name. He damn sure wasn't about to start now.

"Who the fuck you calling a hoe? If anybody is a hoe, it's your lying, cheating, sorry ass!" Mel snapped, pointing both her index and middle fingers at him.

She was pissed off and at that point ready to fight; he had her fucked up.

"Look at the muthafuckin kettle calling the pot black, fuck outta here. You a hoe, got niggas calling my phone, clowning me about some nigga creeping out your momma crib!"

"So what, I had a little company. At least I haven't been fucking him for years behind your back," Mel snapped, folding her arms across her chest.

If looks could kill, she would've been deceased. She was speaking his language and he couldn't take it.

"Fuck you Mel, don't come looking for me when that nigga breaks your heart. You ain't never gotta worry about me again."

"Just like a nigga to fuck up and play the victim. You wanna talk that love shit, huh? Let's talk about it Corey. Remember I loved you when you embarrassed me with the same bitch for years my nigga! For years!" Mel yelled while clapping her hands, stating facts.

"Mannn."

"Shut the fuck up! I loved you when you gave a bitch one up on me, and you thought I didn't know about the abortion? Nigga, you been playing in my face and my dumb ass been letting you, so I guess we even!"

"It's cool, I'm gone. Don't let me catch you with that bitch ass nigga."

"Please Corey, worry about you and your bitch. I'm no longer your concern."

"Yeah aight."

The entire time he moved his stuff out, Mel was a little closer to a peace of mind. She was glad he decided to leave on his own because she didn't want to just put him out. Though things were officially over between her and Corey, she didn't wish any bad on him. She sipped a glass of wine as he took the last of his things and tossed the keys on the table, walking out of the door for the last time.

When reality finally set in, Mel sat in the middle of the floor and cried like a baby. She never in a million years thought she would see the day, her and Corey go their separate ways. She would be lying if she said it didn't hurt her to see him walk away for good, but it had to happen. She was losing herself trying to love him. Downing her fifth glass of wine, she was tipsy and needed someone to tell her she was ok. The first person she called was Blessing when she didn't get an answer, she shot Black a message.

Mel: I'm missing you Black.

Black: 4100 Drury Lane.

She sat there contemplating on whether or not she was going to meet him. He had never invited her to his house, so she felt a little special. Pulling herself off the couch, she headed to her closet and found the sexist shit she could put together. Opting on a black leather trench coat she got off Fashion Nova, she pulled a sexy red lace lingerie set out. She topped her look off with a pair of red bottom stiletto pumps. She was freshly single and had a month's worth of cum backed up in her. She honestly didn't know what she was looking for in him, but he was doing a great job deterring her from Corey.

Mel: I'm on my way.

Once she showered and got dressed, she completed her look with a red matte lipstick. Her heels clicked against the marble floor in the lobby of her building, echoing throughout the room.

"Wow Mel, you look stunning," Joseph complimented her as she made her way out.

"Thanks."

She walked to her car and hopped inside; it was like she was craving Black though she never had him. Forgetting how cold it got in the windy city that time of year, Mel had to put a little pep in her step. The last thing she wanted to do was get sick all over again. Immediately turning the heat and seat warmers on in her car, she pulled out and headed to Black's house. She listened to slow cuts the entire ride and all she could think about was Black touching every part of her body, she had it bad. Everything between the two was moving at a rapid pace, and she was fine with that. Mel had wasted enough years being unhappy and if Black was willing to step up and treat her right, she was all for it.

After driving twenty minutes, she was finally pulling into the parking lot of the Renaissance Hotel. She didn't know how to feel; here she was dressed in practically nothing because she thought she would be in the comfort of his home. She was ready to turn around and drive right back to her house until Black facetimed her phone.

"Where you at?" he asked, looking directly at her.

"I'm in the parking lot," she replied, dryly pulling into a park.

"Ok, come straight to the top floor."

"Alright."

She really wished she had worn something different; there she was looking like a hoe getting ready to walk into those people establishment. She quickly walked into the building, and it was like all eyes were on her as she moved about the lobby trying to find the elevator. Older wealthy looking men undressed her with their eyes while their snobby wives sent dirty stares in her direction. The closer she got to the top floor, the more the regret sat in. Stepping off on the very top floor, she was taken away by the décor. She had to admit it was beautiful, but it still wasn't what she was expecting.

She walked up to the only set of doors on the floor besides the elevator doors and knocked lightly. In the matter of seconds, Black came to the door shirtless with a huge diamond chain that read "Affiliated" and a blunt hanging from his mouth.

"What's up baby?" he asked, allowing her to step inside.

"Nothing much."

It was crazy to her how well Black was learning her attitude because he instantly knew something was bothering her.

"You good?"

"Yeah, I'm ok. I just thought I was meeting you at your house, I wasn't expecting a hotel."

Mel didn't want to sound like a brat or anything, but she had to tell him how she felt.

"I had a business meeting not too far from here and decided to grab a room instead of driving to my house. When you texted me, I thought nothing of it, I just dropped the location," he explained while Mel pretended to listen.

"It's cool."

There was an awkward silence between the two. Black stared at her as he inhaled a huge cloud of smoke, she was secretly starting to love the smell of weed.

"You looking sexy as fuck, Ms. Caston, you dressed it up for me?" Black asked from his seat on the couch with his eyes so low they looked closed.

Mel tried her best to push her disappointment to the back of her mind, but that it was bugging her. She wasn't just some bitch he could bring to a hotel and fuck, and she needed him to understand that before they moved any further. Not being one to control her facial expressions and her tongue at times, she attempted to speak on it for a second time.

"Yeah, I did, but..."

"Let's slide."

Not giving her a chance to finish her sentence, Black stood up and threw his shirt over his head and started grabbing his belongings as

Mel stood there confused, trying to determine if she should finish speaking.

"I'm sorry, I didn't mean to kill the mood," she apologized as he double checked to make sure he had everything and walked to the door.

Mel felt like shit; she knew she had probably just turned him completely off and those weren't her intentions. Black allowed her to step on the elevator first before following as she glanced at him out the corner of her eye. Stepping off the elevator, they both walked through the lobby in silence. Melody's feelings were hurt as he walked her to her car, and the cold air that she felt on her way in was nonexistent as she stood there staring at Black.

"I guess this is it, huh?" Mel asked, breaking eye contact looking off at nothing.

"It? You can't get rid of me that easy, baby. Let's drop your car off to your OG house so you can get in with me."

Mel couldn't hide the smile that spread across her face if she wanted to. Before she knew it, she had pulled him in and kissed his lips. That same electricity that always filled her body shot straight to her pussy this time.

"Let's go," she said in between kissing his lips.

Mel took the ride to her mother's house with Black in tow. When she pulled up and saw a group of guys in front of Corey's mother's house, she cursed herself because she knew they were there for him. Running into Corey was the last thing to cross her mind, yet there he was with his eyes glued to her car. Out of respect, she put her car back in drive and attempted to pull off, but she looked closer and noticed an unknown female rubbing his shoulder. At that moment she no longer gave a fuck, she threw it right back in park. She realized he was definitely for the streets and tonight, she was for Black.

She grabbed her purse and exited the car, demanding everyone's attention.

"Hey Mel," A few of the guys spoke as she waved and made her way to Black's car.

"That Maserati so cold!" she heard one of Corey's friends admire Black's car.

"Straight hoe shit," she heard Corey say loud enough for her to hear.

Black did as he always did and opened the door for her. Deciding to ignore Corey's comment, she climbed inside before setting the alarm on her car. Sinking down into the plush leather, she sat back and enjoyed the ride. Black reached over and grabbed her hand while weaving in and out of traffic. Vibing to the music and inhaling the smoke from his weed had her body relaxed, everything was perfect. She had unknowingly closed her eyes and caught a contact; it wasn't until she felt the car slowing down, she opened her eyes.

"You live here?" Mel blurted out at the sight of the mansion that stood behind the huge gate that read "Bryant."

Black looked over at her and chuckled before responding.

"Yeah baby. Black plus one," he said into an intercom before the gate opened, allowing them access.

It was not only one, but three mansions she noticed upon entry, and Mel couldn't believe her eyes.

"Plus one? You have to announce your company?"

"Yeah, can't just give anybody access to where you lay your head."

"Glad I'm not just anybody."

"You definitely not," he assured her before pulling in front of the mansion to her right.

Mel stepped out and couldn't believe the size of the houses. The closest she had ever been to a house this size was when she used to watch MTV Cribs back in the day. She quickly followed Black up the stairs as she was anxious to see the inside. She stepped through the door, and her mouth immediately hit the floor. The house had to be built for a giant. The ceilings were so high she was sure he had to hire people to come out and change his lightbulbs.

"Get comfortable, ain't shit off limits to you. Mi casa es su casa," he replied, removing his shoes.

"I appreciate that," she replied, stepping out her heels.

"Nah, leave those on," he ordered, referring to her stilettos.

She gave him a sexy smirk before replying, "I wouldn't dare walk through your house with my shoes on Mr. Bryant."

Black looked back over his shoulder just as she dropped her coat, revealing the lingerie she was wearing.

"That mean I gotta fuck you where you stand then Ms. Caston."

Mel had never been so turned on in her life, she was ready to let him fuck her anyway he liked.

"Well why you still standing there?"

"Because I want to make sure you understand my terms and conditions," he shot back, walking toward her.

"And what's that?"

"I'm a selfish ass nigga. When I touch that pussy, it becomes mine."

"Yours, huh?"

"Mine," he replied sternly, sending a chill down her spine. Something told her he meant every word he said, and she was all for it

❄ 22 ❄

Blessing sprayed the Chanel No. 5 perfume in the air and closed her eyes before stepping into it. Dressed in a black painted on bodysuit from Fashion Nova, she spiced up the plain look with a gold Chanel rope chain belt and a pair of YSL heels with the large bag to match. With a slick chic ponytail to the back, Blessing rocked a pair of diamond gold hoops with the identical chain and bracelet. Twirling in the full-length mirror, she was pleased with her look and officially ready for her date. After agreeing with Boss, Blessing thought of all the reasons in the world to cancel, but the thought of Ari being back on the team changed her mind. In the small amount of time they'd spent together, the two had formed a tight bond. Ari was so full of life, outspoken, and vibrant; the exact same way Blessing was at her age. On top of all that, the love they shared for dance was like no other.

Making sure she had everything she needed, Blessing put on two coats of clear Fenty lip gloss just as her phone chimed. Reading over a text message from Boss, she let him know she was on her way out after cutting off all the lights. She had no idea what the plans for the night consisted of especially since every time she asked him, he told her to chill and let him do his thing. After their date over milkshakes,

Blessing and Boss exchanged numbers and talked every single day since then. Pleasantly surprised by his conversation, she was most definitely impressed by his business endeavors and the bond he had with his daughter. Being raised by a single father herself, Blessing was able to relate to the stories he told.

"What's up beautiful," Boss spoke while he stood outside the car with the passenger's door open. Dressed in all black as well, she loved how he unintentionally matched her fly.

"Hey Mr. Bryant." She smiled, shocked by the sweet gesture and his gentleman ways.

Stepping inside the white Bentley, Boss waited until she was situated before he closed the door shut. Admiring the custom interior and foreign looking buttons, Blessing tried her best not to sound basic, but she couldn't help it.

"This a nice ass car," she admired aloud the second he joined her inside.

"It's aight. What color you want yours?" Boss looked over at her and asked with a straight face.

"Boy, stop playing." She smacked her lips and giggled.

"I'm serious than a muthafucker baby." He smirked before pulling off and into the flow of traffic.

Curious as to where they were headed, Blessing wanted to pry more but instead decided to sit back and enjoy the ride. The temperatures were in the low sixties, and the little breeze coming through the cracked window set the mood even more. Occasionally glancing over at Boss who whipped the wheel, Blessing couldn't help but be turned on by his presence alone. Unsure if it was the beard or the gold Rolex glistening on his arm, either or, she was dangerously attracted to that man.

"O'Hare? Where the hell we going?" Blessing sat up and asked the moment she noticed Boss turning into a private lot owned by the airport.

"On our date. What you mean where we going?" he replied, killing the engine and hitting the locks.

"I mean... yeah I know that, but why we here?"

"We here cuz this part of the date now come on, I hate being late," Boss locked eyes with her and stated, causing her to move instantly.

Grabbing her bag and phone, Blessing waited for Boss as he made his way to her side. Opening the door for her, she gladly grabbed his hand as he helped her exit the ride. Adjusting the straps on her shoulder, she walked hand-in-hand with Boss towards a small plane with the word "Bryant" written across in bold black letters.

"You gotta be shitting me. Where the fuck we going?" she pulled him in closer to her and mumbled.

"Baby, chill. Let me do my shit." Boss looked at her and smiled before helping her onto the private plane.

Just like with the car, Blessing was blown away by the interior of the aircraft. She had never been on one, and the only time she seen them was on celebrities' Instagram pages. She knew Arianna's family was on the wealthy side, but she had no idea they had Kardashian money. Taking a seat in the leather chair assigned to her, Blessing watched as Boss instructed the crew before finally taking his place next to her.

"We'll be there in bout an hour. You good? You hungry? Want a drink?"

"I'm good on the food, but I'll take a bottle of water."

After flagging down a crew member, Boss ordered himself a double shot of Henny along with her bottle of water. Taking off ten minutes later, the lights were dimmed and the two watched a movie as they cruised the skies to an unknown destination. Changing her mind and ordering a shot of cognac after all, Blessing was enjoying herself and their date hadn't even begun. Feeling themselves descend from the air, Blessing felt butterflies forming in her stomach. It was definitely a first for her. She wouldn't have thought in a million years that she'd experience a first date such as that one.

Taking his hand, Boss lead them off the plane and into the hot muggy Las Vegas air. Excitement replaced those butterflies as she thought about the night ahead of them. It was her first time in Nevada and although drinking and gambling wasn't her idea of a first date, she was still all for it.

"We finna go to the casino?" Blessing asked as they made their way to an awaiting Rolls Royce.

"Casino? Nah, I don't like losing money baby. We going to the fight."

"Fight? Wait, the Mayweather fight is tonight. It slipped my mind that fast," she excitedly said.

"I got tickets after finding out you love boxing and shit," he casually replied, driving out the airport and to MGM Casinos.

Blessing was stunned to the point of silence. Floyd Money Mayweather was her favorite boxer and the fact that Boss received that information and acted on it, earned him more brownie points than he knew. Holding and caressing her hand the entire ride, Blessing basked in the moment. He was definitely making it a date to remember. Only ten rows from the ring, she played her role well by not acting star struck. She maneuvered through the crowd on his arm, blending in like it was a regular event for them. Like a kid in a candy store, Blessing was in awe at all the legends amongst her. It was a once in a lifetime thing, and she had a boss nigga to thank for that. After watching seven rounds of Floyd kill, he knocked his opponent out early in the eighth, sending the crowd in an uproar. Lingering around and taking a few pictures, Boss introduced her to a few big shots before they retreated back to the car.

"You hungry? I can have the chef hook you up sum on the plane," Boss looked over at her and asked as they sat in traffic.

"Yeah, that's fine," she replied in a low tone.

"What's wrong? You ain't enjoy yourself?" he wondered.

"What? One of the best nights in my life. It's just that...." Blessing paused, looking down at her phone and then ahead out the window.

"It's just that, I don't want it to end. The thought of going back to Chicago makes me sad," she truthfully admitted.

"Sad? Then let's change yo climate cuz shouldn't shit be making you sad," Boss grabbed her hand and said.

"But as far as tonight, it ain't gotta end. I can get a penthouse, and we can fly out in the morning..... But that's yo call," he glanced over at her and explained.

Without having to think twice, Blessing knew exactly how she wanted to end her night. Getting stopped by the light, she looked over and locked eyes with him before licking her lips. It had been a little over a year since the last time she had sex and although it wasn't like her to fuck on the first night, Boss was getting both pussy and throat that night.

"Get the room, I'll google some shit and find a drive-thru," she ordered just as he bust a U in the middle of the street.

❄ 23 ❄

"How we let these niggas get us open like this?" Blessing asked Mel as they got ready to head out for their lunch date.

"It's the dick for me," Mel replied as they high fived one another and laughed like two old ladies.

Mel instantly replayed her night of passion in her head. Black had done some things to her that her body had never experienced. He took his time learning every inch of her body, and she was hooked for sure.

"Mannnnnn listen, it's *everything* for me. Boss is a different breed of man."

"Tell me about it! If I could hug their parents, I would. They snapped when they birthed those niggas."

It was like they had finally lucked up on the perfect men. It felt so good to see Blessing smile and be truly happy.

"Snapped!" Blessing agreed as they made their way out the door and down to the elevator.

"I swear, oh and we're taking your car bec..."

Mel stopped in mid-sentence when the elevator doors opened, and she locked eyes with Black as he stood disturbingly close to her neighbor, Cresha. The laugh the two were sharing stopped, and Black's smile quickly faded as he stared at Mel. Blessing had to literally grab her by the arm and pull her onto the elevator. She was speechless, but Cresha wasted no time greeting them.

"Hey y'all, this is my boyfriend, Black. Babe, these are my neighbors, Melody and Blessing. I was trying to get our lil mama on Blessing's dance team, but she's not holding auditions until January."

"Nice to meet you Black," Blessing replied while Mel remained silent and stuck.

Blessing wore a mug while looking over at her best friend. Mel was on the verge of tears; she felt so played. She asked him multiple times if he had a girlfriend, and he blatantly lied. She knew it was too good to be true. it's crazy he was just fucking her in every room of his house, now this. A part of her wanted to put his ass on blast, another part of her wanted to breakdown, but instead she played it cool. The usual five second ride down to the lobby seemed like it was an hour long. When the doors opened, Mel was the first to exit. She quickly walked to the car as Blessing tried to catch up.

"Unlock the door Blessing!" Mel yelled as she hit the alarm on the car, doing as her friend asked.

Her breathing was heavy, she looked out the window as her chest caved in and out. The sight of her nigga walking out the building with her neighbor was beyond her, and the fact that he left out the part about having a daughter spoke volumes to Mel.

"Friend, calm down, it's ok," Blessing said, finally hopping in the driver seat of her car.

"Like why me bro? I asked that nigga on several occasions did he have a girlfriend, and he lied!" Mel replied, clapping her hands.

Mel followed Blessing's eyes as she looked at Cresha and Black engaging in what looked like a heated argument as they hopped inside his car and pulled off. She no longer had an appetite; she wanted to climb in her bed and forget today happened.

"You have to see what's to it, friend, I'm sure he would've told you if he had a child."

"It's true because why the fuck wouldn't he say something. He stood there looking dumb as fuck in the face! I have no luck when it comes to these niggas," Mel replied, shaking her head as they pulled out of the parking lot.

The first thing she did was blocked Black's number. She didn't even want to hear what he had to say. Her only regret was that she gave herself to him on a sexual level, but that was her own fault.

"You do, friend, and I'm not taking his side when I say this, but maybe just maybe she over played her part in that elevator, and he didn't respond because he didn't want to cause any conflict."

"Fuck him, her, and that elevator, it's all good."

Mel reached over and turned the radio up because she didn't want to talk about the situation any further. Though she was in a really bad mood, she went out and had lunch like planned. Call her crazy, but though she had blocked his number she found herself checking her phone every few seconds to see if he had reached out.

"You blocked him, didn't you?" Blessing asked from across the table where she was sitting.

"I sure the fuck did."

"Yet, you've checked your phone at least ten times since we've been sitting here. Make it make sense, friend."

"I blocked him; I don't have time. There you go, I made sense of the situation."

"Don't get cute," Blessing replied, followed by the rolling of her eyes.

"I'm just saying. I could've stayed with Corey for this shit."

"A lie, you can't even compare him to Corey's ass."

"Hmph, could've fooled me."

The rest of their lunch date consisted of occasional laughs and Mel removing Black from the blocklist. After pondering on the situation, she realized that he owed her nothing, no explanation, no call or text. She had once again made a fucked-up decision, and it was no one's fault but her own. She was too old to be so naïve.

Blessing kept her occupied for the most part, but as soon as she stepped foot back in that elevator, she was pissed all over again.

"Go take you a nice bath and pour your wine, so we can watch our shows on facetime," Blessing said to Mel as they stepped off on their floor and parted ways.

"Ok, I'll call you in a lil bit."

Mel walked inside of her apartment and the very first thing she did was find Cresha's Facebook page. She needed answers for her own sanity because her mind wouldn't allow the situation to go away. After scrolling on her page for about fifteen minutes, she was slightly relieved when she found no ties to Black. She closed the app and tossed the phone on the table and headed straight to the shower. She stood under the hot water and the tears started to fall immediately. She wasn't crying over Black, but she felt like her life was spiraling out of control. She cried like a baby; her soul needed that cleanse. When she stepped out the shower, she felt so much better.

After filling the largest glass she could find with wine, she picked up her phone, curled up in her queen-sized bed, and grabbed the remote. After scrolling through the channels, she dialed Blessing's number only for her to respond with a text saying she would call her back. She was probably talking to that damn Bryant. She tossed the phone on what used to be Corey's side of the bed before starting her shows without Blessing. No sooner than she got in tune, her cell alerted her of a text. Quickly grabbing her phone with hopes of it being Black, she screwed up her face when she noticed it was Corey.

Corey: Mel.

Mel: Corey.

Corey: You letting that nigga take my place?

Mel: Ain't no nigga, I'm chilling.

Corey: Can I chill with you?

She rolled her eyes as she read his words, she didn't even bother responding. The phone started chiming back to back, and she knew it was Corey double texting, so she ignored it. Once the alerts stopped, she picked it back up. She sat straight up when she saw Black had messaged her.

Black: Hit my line Melody.

Mel: For what? You had nothing to say earlier, I'm good on you.

Black: Aight.

Mel hated how nonchalant he was, she had so much more to say. She wanted him to keep talking, but then again, she wanted him to leave her the fuck alone.

Mel: "Aight" huh? All I asked you for was the truth and you

couldn't give me that. You made me look real fucking stupid today, but it's all good. BTW what type of nigga lies about having a whole kid? My perception of you was so wrong...

Mel typed her message out and deleted every word before she could press send. As bad as she wanted to give him a piece of her mind, she left well enough alone.

❧ 24 ☙

"So Daddy, look right when Mayweather blocked that right hook, he caught buddy ass with a nasty body shot." Blessing sprung to her feet and demonstrated while her father and Aunt Vera looked and listened on.

"And what's the nigga name you said flew you all the way to Vegas for a date?" Walter asked for the fourth time during the conversation.

"Walt, shut the hell up and listen to the story. Blessing a grown ass woman and any man doing all that to make a good impression is worth a second, third, fourth and fifth date," Vera snapped, waving off her twin brother and focusing on Blessing.

"I like him baby. Matter fact, I like him and whoever that was Melody was creeping with the other night too. Just like I'm happy your divorce is final, I'm glad she waking up and seeing my son ain't shit either," she continued.

"Speaking of that nigga. Where he at? I guess he call himself mad at me for not telling him about Mel and Black but that shit ain't none of my business. I got my own love life to worry about," Blessing noted.

"He ain't been here. I'm guessing he with that other child, but I try to mind my business too," Vera replied.

"Vera, you ain't never tried to mind yo business a day in yo life," Walter blurted out, causing his daughter to laugh.

Blessing listened as the siblings argued back and forth. It seemed like the older her father and aunt got, the more they fought. Sometimes she wished that she had a brother or sister, but then she remembered how life was growing up with Corey and immediately redacted that thought. Grabbing her phone and Gucci bag, Blessing eased her way out before the two came to blows. Slipping out successfully, she ran down the stairs onto the front porch where she ran into Corey.

"Opp," he barked, making his way up the stairs as she stood posted at the top.

"Suck my dick Corey!" Blessing snapped, sticking up her middle finger while refusing to move out his way.

"Uncle Walt! Blessing down here cussing!" Corey yelled out seconds before Blessing heard footsteps marching down the stairs.

"I heard that nasty ass mouth," Walter voiced from behind her, followed by Vera who was close on his heels.

"She think she slick too. Trying to sneak out like we old and senile," her aunt fussed, causing everyone on the porch to laugh.

"Now since the four of us together, we need to discuss Thanksgiving. I invited Charles, Mary Lou, Shannon and Mario nem' said they was coming. I was thinking about renting out a hall or some, but then I figured I can save the money and have it both upstairs and downstairs."

Blessing listened and nodded her head as Vera ranted. Holidays were important to her family but to her, it was just another day. After agreeing to bring pops, paper plates, spoons and forks, Blessing was finally safe and sound in her car. It was 3:45 p.m., which meant she had fifteen minutes to meet Boss. After fucking his brains out in Vegas, the two had been practically inseparable since then. Although it had only been a week, Blessing and Boss made time to see each other six out of those seven days.

As promised, he allowed Ari back on the team, making her life smooth sailing. Bringing the engine to life, she pulled away from the curb, heading to the address given to her. Less than five minutes away, Blessing was pulling in front of Affiliated Clothing. Checking her reflection in the mirror, she applied a coat of Carmex and slicked her ponytail down before getting out. Stepping onto the curb in a pair of wheat Timbs, she tightened the white Mackage coat and proceeded forward.

"Welcome to Affiliated. I'm Nisha, how can I help you?" a pretty brown skin woman approached with a smile and greeted.

"Ohhh girl, I love that bag. I've been on the waiting list since last month," she beamed while her eyes admired the piece from Gucci's Fall Collection.

"Thank you boo, but I'm here to see Boss," Blessing replied with a warm smile.

"Oh ummmm Boss, huh?" She twisted her head to the side and smirked before taking a step back, sizing Blessing up.

"Yeah.... Boss! You need me to spell the shit out for you?" Blessing stepped forward and questioned, just as Boss appeared from the back.

"Nisha, it's some shit in the storage room that needs to be stocked," he announced before locking eyes with Blessing.

"What's up baby." Boss stopped in the middle of the floor and smiled, with his arms opened wide.

"Hey bae," Blessing beamed, shooting Nisha a look before falling into Boss's big arms.

Inhaling her new favorite scent, weed and Burberry Touch, she closed her eyes and basked in the moment. It was crazy how she tried to deny their attraction in the beginning but now she loved and enjoyed every second of it. Not even on no corny shit but, that night in Vegas changed her life. It was the way Boss handled her in and out of the bedroom that drove her insane. No woman in her straight mind would've been able to resist him, especially after a first date like that.

"Let's go to my office," he instructed, turning on his Timbs and leading the way towards the back.

Once inside, Boss closed and locked the door while Blessing took a seat on the armrest of the chair inside the office. Seductively eyeing him as he walked over towards her, Boss licked his lips and returned the stare.

"You missed me?" Boss twisted his head to the side and asked before pulling her up and into his arms again.

"You know I did," Blessing replied, bringing her lips to his, sucking on the bottom one before kissing him passionately.

Thankful that her Timbs were unlaced, Blessing began slipping out of them, knowing that her leggings were next. Boss's touch made her pussy drip and seeing how they had sex every time they laid eyes on each other, she knew that he had to feel the same way. Outside the physical attraction, Blessing and Boss vibed and kicked it like first cousins. Feeling like they were moving too fast, Blessing still didn't want to slow down. She was enjoying the ride that Mr. Bryant was taking her on and didn't see a stop sign in the near future either.

"Take these off," he ordered, pulling at the elastic waist on her leggings.

Moving at the speed of lighting, she did as she was told, removing the black thong underneath as well. Using his fingers to massage her wet spot, Boss and Blessing tongues continued in a game of Twister. Unable to take anymore teasing, Blessing started to tug at the jeans he wore.

"Take these off," she pulled away and stated, causing them both to laugh.

"Stop playing with me man. Turn around!" Boss smacked her on the ass and demanded, pulling down his pants and pulling out his hard dick.

Glancing down at his manhood, Blessing licked her lips as her mouth began to water. His dick was amazing, the sight and the feel, therefore, she couldn't help but get wetter just standing there. Finally turning around, Boss grabbed Blessing by her ponytail and pulled her head back. Kissing on her neck, his fingers continued to roam, making her cum from three strokes on her clit.

"Aight, that was one," he whispered, licking her earlobe while foundling her opening.

Grinning at the thought of what was next, Blessing's facial expression changed quickly when she heard Boss cursing behind her.

"Fuck."

"What's wrong, What happened?" Blessing turned around and quizzed.

"Nun. I ain't got no rubber," he replied sadly, causing her to giggle.

"It's okay baby. I'll see you tonight." She smiled, attempting to turn around but he stopped her.

"Who else you fucking Blessing?" Boss asked, his question catching her off guard.

"Who am I fucking? Nobody but you," she offensively replied.

"Aight, we gone keep it that way," he told her before forcing her back around, bending her over on the desk and slowly sliding his dick in her.

Moaning out in pain and pleasure, she gripped the ends of the desk and tried not to buckle. Although Boss tried his best to be gentle, his strokes were still powerful. Feeling herself about to cum for the second time, Blessing threw it back, causing Boss to speed up. After getting hit from the back, Blessing pushed him onto the chair and straddled him. Riding him slowly back and forth trying to adjust to the pain, it wasn't long before Blessing was bouncing up and down like she was on a pogo stick. Looking into his eyes while he bit down on his bottom lip had her wanting to cum again.

"This pussy a muthafucka," he gripped her hips and spoke, guiding her up and down.

"Nah it's the dick for me bae," Blessing tossed her head back and moaned, her actions causing Boss to nut in her.

Looking him in the eyes, she couldn't help but smile. Whatever connection they had was electric, some may even call it dangerous. A part of her knew she shouldn't have been messing around with one of her Angel's parents. It was like mixing business with pleasure, which was a definite no-no, however Blessing couldn't bring herself to end it.

"I fucks with you shorty," Boss confessed, smacking her on the ass as she stood to her feet.

"I fucks with you too baby, but I gotta go," she glanced down at her Apple Watch and told him while stepping into her thongs.

"I gotta go pick up the costumes for my Angels and the place closes in twenty minutes," she continued, noticing the displeased look on his face.

"I'm glad you cleared that shit up." He chuckled, standing to his feet and heading to the bathroom where he returned with a warm wet towel.

"Thank you."

"Nah, thank you," he replied before kissing her on the forehead and dressing.

After cleaning up and summarizing the plans for their date that night, Blessing and Boss headed out the office's doors and into the crowded store.

Feeling like she was doing the walk of shame, Blessing ignored the stares and smirks that she got from both the men and women shoppers. Half of them spoke to Boss who led the way like all the attention didn't bother him. It was clear as to what they were doing back there, especially seeing as to how her leggings were on inside out. Finally making their way to the door, Blessing locked eyes with Nisha who stood behind the register, looking like she wanted to cry. Smiling and waving goodbye, she continued to follow Boss out the doors and to her car. Hitting the locks, he opened the door for her before opening his arms for a hug.

"I'll see you later tonight. Aight," he confirmed, pulling away and helping her inside.

"Yup."

"Aight and don't forget what I said in my office. That's *my* pussy," he publicized, making sure to give direct eye contact.

"Yeah Boss, all that's fine and dandy, but I got a demand too."

"Oh word? What's that?"

"Make sure *my* pussy is the last pussy you get in that office or you'll be looking for another store manager," Blessing warned, running the same game on him.

25

"So, which one of those bitches you fucking Black?" Cresha asked, standing at the island in the middle of her condo as the fumes from the breakfast she was cooking filled his nostrils, causing his stomach to growl.

Black didn't even want to step foot back into the building after running into Mel last week, but he needed to bag up some work that he had stashed at Cresha's house. He came early as possible trying to make sure he didn't run into neither Mel nor Blessing. The only reason he was there that day was to grab Cresha and handle some business. He often had her to collect money from the trap houses to keep the police that wasn't on their payroll under wraps. For some reason, they weren't quick to fuck with females but would slam the first nigga they saw to the pavement.

"You worried about the wrong shit, Cresha, and you know firsthand I don't answer to nobody," Black replied while sitting at her table, never looking up from the small bags he was filling with pure cocaine.

"Black you got me so fucked up! You gone have me to act real crazy with them hoes, and I'm trying to keep the peace."

"You gone fuck around and get yo ass beat."

Cresha hit him with a stale face. He knew that was coming because she thought she was tough. Though Black had seen Cresha stomp a few hoes in the past, but he could tell just by play fighting with Mel sometimes, her hands had structure.

"Come on now Black, them preppy hoes could never whoop me. Now you can either tell me what's up, or I'm gone figure it out on my own and when I do, it's gone get ugly."

Black chuckled at her choice of words because she knew better than to fuck with him. He wouldn't think twice about putting a bullet through her lace front.

"Oh, you think I'm bullshitting huh? I'll go downstairs and bring both of them bitches up here!" Cresha said, walking to the front door as if she was going to walk out.

"Man, sit yo goofy ass down somewhere, that's exactly why you'll never be my bitch and since we on the subject, make that your last time referring to me as your boyfriend."

She frowned her face as he laid down the law to her. Like he said, he had been giving Cresha plenty of passes because of the time she did for him, but that shit was over. He let her get too comfortable, and it was starting to show.

"Please, I was the one that sat in a cell for your ass, remember that shit! Hoes can't walk a mile in my shoes! I been your bitch and gone continue to be until I say different, nigga!" she spat with much venom as she made her way over to him.

She fucked up when she pointed her fingers in his face, and in one swift move, he jumped up from his seat and wrapped his hand around her neck applying pressure. She tried her best to free herself from his hold, but she had no wind.

"I told you to stop talking to me like you ain't got no sense!"

He released her and let her body drop to the floor as his phone rang. Lucky for her, Ari had just saved her ass by calling. She coughed uncontrollably and cried as he walked to the back of the house to answer his niece's facetime.

"Hey Uncle, you didn't forget you have to take me to school today, did you?"

"Nah, I'm on my way to grab you now," he assured her before ending the call.

He walked back into the living room, and if looks could kill, he would have been a dead man. Not really giving a fuck how she felt, he grabbed his shit and walked out. He wanted to knock on every door in the building until he found Mel; he was missing her. He tried reaching out to explain the situation to her, but she blew him off. He didn't know what he was feeling because he had never had real feelings for a female like he did for Mel. He found himself thinking about her more and more as the days went by, but he was too stubborn to reach out.

Thoughts of her plagued his mind as he flowed through the early morning traffic. Finally pulling into their estate, he parked in front of Boss's house and waited for Ari to come out. The front door opened, but Boss came down the stairs, walking toward his car instead of his niece.

"What's up lover boy?" Black teased his brother about his new dealings with Blessing as he climbed in the passenger seat.

Him and Boss often talked about both ladies, so he knew firsthand how deep she had her hooks in his brother. Black couldn't help but think of the saying his mother swore by, "It takes a special kind of woman to love a Bryant."

"Fuck you, we got a shipment coming in at 2:30. I need you to grab Ari after school and take her to dance class for me."

"Aw you let her back on? I guess that lil pussy got some power," Black replied, causing them both to erupt in laughter.

"What? Power ain't the muthafuckin word my nigga. But um, I need you to fix whatever you got going on with Mel because you fucking up my shit. My lady all sad and shit because her best friend sad, you know how it go with females."

"How the fuck I'm supposed to fix some shit, and she won't talk to me, bro? I'm not about to kiss her ass."

"You gone learn that sometimes you have to kiss a lil ass when you fuck up the home front. Now, if she was just another bitch on yo hit list then by any means, disregard every word I just spoke," Boss said as his daughter came running down the stairs.

"I hear you."

Boss got out and gave his seat to Ari before kissing her forehead and disappearing into the house.

"What's up favorite uncle?" she greeted him before securing her seatbelt across her body.

"What's good favorite niece? Where is your bookbag?" he asked, noticing she didn't have it.

"Oh, we have a field trip today. We're going to the Museum of Science and Industry."

"Word?"

"Yup."

They turned the music all the way up as they always did when they rode together and rapped along with Chicago rapper, Polo G. He pulled up to the school and caught a park right behind the line of yellow school buses as Ari removed her seatbelt. He stopped her right before she was about to get out.

"Aye, you want me to chaperone your trip?"

"I mean if you trying to see Ms. Caston just say that." Ari laughed at her uncle as he shook his head.

"You too much man," he replied, killing the engine and climbing out of the car.

Spotting Melody standing in front of the school directing her kids to the bus in a knee length Moncler coat with a pair of UGGS to match, he followed Ari as she walked in her direction. She was so wrapped up in making sure her kids got on the bus safely, she didn't notice him standing behind Ari at the end of the line. She stepped up on the bus and directed the kids. When Ari stepped on and hugged her, she locked eyes with Black wearing a blank facial expression.

"Is it room for one more?" he finally asked as she stepped aside and allowed him on the bus.

He took a seat right behind the driver as Mel talked to her class and got them settled. Boss's words were replaying in his mind like a broken record. *Sometimes you gotta kiss a lil ass.* She came and sat next to him and still remained silent. Black didn't have any long speeches or shit like that, so he just said what he felt.

"Look, I'm not good at apologizing because I never felt like I owed anyone walking this earth an apology until now. I didn't mean to hurt you."

"But you did Black, I asked you if you had a girlfriend and kids and you lied about having both."

"I never lied about either. Cresha is not my girl, and I have no kids."

"Ok so what was all that shit in the elevator about, and why didn't you clear it up in front of her?" Mel asked, whispering so that her kids couldn't hear her.

"That was me being a dumb ass nigga. I didn't want shit to kick off, so I remained silent, but I got on her ass about it."

Mel wasn't playing any games, she was laying it on Black thick. He knew he had to be honest with her about everything if he wanted to get her back. He didn't realize how much she meant to him until he saw the hurt in her face that day. After explaining the entire situation with Cresha from beginning to end, leaving nothing out, he was finally back in her good graces.

"I don't know what this thing is that we have going on, but I want it Black. I can't take another heartbreak, so if your intentions don't align with mine, we can leave everything the way it was before you walked on this bus."

He sat there and thought long and hard before responding. Was he ready to be in a real relationship?

"Bet it up then Mel. Moving forward, you my girl and I'm yo nigga, ain't no more in between."

He watched as a smile spread across her face. Forgetting about the kids on the bus, they shared a kiss.

"Look, look, Ms. Caston! It's snowing!" one of her students yelled out, causing them both to look out the window.

He watched Mel smile and look up at the sky. Black always said it would be a cold day in hell when he settled down with one female, guess that was a sign.

❧ 26 ❧

Boss turned up the radio and did sixty on 290, heading towards downtown. In addition to it being Halloween, it was Ari's thirteenth birthday. In a race against time, he headed to his jeweler to pick up the Rose Gold Rolex he got custom made for his princess. Making his exit on Racine, Boss whipped the Porsche like it was a Chevy, arriving at his destination with ten minutes to spare. Double parking and hitting the hazard lights, Boss sprinted inside the jewelry store ready to handle business.

"My favorite customer. What's up Boss?" Hakeem spoke in a heavy Arabic accent.

"What up my boy? You good?" he shot back, making his way to the counter while Hakeem placed two velvet jewelry boxes on top.

"Yup, but make sure you tell Ms. Arianna I said happy birthday. I know she gon love this," he beamed, revealing the rose gold rollie with her name engraved inside.

"Shid, she better. This muthafucker is nice though." Boss picked it up and examined, admiring the details.

"Appreciate it," he looked up and said to Hakeem before placing it back down and pulling out his ringing phone.

"And thennnn, I have the other customized piece you requested.

But Boss I gotta know, who's the lucky lady, cuz I know this one not for your daughter," he pressed, opening the box, revealing the iced out neckless.

Cracking a slight smile, Boss looked up at Hakeem and then back down at the $15,000 diamond chain.

"You a cold ass nigga, but you gotta stay out my business," Boss chuckled before continuing.

"Let's wrap this shit up. I got somewhere to be." He glanced down at the Audemar on his wrist.

Walking away to take the call he'd been ignoring for the last five minutes, Boss finally answered in an aggravated voice.

"What up?"

"Aye Boss, we caught a fish," Lil Mike voice sounded through his ears.

"Aight, handle it. I'm busy."

"Nah Boss, this a big fish. As a matter of fact, we been trying to catch this hoe for a while," he responded.

"Be there in ten."

Boss ended the call before Lil Mike could reply. Heading back over to the register, he pulled out an American Express card and paid for both items. After thanking Hakeem, he was out the door and inside the car before he could blink. Taking the same route back, Boss swerved in and out of traffic, arriving at the trap house in K-Town in less than ten minutes. Thankful that traffic was light, and the police wasn't on bullshit, he was able to stay on track with time. Grabbing the pistol under his seat, he doubled checked for the second one he kept in the glove compartment and got out. Skipping up the stairs two at a time, Boss checked his surroundings one last time before entering the building. Heading straight to the basement, he knocked four times before being granted entry. Greeting one of the workers with a head nod, Boss proceeded down the stairs where he found Murda tied to a chair. Chuckling lightly at the sight of him, Boss spoke to the other individuals in the room before finally addressing the situation at hand.

"Murda. My nigga. What up?" he spoke while twisting the silencer on the piece.

"Where y'all find this nigga?" Boss turned to Lil Mike and questioned.

"Shid, after finding out his OG died last week of cancer, we knew the nigga would come out of hiding for the funeral, so we caught him lacking then."

Shaking his head up and down with a pleased expression on his face, Boss redirected his attention back to his friend and former employee.

"It's unfortunate to hear about what happened to Ms. Fritz. She made the best spicy chili," Boss reminisced.

"But what's even more unfortunate is the fact that her only son gotta lose his life over a few hundred thousand dollars, but I guess looking on the bright side, you can be with yo momma again," Boss told him before putting two bullets in his head.

"Y'all know the routine. Get this shit cleaned," Boss instructed while heading up the stairs.

"Muthafuckers got me late and shit," he mumbled to himself, putting the gun away and pulling out his keys.

Taking the twenty-minute drive to Schaumburg, Boss was finally pulling inside the skating rink's parking lot. Killing the engine and grabbing Ari's gift, he made sure to secure Blessing's in a safe place before getting out. Although the party had only officially started thirty minutes ago, the amount of cars present let him know it was a full house already. Entering what the party planner turned into a haunted house, Boss was pleased with the presentation and even more shocked at how many people came in costume. Spotting his family standing near the concession stand, Boss made his way over to them, admiring the ghost and goblins along the way.

"Hey my favorite son," Sandy, his mother said, greeting him with a hug first.

Speaking to his father and brother next, Boss flagged Ari down, who was dressed as Gabrielle Union in her favorite movie, *Bring It On*. Joining in on the fun, her best friends and cousins wore the same cheerleading outfits.

"Hey Daddy!" she ran up and spoke, trying to wrap her short arms around him.

"Happy birthday again baby." Boss replied, handing her the giftbag that contained her watch.

"Oh my God! Thank you Daddy!" she sang, jumping up and down excitedly.

"You're welcome, but don't open it until you open all your gifts. Go put it with the others," he told her before scanning the room, noticing Blessing and her home girl coming through the door.

"Aye, I'll be back," he announced to everyone before walking away towards them.

In costume as well, Blessing and Melody wore pink and yellow plaid outfits identical to Cher and Dion's in the movie *Clueless*. Thankful that she showed up, Boss found himself wanting to spend all his free time with her. He knew from their encounter at her dance studio that she was special. It was the way she stood up to him and how she went hard for his daughter is what really won him over. Hearing how highly Arianna spoke of her also made Boss fall harder for her. Unlike the other women in his life, Blessing was more than pussy. She was the first woman he could see himself wifing.

"That's yo costume? What the hell you supposed to be?" Boss heard Blessing say, snapping him out of his trance.

"This is my costume. I'm a Boss baby," he quickly gathered and replied, looking down at the gray Nike jogging pants and white air force ones he wore.

After embracing, Blessing reintroduced Melody and Boss before he ushered them off towards the section his family was in. When he invited her to the party, introducing her to his parents slipped his mind. Arica was the only woman who had ever met them, and that was almost twenty years ago. It had only been a month with Blessing, and she had him doing things out of the norm.

"Aye Mom and Pops!" Boss called out over the music, trying to grab the both of their attention.

"Y'all remember Ari's teacher, Melody. This Blessing, her dance teacher."

"Ohhhh so this is Blessing," Sandy sang, standing to her feet and pushing her husband out the way.

"It's nice to meet you. I've heard so much about you from both my grandbaby and son. Seems like they both crazy about you," she said, winking her eye at Boss before pulling Blessing into a hug.

"Nice to meet you too. You as well Sir," she replied with a smile.

Pulling his ringing phone from his pocket, Boss's mood changed at the sight of Arica's name flashing on his phone. It was the third time she had called and like the previous others, he ignored it. Hearing the phone chime one last time, he assumed she left a voicemail but later learned it was a text message.

Arica: I missed my flight. I've been calling Ari's phone all day to tell her happy birthday but no answer. Tell my baby that I am so so so sorry for missing her party. I could fly out later but that'll mean I miss the B.E.T Hip Hop Awards that's taping tomorrow and I can't afford to miss that so tell her that I'm sorry.

Shaking his head back and forth, Boss tried his best not to react, but he hated everything about the mother of his child. Being a mother to Ari always came second, and he was tired of lying to his daughter to protect her heart.

"It's okay. Ari's growing up. She gon' see for herself that lady ain't shit," Blessing's voice disturbed his thoughts, also catching him off guard.

"What? How the fuck?"

"I can just tell. Don't let that bitch fuck up yo day, it's about Ari. Now let's grab some skates, so we can act like New New and Rashad," Blessing grabbed his hand and stated, pulling him away and taking his mind off all the bullshit.

❧ 27 ☙

"Momma you want some wine?" Mel asked, maneuvering around her kitchen as she prepared a huge meal.

It had been a while since Mel invited her mother over for dinner, especially since she started helping out with the after-school program at work. All of her free time outside of that was spent with Black. Every day, she learned something different about him that made her like him more. The fact that they loved all the same movies and enjoyed the same music made them vibe even harder. She still couldn't believe that he had labeled them.

"Sure, I'll have a glass. You keep this place so clean and neat."

"I try," she replied, walking over to her mom with the glass of Red Moscato.

"Thanks sweetie. So what are you whipping up?"

"Baked porkchops, bacon wrapped asparagus, garlic mashed potatoes, mixed vegetables, garlic bread with a side of our favorite, cherry Kool-Aid."

"Well ok, when you start cooking like that miss thang?" her mother sipped her wine and teased.

"Don't do me like that," Mel joined her mother in laughter.

"Hmph, must be that young man that snuck out of my house."

"Huh?" Mel replied, acting oblivious to what her mother was speaking of.

She knew for a fact, this time around it was Vera that spilled the beans. They always sat on the phone and gossiped. The two were good friends long before her and Corey had gotten into a relationship.

"Yeah Vera told me, say he fine too, so when do I get to meet this young man?"

"You will in due time."

"Well, I'm glad you're not sitting around waiting on Corey. Let him give the next heffa hell."

"Nope, those days are officially over," Mel assured her while preparing both of their plates and placing them on the table.

She had a very nice setup for their dinner. She even pulled out the dishes her grandmother bought her when she first moved in her place. Mel cherished her mother; her qualities and love was unmatched, and she hoped she could be half the woman she was one day.

"Good, you're not going to call Blessing over to eat with us?"

Her mom loved Blessing like her daughter, and she always made sure she was included in everything they did.

"No, I put her plate up. She's down there on the phone with her guy," Mel replied, digging into her meal.

"Oh, Vera told me about him too. Y'all both around here cutting up, huh?"

Mel shot her mother a smile while moving her fork in a circular motion. "I meannnn, I wouldn't say all that, but them Bryant men hold weight with us."

"They're related?" Her mother looked up from her plate.

"Yes, they're brothers."

"Lord, Corey and Kevin gone flip when they find this out," she joked, but Mel hoped like hell there wasn't any truth to her statement. She had seen both Black and Boss in action, and it wasn't pretty.

They spent the next hour or so laughing and talking before it was time for her mother to head home before it got too late. She cleaned up their mess before grabbing her housekeys and walking her mom down to her car. Though her and Black had fixed their issue, that damn elevator still pissed her off. She hugged her mother before watching her get inside her car and pull away. Heading back inside with her face buried in her phone, she quickly looked up when she walked dead into someone.

"Ou, I am so sorry," Mel replied before looking up into Cresha's face. She hadn't seen her since the Black incident.

"It's ok, I've been wanting to speak to you about the other day. Do you or Blessing know my guy from somewhere?"

Mel couldn't believe this bitch had the audacity to question her like she was a kid. "Yeah we know him."

"How? Where y'all know him from?" She folded her arms across her chest as she got tight in the face.

"Cresha, make this your first and last time questioning me. That's your nigga, right? Ask him how we know him. Excuse me," Mel stepped around her and headed straight to the elevator.

"Bitch," she heard Cresha say before the doors opened.

"Bad, make sure you add the bad to the bitch, bitch!" Mel corrected her before stepping inside and pressing the button. She couldn't get to their floor fast enough.

She stepped off and headed straight to Blessing's house. She knocked once before Blessing opened the door and let her in like she was expecting her.

"Where my food?" she asked with a puzzled look plastered on her face.

"At my house. Why I walk momma to the car and bump into Cresha in the lobby. Hoe had the nerve to try and question me about us knowing Black."

"What?"

"Yeah, I checked that bitch and left her standing there looking stupid."

"Wanna go beat her ass?" Blessing asked, ready for whatever Mel decided to do.

"Nah, fuck that bitch, but I'm gone tell Black he better control that hoe."

Mel did just that, she pulled her phone out and shot Black a text.

Mel: Bae.

Black: Waddup baby?

Mel: Get that hoe Cresha before I fuck her up.

Black: What happened?

Mel: Her mouth gone write her a check that her ass can't cash.

Black: Chill Tyson, I'll handle it.

Mel: Please do.

Mel looked up from her phone at the sound of Blessing's voice. "Bitch! Why Boss baby momma just request to follow me on IG," she said with her eyes glued to her phone.

"Whew, these hoes on a roll today, huh? Add the hoe."

"You think I didn't?"

"Let me see."

They sat there for the next thirty minutes, looking at Ari's mother's degrading ass pictures.

"I swear to God, I know this bitch from somewhere bro."

Blessing sat there trying to pinpoint where she knew the girl from while Mel waited on her to figure it out.

"Look that bitch be posted up with all the celebrities," Mel said, still scrolling through the photos.

"Right but couldn't make her daughter's birthday party. She's a bum bitch."

"Clearly. I feel sorry for Arianna."

"She's good, that baby ain't missing out on no love, I promise," Blessing assured her before standing to her feet.

"Oh, trust me, I know, but it's still sad."

"Fuck that lady. Come on bitch, I needs that plate like yesterday," Blessing said while stretching and rubbing her flat stomach.

"Greedy hoe," they laughed before heading down to Mel's place.

"My man ain't complaining," she replied, twerking in the hallway.

"And who exactly is your man?"

Both Mel and Blessing followed Cresha's voice as she turned the corner and leaned against the wall. They all stood there looking at one another; they were surprised at how bold she was.

"I'm not gone beat around the bush with y'all, and since somebody reached out and called themselves *telling* Black on me, and I'm not sure which one of you it was, I'm gone address you both at the same time."

Blessing chuckled at her neighbor before responding to her. They all knew fighting in the building was an automatic termination of the lease they were all under, but at this point neither Blessing nor Mel gave a fuck. She came fucking with them.

"I don't know who the fuck you think you talking to but bitch, I will drag you. And nah I ain't fucking Black, I'm fucking Boss. Black is her nigga, now do something!" Blessing snapped, giving Cresha exactly what she asked for.

Cresha started walking back when she noticed she was about to get her ass beat. "Y'all not about to jump me, but just know I'm on that!"

"Bitch and we on whatever you on," Mel spat, meaning every word as Cresha disappeared around the corner.

Mel knew at that moment; she was going to be a muthafuckin problem.

❦ 28 ❦

BLESSING HELD THE BROOM LIKE A MICROPHONE AND SANG HER heart out as she swept the kitchen floor. Beyonce's *Dangerously In Love* had been in heavy rotation while she cleaned her condo. It was six o'clock on a Friday night, and she couldn't have been happier. After arranging a movie night with Boss and Arianna, Blessing lit a few candles and cleaned up her place from top to bottom. She loved the smell of Bath & Bodyworks, especially her favorite, Champagne Toast. With her house smelling good and her feeling better, she looked forward to the night and spending time with Boss and Ari.

After finishing up in the kitchen, Blessing jumped in the shower, throwing on a pair of leggings and oversized tee once she was out. Spraying on a new fragrance, Beautiful Day, she tied up her hair in a scarf and returned back to the kitchen. Going inside the cabinet and pulling out a glass, Blessing poured herself some red wine and retreated to the couch. Snatching up the remote, she turned off the music and turned on the television when there was a knock on the door.

"Who is it?" she asked, grinning at the sight of her guest who she spied on through the peephole.

"It's me Coach B," Ari replied, dancing on the other side of the door.

Snatching the door back, Blessing's heart smiled looking at Ari who danced with two bags of goodies in her hand, and Boss who shook his head back and forth.

"What up baby," he spoke, walking pass her and placing a kiss on her forehead.

"Coach Beeeeeee!" Ari sang before hugging Blessing and following behind her father.

Once in the kitchen, the trio emptied the bags, setting aside the items that they needed for dinner. Going with Ari's idea and making a homemade pizza, Blessing made sure she had every ingredient you could think of. Unsure of how the food would turn out, Blessing took out three T-Bone steaks just in case.

"Aight y'all. We can start making this pizza and watch a movie while it cooks. Ari, you get that text message I sent earlier?" Blessing cut her eyes over at the teenager and asked.

"Yup! I got yo hot popcorn right here Coach B," Ari replied, holding a family size bag of Chester's Popcorn in the air.

"My dawg!" Blessing smiled, dapping her up before she took off running to the bathroom.

The more and more she spent time with Boss and Ari, the more Blessing cared for them. Spending a bunch of time with Arianna at practice, she found herself missing her when she wasn't around. She was attached to all her Angels, but Ari held a special place in her heart, and she knew Boss was a reason for that. Going inside the refrigerator and pulling out the shredded cheese, Blessing froze at the touch of Boss who pulled her in close from the back. Goosebumps forming all over her skin. She instantly got wet, and his dick poking her in the back didn't help.

"So you know I'm still getting some pussy, right? I ain't the one who invited Ari's blocking ass anyway," Boss said in a low tone near her ear, causing more goosebumps to form.

Just as she turned around to respond, Ari came flying down the hallway, abruptly joining them in the kitchen. Sliding across the marble floors in her socks, she came colliding with the barstool, knocking it and herself down.

"That's what yo goofass get. Stop running like you ain't got no sense," Boss barked, sending Blessing's eyes shooting in his direction.

"Nigga and you need to talk to her like you got some sense. That's a young lady, not one of your workers or homies," Blessing checked, her words causing both Boss and Ari to smile.

Although they were cheesing for two different reasons, she thought it was cute the way they acted alike. With Boss, he wasn't used to people checking him nor correcting him when he was wrong and with Ari, no one stood up to him when it came to her. Well nobody but her granny. After clearing the air, Blessing decided to play some music to set the mood while they prepped their meal for the night.

"Alexa..... play crush on you by Lil Kim and Biggie."
I know you seen me on the video (true)
I know you heard me on the radio (true)
But you still don't pay me no attention

"UGH... DON'T NOBODY WANNA HEAR THAT. ALEXA, PLAY GIRL OF my dreams by Rod Wave," Ari said with a screwed face, turning the song and causing both Blessing and Boss to laugh.

Singing along like a night at karaoke, the three of them made personal pizzas and vibed over good music. While cracking jokes and tag teaming Boss, time passed and before they knew it, the food was done. Not too pleased with the presentation, Blessing prayed that it tasted better than it looked. Eyeballing their plates as well, she noticed that the both of theirs looked edible while hers on the other hand, not so much. Waiting for the pizza to cool, Blessing locked eyes with Ari who motioned for Blessing to check her phone.

Ari: Coach B, I think now is the perfect time to bring up the competition.

Locking and placing her phone back down on the counter, Blessing signaled to Ari before stepping over closer to Boss.

"Aye baby. I was thinking that with our next competition being around the corner, I think it'll be great if you come," she spoke softly while rubbing his back in a circular motion.

"Mannnnn, I still ain't fully on board with this dancing shit and now y'all want a nigga to come and sit in the stands?" Boss twisted his head to the side and asked, looking back and forth at Blessing and Ari.

"I mean Daddy, why not? I want you to see for yourself that dancing not what you think it is. I swear we not swinging from poles and giving lap dances Daddy," Ari looked up and pleaded with bright eyes.

"Yeah baby, come see for yourself. You might enjoy it anddddddddd, if you come, I promise I'll...." Blessing paused, looking over at Arianna who eagerly listened on.

"Make you cum," she whispered in his ear.

"Ewwwwww, y'all nasty. Never mind. I don't want neither one of y'all there."

Laughing at her silliness, they talked a little more about dancing before cutting and eating the pizza. Happy that it did taste better than it looked, the crew stuffed their faces and enjoyed each other's company. Once they were done, they changed into their pajamas, grabbed blankets and snuggled on the couch. With plans on binge watching *Home Alone*, Boss was snoring before they left for vacation on part one, and Blessing was sound asleep before part two started. Unsure of when Ari tapped out, Blessing however found herself being the first to wake up the next morning. With the *are you still there?* message from Netflix on the screen, she carefully slid from under Boss and into the bathroom. Relieving her bladder and then brushing her teeth, she jumped in the shower and cleaned up. Dressing in a pair of jogging pants and sweatshirt, Blessing headed to the kitchen where she prepared breakfast. Using the steaks from last night, she fried those up along with cheese eggs, rice, and croissant rolls. Setting the table for two, it was Saturday morning which meant Blessing had a date with the boxing ring.

"Where you going?"

Startled by Boss's voice, Blessing jumped, almost dropping the jug of orange juice in her hand. Giving him an evil eye, Boss placed a kissed on her lips before disappearing down the hall and into the bathroom. The moment the door closed, Ari's eyes popped open, and she joined Blessing in the kitchen.

"Good morning baby. How you sleep?"

"I slept pretty good. Well, aside from you and my daddy snoring," Ari replied, and her words sent Blessing's mouth flying open.

"Told you yo ass snore. Good morning Princess," Boss appeared from the back and stated, placing a kiss on Arianna's forehead.

"I hope y'all enjoy breakfast, but I gotta run."

"Run? Run where?" Ari quizzed, stuffing a fork full of eggs in her mouth.

"My dad's boxing gym. I work out every Saturday, and I finally convinced Melody to join me. I would cancel, but Lord knows the next time I'll be able to get her lazy ass to work out," Blessing explained, grabbing her phone and bookbag, and heading towards the door.

"Lock up my shit Boss. I'll call you when I'm done. Love you Angel."

"Love you too Coach B."

Walking three doors down, Blessing knocked twice on Melody's door before fetching her set of keys. Knowing that she was more than likely sleep or backing out again, Blessing wanted so bad to enter but remembered her and Black were on good terms. Raising her hand to knock a few more times, the door flew open and to her surprise, Melody was standing front and center, ready to go.

"I bet you thought I sent you off, didn't you?" she quizzed, grabbing her bag and locking up.

"I sure did. Now let's go."

With traffic on the heavy side, the friends arrived at B&B's Boxing Gym later than they anticipated. Happy to see a packed house, Blessing dragged Melody out the car and straight inside. Speaking to the regulars and even some new faces, she peeked her head inside her father's office to see if he was in there. Noticing the lights off, she returned to where Melody was so they could begin their workout.

"Okay, we gon stretch for ten minutes and then we can start light and jump rope."

"Light? Bitch, ain't shit light about your workouts. This the main reason I stopped coming with you years ago," Melody whined, twisting her body from side to side.

"And that's probably why you got that lil pudge too. Try to keep up, Big Momma," Blessing joked, patting Mel on the stomach before jogging in place.

Sharing a laugh, the duo stretched for ten minutes like stated. Moving over to the jump ropes next, Blessing did ten sets while Melody had tapped out by the fifth. Amused at her best friend's antics, Blessing giggled at her as she laid flat out in the middle of the gym floor.

"Come on, get up and spot me in the ring. All you gotta do is hold your gloves up in the air. I wanna work on my jabs."

Doing as she instructed, Melody climbed in behind her and got in stance. Putting both hands in the air, Mel closed her eyes tight, causing Blessing to laugh.

"Why the fuck yo eyes closed?"

"Cause bitch, I seen you fight and there's a reason I'm always on the side of you and not in front," Melody popped her eyes opened and answered, sending Blessing bending over in laughter.

"You laughing, but I'm serious. I remember that time you fought Ashley off 63rd and her brother, Tony, jumped in? Blessing, you beat both they ass and swung on they momma when she came out."

"Well, her old ass shouldn't have ran up, but stop bringing up old shit. I'm a changed woman and—"

"And you know dem hands deadly, and you ain't trying to catch another case."

Rolling her eyes at Melody, Blessing hated to think about her past, especially when she was a changed person now. She had grown so much since her earlier years and was thankful that it had been years since she allowed her anger to get the best of her. She was no longer in the mood to workout, especially seeing the condition Mel was in.

"Let's go girl. At least we can catch Chik-fil-A before breakfast is over."

"Bitch, I been waiting on you to say that since we walked through them doors. I want two orders of hash browns," Melody pulled off her gloves and replied, climbing out the ring first.

Quickly showering and changing clothes, the besties bundled up and headed to the car. With the parking lot full, Blessing was forced to park down the street. Laughing and exchanging insults with Mel, she was so wrapped up in their fun that she didn't notice Kevin standing by her car until it was too late.

"This nigga," she mumbled, causing Melody to straighten up and get serious quick.

"What the fuck you doing here?" Mel stepped up first and snapped as Blessing pulled her back by the tail of her shirt.

"Bitch you need to mind yo business. Ain't nobody talking to you!" Kevin barked.

"Nigga, is you fucking stupid? You better watch yo mouth and stay the fuck away from me!" Blessing spat, muffing Kevin upside the head.

Ready for a reaction, Melody stood behind her friend just in case something popped off. Just like everyone else around her, her ex-husband was more than aware of how she got down. He could play the crazy role all he wanted, but he knew better than to even flinch. Sick and tired of him and his pop ups, Blessing patience was wearing thin with him.

"Look, I just came to talk. Can we talk?" he held his hands in the air and begged.

"Nigga nooooo! There is nothing to talk about, so I suggest you move away from my car before we have a bigger problem," she warned, looking down at her phone at Boss's name that strolled across the screen.

"Who the fuck is that calling yo phone? Is that a man? That's yo nigga? Who the fuck is that?" Kevin questioned, snatching Blessing's phone and answering Boss's facetime.

CHAPTER TWENTY- NINE

"What's up? You been tucked in here all morning, trouble in paradise?" Boss asked, walking into Black's office as he sat behind his desk at Affiliated.

"Nah, everything good besides that bitch, Cresha, acting crazy."

"Yeah, I heard. You know you gone have to figure out a different living arrangement for her before shit goes left for real. Blessing wants to beat her ass and you know she been boxing her whole life. Her and Mel gone fuck around and hurt her."

Black knew he had to get Cresha out that building and being that the lease on the condo was up next month, she had more than enough time to find her somewhere to go. He got the last of his stash from her house and cut all ties with her, but she wasn't trying to let him go. He knew she was crazy but fucking with Mel was off limits. He always thought niggas that let bitches fight over them was corny as fuck.

"I'm already knowing. Speaking of crazy, what the fuck you do to Nisha? She been tight in the chest all morning."

"Shit, she had a problem ever since Blessing came through this bitch. She'll be aight," he said, taking a seat across from Black.

"Sis round this bitch making hoes uncomfortable, I fuck with her."

"Yeah me too, might have to fuck her lil ex-husband up in the process though," Boss replied, tapping a pen on the desk.

Black looked over at his brother, waiting on him to elaborate on the subject at hand. Both being overly protective of the other, he needed Boss to speak sooner than later.

"What you mean?"

"I was on facetime with Blessing earlier and the nigga snatched her phone and tried to talk to shit, but she ended up snatching her shit back and ending the call."

"Hold up, fuck she doing with her ex-husband?" Black question, trying to put the pieces together.

"She said the nigga popped up at the gym on her. I'm gone handle it."

"It's too late, he treated you already and took his lady back," Black teased, causing Boss to chuckle before standing to his feet.

"Yeah ok, I ain't worried. I put a Boss stamp on that pussy," he replied as Nisha walked in on the end of his statement.

"Hmph, Black where are the extra sensors?" she asked, rolling her eyes at Boss, causing Black to laugh.

"In the back next to the hangers," he replied before both her and Boss headed out to the salesfloor.

Black pulled his phone out and got straight to business with Cresha, he was done playing her game.

Black: Aye.
Cresha: Yeah?
Black: That lease up next month.
Cresha: Ok, renew it like you been doing.
Black: Can you afford 2,100 a month?
Cresha: What?
Black: Exactly. Start looking for something you can afford on your own. I'll pay your first six months, but that's it.
Cresha: So, you putting me and my daughter out of our home?

He knew she was going to play the kid card, but he really didn't give a fuck; he meant what he said. Her fucking with Mel was the last straw, and he knew as long as Cresha was around, there would be nothing but conflict between him and his girl.

Black: You got a month to find a crib and a job, it's time to get on yo shit.

Cresha: You gone do me like this over another bitch after all I have done for you? What she got that I don't got Black?

Black: A job, start looking for you one.

She never responded to his last message, instead she started calling back to back, but he declined every call. He didn't feel like listening to her cry in his ear. A lot of shit in his life was about to change. Black had been with so many females he lost count. Pussy was never out of his reach, but ever since he started fucking with Mel, she was all he wanted.

He hung around the store until it was time for him to meet Melody for lunch. Boss decided to join them since his girl was already with her. Hopping in the car with Boss, they shared a backwood filled with the best exotic weed and enjoyed the lyrics that Rod Wave was spitting through the speakers. Both brothers were lost in their own thoughts, and by the time they turned into the parking lot of Ruth Chris, their eyes were practically closed. They both sat there stuck from the exotic in their systems.

"You gone get out?" Boss asked, looking over at his brother, finally killing the engine.

"Why you worried about me bro? Yeah, I'm getting out, is you?"

"Man fuck you. Come on," Boss laughed, pushing Black with his elbow.

They walked inside wearing the weed aroma like it was a part of their attire. Looking around until he spotted his girl, Black made his way to the table her and Blessing occupied with Boss in tow. Thirsty bitches sized them up as walked through the place like they owned it.

"Waddup baby? What's good Blessing," Black greeted both ladies before leaning down, kissing Mel on the lips and taking a seat next to her.

"What's up Mel," Boss spoke after greeting his girl with a kiss.

"You niggas are so loud," Blessing whispered low enough for only the four of them to hear.

"I swear I was just about to say that, gone get everybody in here high," Mel chimed in with her friend.

"Y'all don't like our cologne?" Boss asked, looking at both women followed by a chuckle.

"Right, this Gucci latest fragrance, D'exotic, the fuck," Black picked up where his brother left off, sending the table into laughter.

"Yeah ok, you mean D'bullshit," Blessing shot back.

"Good one best friend," Mel laughed while clapping her hands.

"Keep that same energy tonight," Black leaned over and whispered in her ear, causing her blush.

With all of the fucking him and Mel had been doing, he was surprised she wasn't pregnant yet. He found himself missing her when she wasn't in his presence; it was to the point where he hated to see her go to her own crib.

"I can't wait," she replied, pulling him in for a kiss.

"Ugh, get a room," Blessing said, pretending to gag at the sight of them kissing.

"I know like hell you ain't talking, you and that nigga be on the verge of fucking," Mel shot back, pointing at Boss.

"And *will*! That's my dick," Blessing replied, reaching under the table.

"Talk yo shit bae," Boss egged her on.

The vibe between the four came naturally; it was all love. For one, Boss and Black had never fucked with females in the same circle, the whole double dating scene was new to them. They ate and enjoyed each other's company the entire time they were there, nothing but laugher came from their table. The waiter walked over and placed the bill facedown, Boss picked it up and looked at it first before putting it back on the table.

"Y'all got on gym shoes?" he asked as a puzzled look covered the girls faces.

"Yeah bae why?" Blessing asked, looking around to see if there was a problem.

Black already knew what Boss was getting at, so he tried his best not to laugh.

"Aight, when I get up and run, y'all better be right behind me."

CHAPTER TWENTY- NINE

They both looked at him like he was crazy.

"I know you fucking lying!" Mel said, looking at Boss sideways.

Boss pushed his chair back as Black did the same, they were just testing the girls to see if they would actually be down to run out on the bill. When they both stood up and grabbed their things ready to make a run for it with them, him and Boss gave one another a look.

"So, y'all some thieves, thieves huh?" Black asked, joining Boss in laughter as the girls flipped them the middle finger. He and Boss both dropped a hundred-dollar bill on the table and walked out with their ladies.

Money could buy a lot of shit, but that vibe was priceless...

❄ 29 ❄

Boss sat behind the cherry oakwood desk in his office on facetime talking to Blessing. With his phone propped up, he freed his hands as he made edits on the website. Since explaining in detail, the history behind her and her ex-husband, Boss didn't find reason to fault her behind Kevin's clown ass actions. And after doing further research on Mr. McCall, not only did Boss learn he wasn't a threat, he also knew that after putting a bug in his ear, he'd be straight. And if not, he'd be dead. Catching feelings for Blessing as fast as he did wasn't part of the plans. The attraction was there, however, he had no clue the feelings would be too. She was different than any of the women on his roster, so different that it had Boss considering retiring.

"Baby, did you just hear anything I said?" Blessing's voice snapped him out of his trance, pulling his eyes away from the MacBook Pro and to the phone.

"Yeah, I heard everything you said," he lied, looking away and towards the door.

"Come in," Boss called out as Nisha peeked her head inside.

"Got a minute?"

"Yeah, wad up?" he said, shutting the laptop while she closed the door.

"I'mma hit you back," Boss glanced down and said to Blessing who gave him the stale face.

"Make sure that's a New York minute, nigga," she spat, ending the call first.

Shaking his head from side to side, Boss chuckled lightly before motioning Nisha over to have a seat. He could see the attitude in her body language although she tried to mask it in the face. Since the run-in with Blessing a few weeks back, she had been tight and giving Boss the cold shoulder. Not giving two fucks, he went about his day like she never existed, but now his nonchalant ways was getting to her.

"I missed you baby. I missed that dick," Nisha flirted, seductively making her way past the chair and around the desk to his side.

"Man, I ain't on that with you no mo'," Boss replied, swatting her hand away.

"Damn, it's like that? Since when?" she snapped, taking a step back and placing her hands on her hips.

"Is there a problem with the store?" he asked, completely ignoring her question.

"So you can't answer me?" Nisha rolled her neck and inquired.

"You know I don't repeat myself," Boss stood to his feet and barked, towering over Nisha's five-four frame.

"Whatever Boss, it's cool. The inventory just arrived, and I got Sharon tagging em," she replied before wiping the corner of her eye and walking away.

Grabbing his phone, noticing the time, Boss secured everything in his office and headed to the car. Shaking his head at Nisha who tossed empty boxes around, he let everyone know he was out and to hit his phone if they needed him. Still early in the day, he drove in the direction to Arianna's school, ensuring he be on time for report card pickup. Turning up the music, Boss nodded his head and rapped along to late rapper, Pop Smoke. Turning into the visitor's parking lot next to Ari's school with five minutes to spare, he wasted no time killing the engine and hopping out.

"Hey baby daddy," he heard Arica's voice say from behind, instantly killing his mood.

"Nice of you to join us. I thought you'd still be shaking yo ass on live," Boss focused forward and replied while Arica jogged to catch up.

"Whatever Boss. If Ari was able to forgive me about missing her birthday party, then you can too. You saw the way her face lit up when I gave her, her gift. She loved those Gucci shoes I got her."

"She already had dem bitches. She just ain't wanna hurt yo feelings." Boss chuckled, pulling open the school doors and walking through first.

Arica smacked her lips, however, she remained quiet. She was clueless when it came to their daughter and although it didn't seem to affect Ari now, he knew that it would eventually. She knew what her mother was doing online, just like she knew the definition of priorities. As crazy as it was and although Boss would never admit it aloud, he was glad she was on Blessing's dance team. It took her mind away from her absent mother.

Knock. Knock. Knock.

"This her classroom right here," Boss called out to Arica who continued strutting down the hall.

"Come in," Ms. Castons' voice called from the other side of the glass door.

Entering the bright classroom first, Arica followed close behind' the both of them making their way towards Melody who stood in the front of the class. Noticing her name written on the chalkboard, Boss's eyes made its way around the room, noticing the holiday decorations next. Finally making his way to the two chairs that sat in front of Melody's desk, he was damn near knocked over by an eager Arica.

"Hello, I'm Arica. Arianna's mom," she pushed through and stated while Melody extended her arm.

"Hello. I'm Ms. Caston. Nice to finally meet you."

"Yeah, I would have been around sooner, but I travel for a living," Arica flaunted, taking a seat and crossing her legs.

"What up Mel." Boss chuckled, looking away from his baby mother and up at Ari's teacher.

"What up Boss," Melody spoke back casually before the both of them took a seat.

"Well, I usually start by showing you all the grades and if you have any questions, let me know," Ms. Caston continued, pulling out a manila folder, handing them a copy to share.

"Ohhhh look bae. Our daughter got straight A's," Arica spoke, her reference to Boss causing both his and Melody's eyes to pop.

"In addition to her grades, Ari has the second highest GPA out of all the eighth graders. With testing being around the corner, she has a good chance graduating valedictorian."

"I'm so happy to hear that. I told Ari, that this year is very important and ..."

"When?" When you tell her that?" Boss looked over at Arica and questioned with a straight face, causing Melody to unintentionally giggle.

Arica darted her eyes at Ms. Caston first and then to Boss whose facial expression hadn't changed. He was seriously waiting on an answer from the mother of his child. This was the first conference she'd attended since Arianna was in the second grade. He knew she was only in attendance now because she knew Melody and Blessing's ties. The same way Ari bragged about Coach B to Boss, she was just as vocal around her mother. After going over a few important details regarding the remainder of eighth grade, Boss insured her that he'd be as active as possible while Arica acted like she was leader of the PTA.

"Well again, it was nice meeting you," Ms. Caston stood to her feet and stated, followed by Boss and Arica.

"Nice meeting you too, and you'll be seeing more of me. In and out the classroom," Arica sassed, her eyes cutting into Melody like daggers.

"That's fine. You just remember that I'm only Ms. Caston inside these doors. I'm a different bit—I'm different on the other side," Mel shot back, matching her stare.

Boss caught the shade amongst the women and was glad that it was time to leave. Arica was childish and tried to get under people's skin with hopes of intimidating them. Knowing how Blessing was built, it wasn't surprising to find out her best friend was the same way.

"Aight Mel, I'mma holler at you," Boss finally stepped in and stated, pushing Arica towards the door.

"Ok. Tell Blessing to call me later!" Melody shouted towards the door, her pettiness causing Boss to laugh.

30

Mel's eyes popped open at the sound of her alarm going off at noon, and though it was Saturday, she still pulled herself out of bed because she had things to do. Grabbing her phone to shut the annoying sound off, she noticed she had a Facebook message notification. Being that she rarely communicated on the app, she was anxious to know who was reaching out to her. Sitting straight up in her bed when she noticed it was Corey's little slut, Kim, on the other end of the message.

Kim: Tell that BITCH ASS NIGGA to stay over there and you can pick up his stuff. I'm not doing this back and forth shit with y'all!

Mel read the message multiple times before responding. She was tired of bitches trying her. Between Cresha and now Kim, she was for sure going to be beating some ass before the holidays.

Mel: Let me guess that nigga didn't come home last night, had you up worried sick, lol. I know that feeling oh so well, I used to be the same way when he stayed out all night playing house with you, Smh. Don't let that nigga stress you out girl.

She sent the message and was glad to see a green dot next to Kim's name, letting her know she was active online. The three dots popped up immediately, letting Mel know she had received and read her response.

Kim: Girl bye, I'll never take advice from a dumb bitch. And you're being funny, bet it wasn't funny when he left yo ass for me.

Mel: Left me? Lmao, girl fuck you. I ain't thinking about you or Corey! Good luck finding YOUR nigga, that's your problem now.

Mel was literally cracking up; she knew she had Kim hot with the daggers she was throwing her way. She had become blind to Corey's bullshit. Like she said, he was no longer her issue. Never being one to laugh at another woman's pain, she got a kick out of Corey and Kim's situation.

Kim: Let me find out you fucking with him.
Mel: LMAO, is that a threat Kimberly?
Kim: Play with me.
Mel: Play with this dick bitch, fuck off my phone.

Mel was done entertaining her clown ass; Kim hadn't been through shit with that nigga yet.

"Best frieeeennnnnnnddd!" Blessing sang as her voice echoed throughout Mel's condo.

She made a mental note to steal Blessing's spare set of keys to her place off her keyring. Deciding to teach her a lesson, Mel hurried and flipped over on her knees in a riding position. Pulling the covers up over her body she started moaning and rolling her hips as Blessing made her way through the house.

"Fuck me Black! Ouuuuuu, this dick so good!" Mel shouted just as Blessing opened her bedroom door.

"Oh my God! I am sooooooo sorry!" she quickly closed the door and ran out, when Mel heard the front door slam, she fell out laughing.

She felt so bad, but it was hilarious. She was bent over laughing to the point her stomach was hurting. Mel didn't bother calling Blessing to explain the joke, instead she showered and dressed down in a black lounge set she got off Pretty Little Things with a pair of black UGG boots. Finally grabbing her keys and purse, she headed down to Blessing's house. Unlike her friend, she never used her spare key unless it was an emergency.

"Blessing, you hear me knocking!" Mel yelled from the hallway.

"Hold on, I'm washing my eyes out with soap!"

"Girl, open this door!"

Blessing finally pulled the door open, Mel busted out laughing at the sight of her.

"G don't laugh, it ain't funny because y'all bogus as fuck!"

"I'm sorry best friend, it was just a joke, but I bet yo ass won't walk into my house unannounced no more."

"Sure the fuck won't, and you can have your keys!"

Mel was literally in tears listening to her best friend fuss. Blessing stood there with a straight face before throwing her hands on her hips.

"You play with me too much," Blessing rolled her eyes, snatching her Carmex off the coffee table and applying a coat.

"Come on man, so we can beat the old people to the electric carts at the grocery store," Mel said, looping her arm around Blessing's.

"You done messed my day up, fuck you and Thanksgiving shopping."

Once Blessing got over her fake anger, they actually made it to the store in a timely matter and was in and out. Loading the car with cases of pops and several bags, they got everything Blessing was responsible for at her family's dinner. Though this was a sad time of year for Mel, she enjoyed seeing people come together. Mel and her mother were always welcomed with open arms to join Blessing's family, but she thought it would be best if she skipped this year being that her and Corey had ended their relationship.

Pulling into a park on their parent's block, Mel turned the car off as Blessing called inside for help. When Corey came out along with Blessing's dad, Melody let out a sigh.

"Aht aht, fuck him," Blessing said, instantly picking up on Mel's energy.

"You right," she replied as they both got out and helped the men unload the bags from the car.

Though it was November, mother nature was being extra courteous with the weather that day. Blessing grabbed the last bag from the trunk and ran it up just as Corey was coming back down. Not wanting things to be awkward, Mel unlocked her doors and attempted to get in before Corey softly grabbed her arm. She looked down at his hand then back up at him because she wanted to know why he was touching her.

"What Corey?"

"I'm not on no bullshit Mel. I just want to holler at you."

"I'm listening," she replied, folding her arms across her chest.

For the first time in a long time, Corey was talking like he had some sense.

"Look, I know how hard this time of year is for you and I wanted you to know that I'm here. We we're friends before anything, let me at least be that for you."

Mel was touched by Corey's delivery, though things were over, she had to admit that he was there for her through everything. When her grandmother passed last year, he wouldn't leave her side. At one point, he was her strength.

"I appreciate that Corey. I'm going to the cemetery on her anniversary day, you can meet me there if you like."

"I wouldn't miss it for the world," he assured her just as a black car came up the block speeding but slamming on brakes right where they were standing.

Off instinct Corey, pushed Mel behind him as the driver side door flew open.

"You lying ass bitch!" Kim yelled, running up to where Corey and Mel were standing.

Corey grabbed her while Mel stood there laughing in her face; their roles had completely switched. She was trying her best to get to Melody, but Corey wasn't having it. Blessing along with everyone else in the house came running out due to Kim's yelling.

"Mel, you good?" Blessing asked, making her way down the stairs.

"I swear to God, Corey let me go! I'm about to beat this bitch!"

"What yo mouth Kim, like you don't see my daddy and auntie standing there," Blessing warned.

The fact that Mel was unbothered by the situation had Kim making an even bigger fool of herself. Melody refused to feed into her and Corey's shit.

"Let me the fuck go bitch!"

When those words left Kim's mouth, followed by her hulking up spitting in his face, Mel knew Corey was about to fuck her up. He paused and wiped his face with the bottom of his shirt before wrapping his hands around her neck. Both Blessing and Mr. Taylor ran over to get him off her.

"Corey let her go!" Vera yelled from the bottom of the stairs.

When Mel saw that he wasn't listening, she walked over and grabbed Corey's arm. She didn't want to see him go to jail behind that bum bitch.

"Corey, look at me, let her go."

It was like Mel's voice had snapped him out of a trance, he released her and let her body fall into Blessing's father's arms. Corey turned and walked in the house with his mother in tow as Mr. Taylor put Kim in her car, but not before she got her words across to Mel.

"I promise, I got you!"

Mel once again laughed in her face. "Girl please, don't get me, get yo nigga!"

❧ 31 ☙

"**G**ood morning. Can I have ten sausage biscuits, ten sausage McMuffins, twenty hash browns and a large coffee, eight and eight."

Blessing placed her order through the intercom and sat back while Boss drove forward and paid for it all. It was tradition before every competition, she got her Angels breakfast, and that day was no different. With Ari in the backseat listening to music through her Air Pods, you wouldn't believe this was her first competition. Practicing for weeks on out, Blessing was confident in her just like she was with the rest of her Angels. Finally convincing Boss to join them, made it even more special for Blessing. After getting their food, Blessing went over the checklist in her head a third time. She hated forgetting things and although it didn't happen often, it still made her nervous. Pulling in the lot and finding a park, Blessing was happy to see that everyone was present, including the team's bus. All her girls were lined up outside waiting patiently, running their mouths and gossiping with one and other. Jumping out, she went around to the trunk and pulled out the things she needed to take with her.

"Good morning Angels!" Blessing smiled, walking through the parking lot with Ari in tow.

"Good Morning Coach B!" they yelled back, and their excitement caused her to laugh.

"I love that energy ladies. Can we keep it up through the day and murder these other squads?" Blessing asked, handing Ty her belongings and unlocking the studio.

"Say less Coach B!" All twenty screamed as they made their way past her and through the doors.

"Y'all know the routine. Go use the bathroom, y'all can eat on the bus. Make sure y'all got everything... I'm talking bout, pads, tampons, Tylenol.... EVERYTHING!" she explained before going inside her office.

Snatching up her laptop along with some much-needed paperwork, Blessing headed right back out, running into her assistant, Ty.

"Everything packed, ready and on the bus. It's a few girls still in the bathroom."

"Okay, I'll wait on them and meet you out there."

Just as those words left Blessing's mouth, Leah and Heaven came running out of the back.

"Anybody else in there?" Blessing questioned, walking towards the restrooms to check for herself.

"Nope Coach B," one of them answered as she peeked her head inside anyway.

"Ok, come on y'all. They waiting on us," she told them, shutting off the lights and heading to Olive Harvey College.

On the bus with her Angels, Boss along with Black and Melody were meeting them at the school. With her MacBook on her lap, Blessing sat in the front seat going over paperwork while her girls rapped Cardi B's *Bodak Yellow* a cappella loudly. Catching herself rapping along here and there, she tried her best to remain focused on the hour ride. Pulling in front of the college, Blessing made sure that everybody's mess were cleaned and that they knew playtime was over.

"Okay listen up Angels," she stood in the aisle at the front of the bus and stated, immediately grasping their attention.

"Like I told y'all a few months back, this competition right here ain't shit but practice to us. We got our eyes on the prize, which is at the end of the year. However, I want y'all to show the fuck out. I heard that The Diamonds of Chicago, Royalty Team, Tigers of Maine and a few other lil dogs were performing today but none of that matters to us. And why is that?" Blessing calmly asked her girls.

"Cuz we the big dogs!" all of them yelled out in unison before jumping up and acting crazy.

Getting them together after a small turn up session, Blessing and her Angels exited the bus, all dressed the same and on one accord. Strutting through in their signature colors, purple and gold, they all stood aside and in line while she went ahead and got them checked in. After doing so inside, Blessing spotted Boss, Black, and Melody getting out their cars in the parking lot and headed their way.

"Ohhhh shit best friend. You make anything look good," Mel sang, referring to Coach B's jogging suit and Air Force Ones.

"Girl fuck you. What up Black. Heyyyy baby," Blessing said, finishing off with a hug from Boss.

"Damn, didn't y'all wake up together?"" Black turned around and asked with his face bunched up.

"I told you bae. I told youuuuuu, that's how they ass act," Melody looped arms with him and said, causing both Blessing and Boss to laugh.

Parting ways with the three of them, she made her way back to her team, and they made their way to the dressing room assigned to them. With help from a few moms, Blessing wasted no time breaking her squad down, sending half to hair and the other half to makeup. With Ty handling uniforms and costumes, everything was starting to come together. Thirty minutes until showtime, Blessing's Angels were going on fourth, giving them a little more extra time to prep.

"Okay! Okay! Okay! I know it's small in here, but I need y'all to figure it out and stretch. We got bout fifteen minutes, and I wanna go over it at least one time."

Doing as they were told, Blessing counted off while her squad put on a pleasing show. She had confidence in them and knew that all their hard work and dedication was going to pay off. She had a squad full of amazingly talented young black girls, and she couldn't ask for a better crew. After forming a circle and holding hands, Blessing prayed with her Angels before lining up and heading into the hallways.

"I want y'all to kill it. Leave it all on the floor. This hip-hop category ain't shit to y'all so go out there and do it to em'. I wanna see face, attitude, all that. Stay in the lines. Don't give the judges any reason to take off no points. They calling y'all name. Go! Angels, I love y'all."

"We love you too Coach B," the girls said in unison before walking onto the floor and doing exactly what she told them to do.

Once it was over and said and done, Blessing's Angel's was bringing home first place with a perfect score from the judges. Everything she asked of them, they did, making the long practices worth it. After the celebration on the floor, they retreated back to the dressing room where they quickly changed and began packing up. Pulling Melody from the stands to help out, they were able to move faster with the extra assistance. Grabbing the last of the things and putting them on the bus, Blessing had to do a double take when she walked back in and spotted Ari hugging her mother.

"She was here the whole time?" she turned to Melody and asked.

"I don't know. I ain't see her when we were watching. Maybe she came with Mr. and Mrs. Bryant."

"Bitch can come to a competition but not her birthday party. These hoes sum else but I'mma be quiet," Blessing slowly shook her head from side to side and replied just as Boss's parents approached.

"Congratulations beautiful. You do an amazing job with these girls," Sandy handed Blessing a bouquet of pink flowers and said, pulling her into a hug.

"Oh my God, thank you so much and thank y'all for coming."

"Ari wouldn't let us miss it." Mr. Bryant hugged Blessing and chuckled.

She loved the way their family supported one another and how they welcomed her with open arms. Blessing didn't have a close relationship with Kevin's family because they weren't relatable. The McCalls were snobbish, thought money ruled the world, and the furthest thing from down to earth. Blessing hated spending holidays or any time for that matter with her ex in-laws, however, the Bryants were the total opposite.

"Let me get a picture with Ari and Coach B," Sandy said, her voice snapping Blessing out of her trance.

"Oh and there go Boss right there. Get in this picture too son," she continued, motioning for Boss and Black who had entered the building with bloodshot low eyes.

Handing the trophies to Melody, Blessing fixed her hoodie before walking over to where they were standing. Ready for the photo-op, Blessing stopped when Arica stepped up and spoke.

"How about a picture with Ari and her parents instead," she rolled her neck and snapped, eyeing Blessing the entire time.

"You right, Momma. Do yo thang. I'm sure me and Ari got more pictures together anyway," Blessing stood to the side and stated while Boss put his arm around her shoulders.

Arica and Ari took a few pictures before Blessing and Boss stole the show. Seeing the shitty look on Arica's face made everything about that moment so much better. Everyone knew she was only there because Blessing was in attendance and although it was her idea to put Arianna on the team, she was definitely regretting it now.

"Okay y'all, the bus is ready to leave. Y'all can meet us back at the studio. I'm rewarding the girls with pizza and wings," Blessing said to everyone in the circle before being pulled away by Boss.

"What's up baby? You good? You high as fuck," Blessing giggled.

"I'm good. I just wanted to pull you aside and tell you how dope you are," he bit down on his bottom lip and replied, staring into her eyes.

"Awww thank you baby," she gushed.

"I forgot to grab flowers, but I did grab you this," he said, pulling out a black square box and handing it to her.

Smiling from ear to ear, Blessing eagerly opened it. Her mouth dropping at the sight of the diamond studded chain and the words on the medallion. Slowly pulling it out, she handed it to him as she pulled her hair off her neck while he placed it on.

"I love it Boss. Thank you," she squealed, placing a kiss on his lips like they were the only ones in the room.

"But is this like an official stamp or something?" she asked, her fingers sliding across the ice on her neck.

"It's been official, but anybody looking at you now will know that you *BOSS LADY*.....

❦ 32 ❧

"**G**ranny pleaseeeee, don't goooo!" Mel cried and talked in her sleep, squirming around the bed like she was trapped in a bad dream.

Today was the one-year death anniversary of her grandmother, and it was taking a toll on Mel. She never talked to Black or anyone else about the way she was feeling, instead, she tried to use him as a coping mechanism. Mel thought that if she stayed at his house and geared all of her thoughts and attention toward him, she wouldn't think about it, yet there she was dreaming out loud.

"Baby wake up," he quickly grabbed her and wrapped his arms around her.

Grasping for air, Mel's eyes popped open, and she couldn't stop the tears. She had never cried in front of Black, but she couldn't control her emotions. She sat in the middle of his bed and covered her face with her hands.

"Talk to me, what's wrong?" he asked, also sitting up.

"I'm sorry," she replied, wiping her puffy eyes.

Mel wasn't looking for sympathy, but she appreciated how concerned he was.

"Sorry for what bae? Tell me what's up."

Finally getting herself under control, she began to talk because she knew Black wasn't going to drop the issue, especially when he saw the tears.

"My grandmother died on this day last year. I have been waiting on her to come and visit me in a dream, and she finally came. It was like she was right there and then she left me again. A year later and it still hurts me to my soul to even think about her," she explained as he listened to every word.

"Death is a part of living baby, she's at peace."

"I know, it's just hard to go on without her, it's like a wound that never heals. I'll be ok though, I'm going to visit her in a lil bit," Mel said, flipping the Versace comforter back before heading to the adjoined bathroom.

She grabbed a change of clothes and started getting herself together. Once she was done handling her hygiene, she returned to the room just as Black got up and started to get himself dressed. Mel made the bed and once again got lost in her thoughts until her phone alerted her of a message.

Corey: Good morning beautiful.

Mel quickly read and closed the message until Black disappeared into the bathroom.

Mel: Good morning, I'll be at the cemetery in a little bit.

Corey: Ok, I'll grab flowers and meet you there.

She smiled at Corey's response before exiting out of the thread. He had been texting to check on her every day, leading up to that day. He was giving her the old Corey, the one she fell in love with, but going back wasn't an option, and she made that very clear.

Looking down at her phone as another message alert appeared, this time it showed Blessing's name.

Blessing: I love you.

Mel wasted no time returning the love as Black walked out of the bathroom, dripped in Gucci from head to toe.

"You look nice," Mel complimented her man as he brushed his hair before completing his look with a Gucci skull cap.

"You like my drip, huh?" Black joked, walking over to his closet, pulling out two large Gucci shopping bags and handing them both to Mel.

"Early Christmas gift?" she asked as her face lit up.

"Christmas? Nah this what we wearing to my people house tomorrow." Mel was shocked, she had only been around his family outside of Boss, at school or dance events with Arianna.

She wasted no time pulling the items from the bags. A smiled spread across her face as she removed a Gucci sweater dress, the signature double G waist belt and a purse to match. Mel knew for a fact that a woman had to have put the pieces together. She jumped up and ran over to him wrapping her arms around his neck, placing kisses all over his face.

"Thanks babyyyy! I'll come to dinner with your family if you would agree to dinner with me and my mom tonight," she countered

"Fasho, you need me to bring anything?" he asked as Mel looked into his eyes and shook her head.

She was falling deeply for that man. Everything he said and done was on point when it came to her. Black had made a fool out of whoever created the saying "The grass ain't always greener on the other side." He was the perfect ratio of thug and gentleman; any female would love to be in her shoes.

"Just bring you."

"Aight."

They walked out into the cold November weather and kissed before hopping in separate cars. Mel followed Black out of the estate and heading straight to the cemetery. Passing all the stores because Corey was bringing the flowers, she hopped on the expressway and flowed with the traffic. Her emotions started getting the best of her the closer she got. Mel hadn't been to the cemetery since the day they put her grandmother in the ground. Death was something that had never sat well with her, especially when it hit home.

Her grandmother was buried right at the entrance of the graveyard which Mel was glad about because she had a slight fear of cemeteries. Pulling her phone from her purse, she dialed Corey's number only to get the voicemail. She thought nothing of it, Corey knew what that day meant to her, so she knew he would be there. The sight of a family burying their loved one right next to her grandmother brought a sudden sadness over Mel because she knew their pain well. Saying a silent prayer for the unknown family, she exited the car. The closer she got to her granny's tombstone; the tears started to flow. Mel knew the flowers that were already there had come from her mother who visited often unlike herself. Wiping her face, she grabbed her phone and shot Corey a message.

Mel: I'm here, I need the flowers.

Mel was numb to the November cold as she stood over her granny. She stood there crying and pouring her heart out, not sure if the dead could really hear, she kept on talking anyway.

"Granny, I am not ok without you. Coming here today was a big step for me, but it's too much. I'm not sure if you can hear me, but I need you to tell me everything is going to be ok. I'm trying to be that strong woman that you and Ma raised me to be, but I am really missing you lady."

Kneeling down to remove the leaves that were piling up around the headstone, Mel quickly jumped at the sound of a woman's voice.

"She hears every word you are saying."

Mel stood up and was face to face with the unknown older woman that had invaded her privacy. Never being one to talk to strangers, she couldn't ignore the sweet looking lady. Melody gave her a smile before burying her hands deep into her pockets.

"That's what I heard, but I wish it was true."

"It is sweetie, I lost my mother many years ago, and I still talk to her. I just buried my daughter today and I'm ok, you'll be ok too," she replied, looking over at the freshly dug grave.

Mel's heart instantly went out to the woman, but she still wondered why she came over to her especially while she was there burying her child.

"I am so sorry for your loss."

"It's ok, to be absent with the body is to be present with the Lord. You'll be alright, and I will too."

The woman smiled and turned to walk away, but Mel still wanted to know her reason for coming over.

"Ma'am, what made you come over to me?"

The woman stopped and turned back to Mel before speaking. "Your spirit, you stay sweet," she replied before walking away.

When she spoke those words, Mel's mouth dropped. For as long as she could remember, her grandmother always told her to "stay sweet." Melody wanted to run after the woman because there was no way her choice of words was a coincidence. Her heart was full with her chest caving in and out heavily, and she knew it was time for her to go. She shouldn't have gone there, she wasn't ready. When she turned to go to her car, she walked right into Black holding a bouquet of flowers. How did he even know where to find her? Blessing had to have given him the exact location. Without saying a word, he allowed her to fall into his arms and cry. This was the cry that she needed, the kind that cleansed the soul.

"I can't do this; I shouldn't have come here!"

"You needed this baby, it's a part of the process."

Black hugged his girl tightly as she released her emotions. She loved the fact that she could be herself around him without holding anything back. Mel calmed herself down and finally got her feelings under control.

"I'm sorry bae, these flowers are beautiful. Thank you so much," Melody said before smelling the bouquet that he handed her.

"You don't have to thank me. She got you up there, and I got you down here."

At that moment, him being there, his words, just his effort to make sure she was ok made her realize he was all she needed and all she wanted. She was glad that Corey stood up because her man stepped right in and showed out.

"I love you Black."

"I love you too Melody."

❦ 33 ❦

"Corey, you reneged. You were cutting hearts from the jump!" Blessing screamed, springing to her feet and slamming down the cards.

"Man you a lie. I ain't cut shit. You stay trying to cheat," he looked up at her and replied with a straight face.

"Nah nigga, you the lie. It's the second book. I played the king of hearts and you cut my shit with…"

"Blessing stop cursing!" Walter yelled out from the kitchen just as she was about to prove her point.

"Turn that book over Corey, you'll see that you cut my king with a low spade," she continued, tapping the deck of cards with her long stiletto nail.

"I ain't turning over nun. If I said I ain't cut, then I ain't cut. Play man, you just hate losing."

"Nah Corey, you gotta show us that book, especially if she saying you cut," Tisha, their oldest cousin, added in from across the table.

"You just saying that cuz she yo partner..... Ma! Do I gotta show Blessing my books just because she accused a nigga of cheating!" he yelled out to the back of the house just as Vera made her way front and center.

"Yeah son, and if she wrong then y'all take three of their books."

"Thank you Aunt Vera. Now show me lil nigga," Blessing stuck out her tongue and teased just as her phone rang.

"Hold on baby," she answered Boss's facetime and stated before overturning Corey's cards, proving her point.

"Exactly. Dog ass nigga. Tisha collect our books, I'll be back," Blessing said to her three cousins before maneuvering through her father's crowded apartment.

It was Thanksgiving Day and no matter how hard Blessing tried to downplay the holidays; she enjoyed the time spent with her family. With both floors filled with Taylors and Whites, not only was her belly full, but she was up a hundred dollars in the game of Spades going on in the living room. The only thing missing was Melody and although Blessing understood where she was coming from, she still didn't like the fact that she allowed Corey to win again. With plans to link up with her later at the Bryant's house, she looked forward to spending the remainder of the night with her bestie.

"Hey baby!" Blessing sang after finally finding an empty room and shutting the door.

"What up. I'm down the street, you can come out," Boss replied, glancing down at the phone that rested in the cupholder.

"Okay. Here I come."

Ending the call, Blessing stopped off in the bathroom where she relieved herself and cleaned up a little. Checking her reflection in the mirror, she fixed her wig and applied a coat of lipstick before making an exit. Grabbing her car keys and purse out of her dad's room, Blessing finally joined the majority of her family back in the living room.

"Where you going?" Corey stood up and questioned, causing everyone eyes to dart in her direction.

"You in my business. Don't do that," Blessing pointed to him and stated before turning and saying her goodbyes to the rest of the family.

Heading down the stairs and out the front door, she noticed Melody's car parked in front of her mother's house. Making a mental note to shoot her a text message once she was out of the cold, Blessing rushed to the car all the while praying she didn't slip on a sheet of ice.

Getting inside the warm ride, her ass melted in the heated seats, instantly making her feel better.

"What up beautiful," Boss leaned over and spoke, placing a kiss on her awaiting lips.

"Hey baby. You look good." She smiled, admiring the all black Gucci sweater on him.

"Me? Mannnnn..... you the coldest muthafucker walking." Boss looked over at her and smirked before pulling away from the curb and into the flow of traffic.

Grabbing his hand, Blessing held it almost the entire ride to their estate. Noticing him taking a different route, her curiosity really got the best of her when he stopped in front of a brick duplex. Putting the car in park, she remained quiet while Boss hit the horn twice before pulling out his phone and placing a call.

"I'm outside," he said before ending the call.

"Where we at? Who house is this?" Blessing quizzed, looking over at Boss whose facial expression went from calm to annoyed in a matter of seconds.

Turning around in the passenger's seat, she followed his eyes, landing on an angry Arica who came storming out the front door.

"So this what we doing now Boss? We being disrespectful now and bringing bitches to my crib!" Arica yelled, as she made her way down the stairs and towards the car.

Blessing's eyes shot back and forth between Boss and his baby mother who was clearly out of her mind. Without saying a word to him, Blessing rolled down the window before addressing the mother of his child.

"You better watch that bitch word before I embarrass you in front of my nigga and yo daughter," she warned with promising eyes.

"Boss, you better control yo hoes cuz this ain't got shit to do with her," Arica cut her eyes at Blessing and stated.

"I told this bitch..." Blessing snapped, reaching for the door handle but Boss stopped her.

"Chill bae," he grabbed her arm and stated before getting out the car and addressing his child's mother.

Making sure to keep the window rolled down just in case things got out of control, Blessing sat in the front seat, still taken back by the fact Arica had just tried her. She had never in her life dealt with baby momma drama and didn't want to start now. Knowing the type of man Boss was, there was no doubt in Blessing's mind that he was going to handle the situation, however, it still didn't sit well with her. Pinning her ear closer to the window, she missed whatever it was that Boss said, but she did catch Arica's reply.

"I apologize for calling her out her name, but Boss, you brought her to my house. I'll never bring a nigga to where you lay your head." She began to weep.

"Mannnnn, you know what a happen if you brought a nigga to my crib," he chuckled lightly before continuing.

"But you can't move like I move. You bet not ever have a nigga around my daughter let alone bringing one to my house. Look, I don't give a fuck how many dicks you do when Arianna's not around but make this yo first and last time disrespecting my lady," Boss stepped in closer to her and stated, however Blessing was still able to hear.

"As a matter of fact, Arica," Boss said, turning to walk away but doubling back immediately.

"I never thanked you. If you weren't being sneaky and shit by placing Ari on the team behind my back, I would have never run into shorty," he said, pausing and looking over at the car while Blessing quickly looked away.

"After Arianna, I thought you was done blessing the kid, but I was wrong. Thanks baby momma and happy holidays." Boss smiled, winking his eye just as Arianna came flying down the stairs.

"Hey Daddy. Bye Ma. Oh my God, BLESSSINNNGGGG!" Ari screamed, causing her to smile from ear to ear.

"Hey my girl!" Blessing rolled down the window and replied, hitting the locks so she could toss her belongings in first.

Completely forgetting about Arica and their drama that fast, Arianna now had Blessing's full attention. She listened as she rambled on about school, dance, and whatever her favorite rapper NLE Chopper had going on. Still tuned in, Arianna continued her rant once her father returned to the car. Glad to see that his mood hadn't changed, Blessing grabbed his hand and gossiped with Arianna the entire ride to their estate.

"Ohhhh, Uncle Black and Melody here too!" Ari squealed, jumping out the car and running inside Boss's parents' house.

Unbuckling her seatbelt, Blessing prepared to do the same but once again was stopped by Boss when she reached for the door handle. Halting all movement, she turned around and smiled. The sight of him alone did that to her. It had only been two months, and he had already torn down the bricks she built around her heart. Was she too venerable? Did he catch her at a weak moment, and she was actually naïve? Lost in her own thoughts, she didn't hear Boss until he called her name a second time.

"My bad baby. What up?" she quickly snapped out of the trance and asked.

"You good? You feel ok?"

"I'm straight. I promise. What was you going to say?

"I was just gon apologize about what happened back at Arica's crib. I don't play that disrespect shit, and I guarantee you that it'll never happen again. Not with her or nobody else," Boss assured, staring into her eyes.

"It's cool. I ain't tripping on that shit," she replied, laughing it off because to her it really wasn't a big deal.

"As long as you know I don't play about the people I love, and Blessing, I love you."

34

"I can't believe I let you and Mel talk me into this shit," Black said to Boss as he rode shotgun in the passenger seat.

Melody and Boss had joined forces to plan Blessing a surprise birthday party, though he was all for birthdays, tagging along with them to look at venues wasn't part of the plan. Not wanting to hear Mel's mouth, he agreed to join them.

"It's gon be fun nigga, get in touch with your creative side."

"Fuck you, y'all better push this same energy out when my birthday come around," Black said, searching around the car for a lighter to flame up the blunt.

"You jealous bro?" Boss chuckled before asking.

"Shid, a lil bit," he joked, causing them to share a laugh as they finally pulled up to the address the GPS guided them to.

Seeing Mel's car already parked, they finished smoking before heading inside. If it looked anything like the outside, they were locking this venue in. Both Boss and Black walked in, looking around at the modern layout before they were greeted by Mel and the party planner that handled all of their events.

"Good afternoon my favorite family," Misty greeted both men followed by a handshake.

"Hey y'all. Boss, this is the one!" Mel said while clapping her hands in excitement and looking around.

Seeing Mel smile was everything to Black, even though it wasn't her event being planned she was just as happy for Blessing.

"If you say this the one, then it's the one. Misty use the American Express card on file, there is no budget. Mel will give you all of the party details and how she wants it set up," Boss assured her, still looking around.

"Wait, so I can do whatever I want to this place?" Mel asked Boss to confirm what she had just heard.

Both Boss and Black laughed as her eyes lit up like a kid on Christmas.

"Yeah Mel, it's all on you," Boss assured her before checking out the bar area.

They all walked around the spacious venue as Mel and Misty put a winter wonderland theme into play.

"Ok so Misty, I'm thinking all white, winter wonderland. I'm talking about ice sculptures, pretty blue lights, and angels, she loves angels!" Mel explained her vision as they walked.

Black knew he had his hands full with Mel, but he wouldn't have it any other way. She was the most loving and caring person he had met besides his mother, and the fact that she also took a liking to Mel was a plus. He was definitely locked in with her. Meeting her mother was a big step for Black. He had never met anyone's people, not even Cresha's.

"Alright guys, I'm excited to start the process of this party. I can assure you, Mel, that your vision will be brought to life as both Mr. Bryants can vouch for me," Misty assured Mel, holding her clipboard that she used to take notes close to her chest.

"Now that we have the easy part out the way. How are we going to get Blessing out of the house on Christmas to attend this party?" Mel turned to both Boss and Black and asked.

Both men stood there with a confused look on their faces.

"It's her birthday, why wouldn't she come out?" Black questioned.

"Um Blessing's mom passed away giving birth to her on Christmas day. As soon as she was old enough to understand, she pushed birthday celebrations and all things Christmas behind her. She always felt like she was the cause of her mother's death."

Hearing Mel tell Blessing's story tugged at Black's heart, he felt bad for her. At that moment, he realized how blessed he was to still have both of his parents.

"I'll handle that, she'll be here. We gone break that cycle this year and every year following," Boss assured them.

"I hope so, I haven't seen her smile on her birthday since we were kids."

After chopping it up with the Mel and the planner a little longer, Boss and Black were back in the car headed to their next meeting.

"I love Mel bro," Black said to his brother as he turned out into the flow of traffic.

"I know," Boss replied, never taking his eyes off the road.

"How you know? I ain't never said shit about love to you."

Boss chuckled at his little brother before responding. "For one, she's been inside of the estate, and two she's turning young Black into a man right in front of my eyes."

Black flashed a smile before running his hands over his face. His brother was right, Mel was changing him.

"Look at you blushing and shit," Boss joked, pulling up to the red light as they both laughed.

Looking over to his right out the passenger side window, he quickly turned his back and shielded his brother when he saw the barrel of a gun pointed at them.

"Boss drive!" Black yelled before shots rang out.

"What the fuck!"

Boss sped off as Black cursed himself for lacking; they had never been caught slipping like that.

"Ahhh shit bro, I'm hit!" Black said as he felt a burn in his right shoulder.

Boss checked his brother while still pushing the car to the limit.

"Aight, just hold on."

"Goddamn, this shit hurt," Black said as his once white Burberry sweater turned red; he was bleeding out bad.

Passing every single hospital he saw, Boss jumped on the phone and had the doctor on their payroll to get to the estate as soon as possible. The Bryants didn't believe in leaving paper trails, they had people of all calibers working around the clock for them. Pulling up to the gate of the estate, Boss announced himself and pulled straight up to their parents' house.

"Where you hit at? Can you walk?" Boss questioned, rushing around to the passenger side as both of their parents came running out.

"My shoulder, yeah I can walk. Where the fuck is Doc at!?" Black asked through pain as he climbed out the car with the help of Boss and their father.

"He at the gate now. Ma, grab some hot towels," Boss said, helping Black into the house out of the cold.

"Oh my God, what the hell happened!" Sandy yelled at the sight of all the blood covering her baby boy before rushing off to get the towels.

"Darrius, how did this happen?" Dino asked his oldest son as they laid Black on the floor.

"Somebody upped on us at the red light. I'm gone handle it," Boss said before stepping out the way as the doctor took over.

"Ahhh fuck!" Black yelled out in pain as the doctor began to work.

It felt like fire was inside of Black's shoulder. He had never felt such pain in his life. He was shocked that he was shot, but even more so in disbelief that someone had actually shot at them. Though the snow outside had the city pretty and white, he was ready to paint it red.

❧ 35 ❧

Boss sat inside his father's basement thinking about the shooting that had just taken place less than two hours ago. Although Black was good, he couldn't help but think about the other possible outcomes. What if it was more serious than a grazed shoulder or even worst, what if it was Ari or Blessing riding in the car with him. Lighting the blunt in his hand, Boss hit it hard twice, inhaling the Za and releasing a heavy cloud of smoke in the air. He listened to his father ramble on and on about the old days and how he would have handled things had it been him in the situation. Instead of being combative or disrespectful, he tuned in quietly all the while knowing he was going to handle things his way regardless of what his father had to say. Starting at the top, Boss filtered out those actually stupid enough to shoot at him. Coming up short on the list of dummies, he knew whoever was behind the trigger had to have personal beef with them. No one in the drug game had the balls to start a war with them, which pretty much left one category of people, family.

"Darrius, did you hear me son?" Dino asked as the doctor patched up Black's shoulder.

"Yeah, I heard you Pops," he lied, going inside his pocket and pulling out his ringing phone.

"What up Boss, this Detective Martin. I was able to get ahold of some surveillance footage from the strip mall across the street from where the shooting took place. I haven't turned it in to the captain. What you want me to do?"

"What's on it?" Boss asked.

"Nun much. Black Regal with no plates. Most likely stolen," Detective Martin confirmed.

"Aight, no paperwork. I'll make it go away. I'll have someone meet you at the spot for yo bread. Good looking," Boss said before ending the call and picking up his main line.

"What up baby?" he answered for Blessing just as his mother joined them in the basement with bottles of water.

"Hey, I was just calling to see if you were okay. I just woke up from a nap and let's just say that the dream I had was more like a nightmare, so I just needed to hear your voice and make sure you were good."

"I'm straight baby. At my folks crib talking to Pops and Black about some shit. You good?" he asked, lowkey taken back by the reason for her call.

"I am now that I know it was a dream," she said before continuing. "But I'm cooking tonight and wanted to know if you and Ari wanted to come over."

"Yeah baby, I'll be through later. Take her home with you after practice, and I'll meet y'all there," Boss explained before telling her that he'd call her back when he left there.

He knew better than to tell Blessing about the shooting and for that, he had several reasons. One of the things he loved about her was the fact that she didn't pry into his business or street dealings. Never not once asking what he did for a living, Blessing still moved like she knew all the ins and outs. Boss truly believed the less she knew, the better off she'd be just in case the wrong people came around asking questions.

"I see you and Blessing getting serious," Sandy handed him a bottle of water and stated before taking a seat next to him.

"Yeah, she cool," Boss replied, untwisting the top and downing it with one gulp.

"Cool, huh? Son you ain't fooling me. I know you love that girl; your father was the same way with me."

"What you mean, the same way with you?" he looked over at his mother and quizzed.

"I came into Dino's life and the nigga ain't know what hit him." She giggled, crossing her legs and looking off into empty space.

"I'mma just put it like this, Blessing is a blessing, son. Not too many young women are like her nowadays. She doesn't give a fuck about your money, the family legacy, none of that shit and what I like most about her is that she loves Ari more than she loves you and women like that don't come a dime a dozen."

Dino's words may have gone in one ear and out the other, but Sandy's words would forever be engraved in his mind. His mother was right about everything she said about Blessing but hearing her say it put a stamp on it. Boss couldn't believe his mind was so gone over a female in such a short time. Outside of Arica, he hadn't been in love, however, he was loving the feeling he was getting from Blessing.

"Now, give me some more grandbabies before I get too old to spoil them," Sandy finished, placing a kiss on his forehead and standing to her feet.

"My oldest baby in love and my youngest one getting shot at. Lord, Jesus fix it." She made her way back up the stairs, sending everyone including the doctor into laughter.

Standing to his feet, Boss placed both phones in his pocket and stretched. Looking at the Rolex on his arm, he noticed he had an hour to make it to his next meeting. Saying his goodbyes to his brother and father, Boss ran upstairs and grabbed the keys to his mother's Jeep. Knowing more than likely traffic would be backed up, he didn't wanna waste any time and chance missing his appointment. Hitting the E-way and merging into the express lanes, Boss did seventy miles per hour towards downtown. Arriving at McCall's Realty Agency with fifteen minutes to spare, Boss parked the truck and jumped out. Heading to the elevators, he took it to the fifth floor where he followed the arrows leading him to a set of glass doors. Pulling on them both, Boss was greeted by a white middle-aged woman sitting behind a receptionist desk.

"Welcome to McCall's Realty Agency, where we turn any home into your dream home. My name is Lisa, how can I help you?"

"Yeah, I got an appointment to see a Mr. Kevin McCall."

"Great! I'll like to let you know that Kevin has won realtor of the year for the past three years and in addition to that, he is the youngest realtor tycoon in the Midwest. Great choice. I'll let Mr. McCall know that his four o'clock is here." Lisa smiled, displaying a set of stained yellow and white teeth.

Acknowledging her with a head nod, Boss took a step back while she placed the call. Looking at the awards on the wall had him really considering the company for a new business venture he had in mind, but he had to handle a personal issue first.

"Mr. Bryant, Kevin will be out any second," Boss heard Lisa say just as an office door opened and out walked a tall, skinny nigga in khakis.

"Hey, I'm Kevin McCall. Follow me this way," he spoke, extending his arm for a handshake.

"Let me rap to you in yo office real quick," Boss looked down at his hand and then up at his eyes and replied before walking away and leaving him hanging.

"I ummm, apologize if you were waiting long. Can I get you anything to drink? Soda or a bottle of water?" Kevin offered, closing the door shut and walking behind his desk.

"Nah, I won't be long at all. I don't believe in wasting people time, so I'll cut straight to the chase. Blessing Monica Taylor is not to be contacted again, not by phone, person, mail, or kite nigga. If I get word that you fucking with my lady, I'mma come in this bitch again but next time, you'll be leaving out in a body bag. Are we on the same page?" Boss hovered over him and asked as Kevin shook his head up and down slowly.

"Aight! Now, Merry Christmas nigga," Boss said before turning to leave. He was officially in the holiday spirit.

❧ 36 ❧

"Alright guys, if you want to exchange gifts now is the time," Mel said to her class ten minutes before she was dismissing them for their two-week winter break.

Melody watched as her students passed gifts around the classroom, and she couldn't help thinking of one day starting her own family. Holidays were meant for families, and Mel always dreamed of having a big one, being that she was an only child.

"Here Mel. I mean Ms. Caston," Arianna handed her a small gift bag.

Ari had gotten so used to seeing Mel outside of the classroom, she often forgot that she was "Ms. Caston" during school hours.

"What's this Ari?" she asked, reaching inside the bag.

Melody laid eyes on a diamond studded teacher's charm to add to the Pandora charm bracelet that Ari had given her a few months back at open house.

"It's beautiful, you know you give some of the best gifts Ari," Mel boasted, causing her student to smile.

"This is nothing wait until you see your other gifts under the big tree at Paw Paw and Grandma Sandy's house!"

"Oh really? I can't wait," Mel said before pulling Ari and a few more of students in for a hug before they made their way out the door, laughing and talking.

Mel had no idea where to start with buying gifts for the Bryants, they had everything, especially the little Bryant she was standing next to. Hopefully, she could at least get Blessing to do some shopping with her next weekend.

Once all of the kids were gone, she sat behind her desk going over some paperwork. With her head buried deep into her work, she hadn't noticed Corey standing in the doorway of her class until he slightly knocked to get her attention. He stood there holding a card and a bouquet of flowers. Blowing air from her nose, she quickly addressed him.

"Corey, why are you at my job and how did you get past security?"

"Mel, what was I supposed to do? You won't return any of my calls or text messages," he said, trying to hand her the flowers.

"Apparently, that means I don't want to be bothered. Besides, we have nothing to talk about and you a couple weeks late with the flowers," she replied, gathering her things to leave and start her mini vacation.

Mel had been avoiding and ignoring him since he stood her up at the cemetery. Standing up on her stilettos, she proceeded to put on her coat and exit the classroom, but Corey blocked the way.

"Mel, it's this easy for you to walk away from me, from us? I gave you time and space, but I want you back. I'm ready to start a family and put all this shit behind us."

Mel shook her head at his words as they went in one ear and out the other.

"Corey, we are over. I found someone who loves me and only me, no cheating, no lying, none of that weak ass shit, and you know what? I love that nigga back!"

Mel was fed up with Corey and his shit, she was done sparing his feelings when he hurt hers freely. They stood there, face to face with only inches between them. The mood was intense, but Mel stood on her words.

"So, you love him? Look me in my eyes and say it, Mel, " Corey said through clenched teeth, sounding like he was on the verge of tears.

"Yes, Corey. I love him!"

Mel stepped around him and walked out. She felt free from the hold Corey had on her for many years. He followed her outside, still talking as she made her way to her car. Blocking out all of the disrespectful shit Corey was yelling out, she kept walking and never looked back.

"Is everything ok, Ms. Caston?" the school security guard asked as Corey made a fool of himself.

"Everything is fine, enjoy your holidays," she replied with a smile before hopping in her car driving off.

She couldn't wait to get home and catch up on her shows for the week. Stopping by the store to grab a couple bottles of wine and few necessities, she was finally pulling into her parking garage. Grabbing her bags and climbing out, she raised an eyebrow when she noticed Black's car parked near the door next to a moving truck. She caught an instant attitude because she knew he had to be up at Cresha's place. Mel slammed her door closed with her hip just as Blessing was pulling into her park. Glad to see her friend because she could use her help with the bags, she waited for her get out.

"Nope, I'm not helping you," Blessing said, approaching her friend who was wearing a mug.

Not really in a playing mood, Mel pointed at Black's car as Blessing's eyes followed. She had talked to Black multiple times that day and he said nothing about coming that way. Mel's mind was pulling in all negative directions, she was ready spaz out. She hadn't seen Black in a few days because he said he hurt his shoulder playing basketball, yet he made time to come see that bitch.

"I'm just trying to figure what he doing here."

"Shid good question, let's go see," Blessing suggested before grabbing a couple bags from Mel and heading inside.

On the same page with Blessing, they made their way inside the building. The front door was propped open by a brown box and the lobby held the rest. Looking up at the sound of Black and Boss laughing, both Mel and Blessing stopped walking as their men stepped off the elevator. A thick female wearing a pair of lime green leggings with the sports bra to match also stepped off carrying a box.

"What's up bae. Hey Blessing," Black spoke like nothing was wrong with the scenario before placing a kiss on Mel's lips.

"Hey, what y'all doing here?" Mel asked, digging for her keys that she dropped down in her purse.

"Cresha moving out, I had to be here to make sure nothing was fucked up and sign off on some paperwork. How was your day?" he asked, instantly changing her mood.

"Aye, we about to run up to my house right quick," Blessing said, pulling Boss by the wrist as they made their way to the elevator.

"Ok nasty," Mel shot back, knowing exactly what they were going to do.

Turning her attention back to her man, she didn't even get a chance to answer his question before Cresha came pushing past Boss and Blessing with her homegirl in tow. She had to have went upstairs and told Cresha that Black was talking to another female.

"That's that bitch right there!" was all Mel had to hear before she quickly stepped out of her stilettos.

Done playing games with the girl, Mel grabbed Cresha before Black could while Blessing got on her friend's ass. Connecting every blow she threw, Mel was wiping the lobby floor with her ass.

"Hey...Hey... Hey!" Joseph yelled, trying to break up the two fights going on.

"Black get her off me!" Cresha yelled out for help as Mel stood over her delivering face shots.

Blessing had knocked the other girl completely out; she was literally asleep.

"Beat that bitch Mel!" Blessing yelled out while pulling her hair up into a ponytail.

Doing just as her friend said, she beat Cresha bloody before Boss and Black broke it up. Cresha was yelling and crying as Joseph pushed her in the opposite direction Black was pushing Mel.

"I told you to stop playing with me bitch!" Mel yelled over Black.

Fixing her clothes as Joseph and building security tried to clear the lobby out. Mel knew her and Blessing would probably be homeless after breaking the lease agreement, but it was all worth it.

"I'm sorry, but I have to report this incident for it goes against our policy," Joseph warned both Mel and Blessing, confirming what she already knew.

"Joseph, how much you make working here every two weeks?" Black asked, awaiting an answer as Joseph placed his hands behind his back, causing his protruding belly to poke out further.

"About fifteen hundred dollars," he said proudly.

"Here's three thousand, you didn't see shit and the video footage is nonexistent."

Black went into his pocket and pulled out a wad of hundred-dollar bills. Joseph's eyes grew wide as he accepted the cash payoff.

"I didn't see a damn thing."

"Good," Black replied, walking his lady to the elevator.

❧ 37 ❧

"So you know my mama talking about grandbabies and shit," Blessing heard Boss say from the bed while she brushed her teeth in the connected bathroom.

"Grandbabies? Was she high, drunk, or off a pill?" she joined in the bedroom and asked with a straight face.

"Man, what the fuck that's supposed to mean? Like having a few shorties by me would be a bad thing."

"Awwww, is the Big Bad Boss feelings hurt?" she walked over to him and asked, grabbing him by his beard and shaking his head from side to side.

"Man move." He chuckled, pushing her away and sitting up straight in the king size bed.

"Nah baby but all jokes aside, on top of only being twenty-four, I'll never allow a nigga to baby mamma me."

"Baby mamma you? The fuck that supposed to mean?" he asked with an offended look on his face.

"Exactly what it sounds like. I'll be a fool to *only* have kids by you. Fuck I look like, Arica?" She giggled, laughing at her own joke but stopping once she noticed the serious look on his face.

"Listen bae, I'll give you ten babies and two puppies once I get a ring. I love you but tell Mama Sandy we gon' hold off on grandbabies until a few carats sitting on this finger," Blessing explained while showing him her empty ring finger.

"Princess or emerald?" he looked at her and asked, his question slightly throwing her off.

"What you mean?"

"What type of diamond cut you want? Princess or emerald?" Boss asked again, this time with a smile that made her pussy moist.

Without saying another word, Blessing snatched the sheets off of him and removed his slightly erected dick from his briefs. Licking her lips while she sized up her new best friend, her mouth began to water, and that's when she knew it was time to put on a show. Jacking him off slowly, Blessing hands focused on the tip while her tongue blessed his shaft. After a few strokes, Boss was completely hard, and her lips was wrapped around his dick. Mastering the art of sucking Boss's dick like she did dance, Blessing had him cumming in no time. After swallowing Sandy's grandbabies, she straddled him, slowly sliding down on his manhood.

"Fuuucckkkk," she moaned as he gripped her hips while she reached forward to grab the headboard.

"Nah.... You wanna be wifey, right? No hands then," Boss looked up at her and said, grabbing her hands and placing them at her side.

Never being the one to turn down a challenge, Blessing did her thang, making him nut again but cumming behind him shortly after. Rolling off top and onto her side, Blessing felt Boss's huge arms wrap around her and like a baby with a warm bottle, she was out. Waking up an hour and half later, Blessing felt for her vibrating phone which had fallen onto the floor beside her. Not wanting to wake Boss, she tried her best to squirm from under him but being the light sleeper that he was, she was unsuccessful.

"My bad baby, I was trying to see who was calling me," she turned to him and stated before leaning over the bed and grabbing her phone.

With four missed calls from Ty and one from Melody, Blessing went to call her back first, but another call came in from Ty. Sliding the bar across and answering the phone, she placed the call on speaker before getting back comfortable in bed.

"Hey Ty, what's up?"

"Hey Coach B. I got out of class early and decided to swing by the studio early to practice before you and the girls arrived, but I can't get in."

"What you mean you can't get in? You left yo key or sum?"

"No, I can't use my key. There's a padlock on the door along with a notice stating that we are permanently closed."

"Permanently closed? What you mean permanently closed!" she jumped up and yelled.

"I don't know. I'll send you a picture, but you need to get down here quick."

Ending the call, both Blessing and Boss sprung to their feet and got dressed. He headed outside to warm up the car while she grabbed everything she needed and locked up. With her mind racing a hundred miles per hour, she wondered what Ty's call was about. Constantly checking her phone for a text message from him, nothing seemed to be coming through which only made her anxiety worst.

"Calm down baby. I'm sure everything good," she heard Boss say from the driver's side just as the car came to an abrupt stop.

"Come on man. A fucking accident." Blessing tossed both hands in the air and sighed, noticing the stalled cars in front of them.

"It's cool. Put yo seatbelt on, I got you," he hit the shoulder and assured her, doing his best to get them there in a timely matter.

Without traffic, she was thirty minutes away but judging from the pile up on the Dan Ryan, it was going to take her double that. Thankful that Boss was the one behind the wheel, they ended up making it there in a little under forty-five minutes. Jumping out before he could fully stop, Blessing damn near lost her mind when she saw Ty and a few of her Angels standing out there crying. Panic set over her and her worst nightmare had come true.

"What the fuck is this about?" she heard Boss's voice say from behind her, but she couldn't move, she was frozen.

"Coach B, what's going on? Why this say that the dance studio is closed?"

"Yeah Coach B, where we gon practice at now?" Steph questioned behind Kali.

As bad as she wanted to respond, she couldn't. It was like she was choking on her own tears. The freezing thirty-degree weather suddenly didn't bother her anymore, in fact, she was boiling hot. The cries and questions from her Angels faded out and all she could see was red. Stepping forward, Blessing snatched the green note off the door and read it aloud....

"McCall's Realty Agency," she shook her head and said before balling up the sheet of paper and pulling out her phone.

Dialing Kevin's number, Blessing waited impatiently for him to answer. Although she hadn't spoken to him since the day at the gym, she knew for a fact that his childish ass would pick up.

"You lil dick, petty bastard. I can't believe you'd do some shit like this to me," Blessing said calmly into the phone before walking over a few steps.

"I can't believe you. You thought I'll let you leave me and keep my shit?" Kevin barked.

"Yo shit? The studio is in my name and..."

"And my family owns the lot." He laughed uncontrollably, sending her emotions into overdrive.

Just as Blessing was about to spaz, Boss appeared out of nowhere and snatched the phone. With widen eyes, she looked on as he placed the call on speaker. Kevin continued to laugh but quickly stopped once he heard Boss clear his throat.

"I told you when I hollered at you before what the other outcome would be. You ain't did shit by taking this raggedy ass studio from her but watch how I take yo life. I'mma holler at you Mr. McCall," Boss promised before ending the call and handing Blessing back her phone.

❧ 38 ❧

"**P**leaseeeeeee friend, I'll buy you whatever you want," Mel pleaded, trying to convince Blessing to come out to the stores with her for last-minute gift shopping.

It was Christmas Eve, and Mel had yet to get everyone a gift. She was kicking herself in the ass for waiting until the last minute. Not wanting to tackle the task alone, she begged Blessing though she knew that was like beating a dead horse.

"No Mel, I don't want to."

Melody was about to give up until a light popped on in her head. She still had to get Blessing ready for her birthday party that was taking place the next night. She just hoped and prayed this whole birthday surprise didn't blow up in her face.

"Ok forget it. How about we just use today as a day of pampering. I'm talking about hair, nails, massages, you name it."

Blessing couldn't hide her smile if she wanted to; not only was Mel preparing for her birthday bash, but also for her dinner date with Black later on that night.

"Now you speaking my language, let's go!"

Mel wasted no time hitting the stylist that they had been going to for years up to set up a quick appointment. Once that was confirmed, they made their way out. Mel had been extra cautious of her surroundings since she fought Cresha. Ever since her and Black got rid of their dead weight, things between the couple had been smooth sailing.

Both girls made their way outside into the cold, crisp winter air. Though it was freezing, the sight of the fresh white snow covering the streets was a beautiful sight to see. Mel always enjoyed the feeling Christmas brought upon her.

After about two hours, Mel looped her arm around her friend's arm as they walked out the salon looking like new women. Mel opted on a brand new melted frontal wig that was laid to perfection, while Blessing went with a long sleek, natural looking ponytail. Glad that Blessing picked a style that would complement any type of dress she put on, Mel silently thanked God. Boss was great with keeping Mel in the loop of things. He hired a stylist to dress Blessing from head to toe, so that was a huge relief for Melody.

Everything was going as planned, Mel made sure to keep up with the time because she still had to cook dinner. Finally getting settled in the passenger seat, Blessing pulled the mirror down and admired her own beauty.

"I set us an appointment to get our makeup done in the morning. Hell, I figured we could at least be cute while we watch movies," Mel said, pulling out into the bumper to bumper traffic.

"That's cool," she replied dryly.

"What's wrong?"

"Nothing, I know you want to spend Christmas with Black friend, and I'm ok with that."

"I'm not leaving you on your birthday. We gone do what we always do," Mel replied, causing the smile that she loved to see spread across her best friend's face.

"You the shit."

"I know...I know," Melody joked before turning the radio up.

Mel was overly excited about Blessing's party, especially when Misty sent her a video of the finished job. It looked better than she envisioned in her head, and it was well worth the entire twenty-thousand dollars that Boss paid. She knew without a doubt Blessing was going to love it.

Finally making it back home with another task to cross off her to-do list, Mel felt accomplished. On top of that, Black was coming over to her house for dinner for the first time; the majority of their time was spent at Black's house. He had even added her name to the estate list, so she could come and go as she pleased.

"Ok, I'm about to go in the house to cook dinner. Black is on his way over, but I'll bring you a plate," Mel laid her plans out to Blessing while pulling into their parking garage.

"Actually, I'm gone go chill with Boss and Ari at the estate."

Mel appreciated Boss for the way he was taking care of her friend, seemed like he and Ari was all she had been missing in life.

"Y'all so cute."

"Them my babies," Blessing replied before they both got out the car.

"Hey Joseph," the girls spoke in unison as they walked toward the elevator.

Things around there building went right back to normal after their lobby incident though Joseph had jokes for days.

"Hey Tyson and Mayweather, my favorite girls."

They laughed at the comment the entire one-minute ride up to their floor before parting ways. Mel went inside and got straight down to business in the kitchen. This was her first time really cooking for her man, so she had to show out. Opting on something simple yet, tasteful, she went with T-bone steaks marinated in grilled onions, garlic scalloped potatoes, broccoli with melted cheese, honey glazed croissants, and a caramel cake straight out of aisle five at the grocery store. She had her wine and his Remy on chill while she set the table with fine china and candles.

Once she was done cooking and her kitchen was cleaned to perfection, she headed to the shower. Washing every inch of her body twice, she climbed out and dried off. She walked around her room naked until she chose the perfect black Fenty lace teddy with the thigh high fishnet stockings to match. Black had been going the extra mile to keep her happy and him showing up to the cemetery put the icing on the cake for Mel.

Snatching her ringing phone up, she licked her lips at the sight of her man when she answered his facetime call. All she saw was white teeth and diamonds as he sat in the dark car.

"Hey baby," Mel sang into the phone.

"What up bae. I'm sorry, but I ain't gon make it to dinner."

Mel's feelings were instantly crushed, she was really looking forward to tonight.

"Oh, okay. Um it's cool," she lied while looking down at the lingerie she was wearing, feeling stupid.

"I'm just playing baby. I'm on my way up," he flashed a smile as Mel balled her face up.

"You play so fucking much, I was gone dump you."

"Dump who? Yeah aight, you stuck with me."

"Whatever, hurry up."

Mel ended the call and ran to the kitchen and set the food up on the table before lighting the candles and telling Alexa to play a slow jam station. Dimming the lights just as she heard a knock on the door, she opened it without asking who it was.

"Well damn best friend, don't give it to him like that!" Blessing boasted, causing Mel to cover her body with her hand.

"Bitch I thought you was Black."

"Hmph, I see! Anyway, I was just coming to tell you I'm about to head out."

"Ok, text me and let me know you made it," Mel said just as Black appeared behind Blessing.

He spoke to Blessing never once taking his eyes off Mel.

"Y'all kids be safe," Blessing joked before walking away.

Grabbing Black by the hand, she guided him to his seat at the table before filling his glass halfway with Remy.

"You did all this for a nigga?" he asked, wasting no time grabbing his utensils.

"You know my style, I'll do anything to make you smile," she replied, causing them both to laugh as she quoted one of rapper 50 Cent's lyrics.

"Plagiarism, Ms. Caston, plagiarism."

They laughed and talked about everything from politics to what they were wearing to Blessing's party. With his birthday being the following weekend on New Year's Day to be exact, Mel knew she had a busy week ahead.

"I never asked you what you wanted for your birthday," Mel said, clearing the table.

"You."

Mel blushed at his response; it was no mystery that Black already had her.

"You got me, silly. Why you still sitting at the table?"

"Shid, I'm waiting on dessert."

Mel had completely forgotten about the cake sitting on the island. She quickly removed the plastic cover and proceeded to cut him a slice.

"You want a big piece or a small piece?" she asked, looking up at him awaiting an answer as he downed the glass of Remy.

"I don't want cake, feed me that pussy, Melody."

For some reason, Black calling her by her full name turned her on. Quickly placing the knife she was holding down, she licked the caramel off her fingers as she seductively walked toward him. Sitting back in his chair, he sized his woman up. Grabbing her by the waist, he pulled her between his legs and ran his hands over her body.

"Take this shit off," he demanded, pulling his shirt over his head before tossing it to the side.

Mel did exactly what she was told; she stood there with her freshly waxed pussy in his face. Grabbing her by the waist he sat her on the table and pushed her legs so far back her ankles were perfectly aligned with her ears.

"Look at this pretty ass pussy. You gone feed me, Mel?" he asked, pulling his chair up to the table like she was his meal.

She could barely respond as he stroked her swollen clit with his thumb. Diving in face first, Black put his tongue on her with two fingers, working her soaked opening. The slow cuts playing in the background mixed with sounds of Black licking and sucking on her pussy had Mel about to lose her mind.

"Fuck Black!" she moaned loudly.

Mel was on the verge of tears as he devoured her with every lick. Feeling her body tensing up, she tried to push Black's head back, but he locked on to her clit, sending her body into a trance. Grabbing his head, she grinded his mouth until she wet his face up with her juices. Mel was stuck for a few seconds until she got her second wind. Climbing down off the table, she ran her hand over his dick as it tried to escape the Polo jogging pants he was wearing. Mel bent over and grabbed her ankles in front of him.

"Damn you tryna bring Christmas in the right way, huh?" Black joked, placing his dick at her opening.

"Hell yeah! Ho...Ho...Ho."

❧ 39 ☙

"**H**appy birthday to you. Happy birthday to you. Happy birthday, Coach B. Happy birthday to you!"

"Arianna, you ain't gotta sing the song every time you walk past her in the house!" Boss opened the bathroom door and yelled out before slamming it back shut.

"You a hater. Keep singing baby, I'm enjoying it," Blessing egged Ari on as she danced and sang through their mansion.

Waking up Christmas morning and on her twenty-fifth birthday with Boss and Arianna was the best gift a girl could ask for. Since losing the dance studio last week, Blessing had been in a real funk. In fact, Christmas Eve was the first time she left the house since Kevin pulled that bitch move. With the support from her friends, family, and man, Blessing tried to uplift her spirits but still found herself having her moments. No matter how hard she tried to enjoy the day and live with no worries, her deceased mom always plagued her mind. If you didn't ask, she didn't tell, which was why most people—especially on social media—didn't even know she shared a born day with Christ. It had been a long twenty-five years, but for the first time ever, she had two people in her life that made the day worth celebrating.

"I'll get it. I bet it's just our guest arriving!" Ari yelled as she slid down the bannister on her way to the front door.

Peeking out the window from her spot in the living room, she could see that it was Melody and Black out there. Joining Ari at the door, Blessing was so happy to see her best friend and even more excited to see the Louie Vuitton bags in her hands. With a smile wider than the Joker's planted on her face, Blessing did a one-two step, gliding across the marbled floors in her socks.

"Happy birthday best friend! I love you!" Melody screamed, giving her a hug before handing over the shopping bags.

"Happy birthday sis," Black filed in behind her and said, pulling her into a quick embrace before sliding in and shutting the door.

"Wait. There's another car pulling in," Ari noted as Blessing opened the door and smiled.

"It's my Daddy and Aunt Vera," she beamed, happy that they made it safe and on time.

Standing onto the porch, Blessing ignored the chill breeze and few inches of snow on the ground as she eagerly waited for them to get out the car. It was the first time her family and his family were meeting and although she was nervous, she knew she didn't have anything to worry about. Aunt Vera was her second diary, therefore, she knew all there was to know about Boss. However, her father was a tough cookie to crack. Protective like most dads, he only wanted what was best for his daughter and after the experience with her ex-husband, Walt wasn't willing to take any more chances.

"Hey Daddy. Hey Auntie!" She hugged them both once they were out the car and up the stairs.

"Hey baby girl!"

"Whew, chile you said they was living nice but damn! Boss, where yo uncles at?" Vera asked, walking past them and straight in the house.

After introducing her family to Black and Arianna, Boss finally emerged from the back where he received the same love. Surprisingly, him and her dad hit it off fast after discovering their shared love for late great boxer, Joe Louis. The seven of them sat in the living room, talking about everything under the sun when the door-bell rang.

"That's Maw Maw and Paw Paw," Ari sprung to her feet and announced, running to the door and opening it up.

Completing the bunch, Blessing was even more happy to see her dad and aunt vibe with Mr. and Mrs. Bryant. It was like they'd known each other for years, especially after Mama Sandy promised to hook Aunt Vera up with one of her brothers-in-law. After spending the next thirty minutes getting to know each other, the chef was done, and brunch was complete. They feasted over Belgian waffles, bacon, eggs, sausage, hash browns and assorted fruits. As a flow of unlimited mimosas went around, the gang fed their faces before opening gifts under the tree. With the majority of them belonging to Arianna, everyone enjoyed seeing her excitement as she ripped away at the gold wrapping paper. Getting everything she wanted and plus more, Ari was the luckiest kid Blessing knew, and she deserved it all.

"Thank you Daddy, Blessing, Maw Maw, Paw Paw, Uncle Black, and Melody," Ari beamed while going around the room dishing out hugs.

With more gifts left under the tree, Arianna handed those out as everyone mocked her and excitedly opened their presents. Seeing her father and aunt react the way they did to their Christmas gifts made Blessing's day. With help from Boss, she was able to pay off the taxes on their building for the next twelve months as well as a paid vacation to Jamaica for them both. Opening up a small square box from Ari and Boss next, Blessing gave it a light shake before taking the top off. A *"B"* keychain with four gold keys on them caused her to look up at the two of them with a puzzled look on her face.

"What's this?" she jiggled them in the air and asked the father and daughter duo.

"Keys to *our* house. Merry Christmas Blessing. I LOVE YOU!" Ari walked over to where she was sitting and said as Blessing pulled her down on her lap, giving her the biggest hug possible.

As hard as she tried not to cry, she couldn't help but be a big baby. She thought the professional painting she got made of Arianna and Boss at the hospital the day Ari was born was something. They knocked her little gift out the waters by welcoming her into their home. Although Blessing more than likely wouldn't move in so soon, she still loved knowing that Boss trusted her with full access to him and his daughter. Finishing up the day with games and more delicious food, everyone slowly parted ways, leaving Boss and Blessing alone with each other. With no energy to straighten up the mess they made, the both of them took a quick nap before the birthday dinner Boss planned for the two of them that night. Thankful for Melody and the spa day before, Blessings' hair was laid, and she already had more than enough clothing to choose from. Dressing in an all-white Tom Ford dress that stopped right above the knee, Blessing paired it with a Jimmy Choo stiletto shoe. Matching her fly, Boss wore a black and white tailor-made Tom Ford suit as well, finishing off his drip with a fresh pair of white Air Force Ones. Having to rush out the door after a quickie that lasted too long, the couple finally made their way to the secret location in the downtown area. Knowing Boss had to pull some strings, being that it was Christmas and many people were off with love ones, she began to wonder exactly what it was he had up his sleeve. Parking in front of a skyscraper downtown, Blessing looked around while Boss walked around to her side, helping her out.

"Boss, what the fuck you got going on?" she placed her hand inside of his and questioned, stepping onto the curb.

"I told you, a dinner for us."

"You a *dinner for us* lie. Why my cousin Tisha hiding around the corner like I don't see her?" Blessing quizzed, pointing down the block as Tisha tried to disappear.

"Aight man.. DAMN! Can you go in here and act surprised?" Boss asked, pulling her aside before they entered the building.

"Oh baby, I am surprised. I love you so much. Thank you," Blessing kissed him on the lips and said before entering her Winter in Wonderland twenty-fifth birthday party.

It was like something out of a fairytale book, and she felt like she was standing in the middle of a snow globe. It was the prettiest thing she had ever seen and seeing all her family there made it all better. With her favorite DJ on the turntables, Melody and the party planner did an amazing job capturing all her favorites. From the catered food to all the treats on the sweet table; everything was about Blessing and she loved it. Kicking off her shoes and showing all her guest that she was the best dancer they knew, Coach B came out, allowing Blessing time to rest. Knowing her like the back of her hand, Melody had a pair of shorts in her purse ready. She knew better than anybody how Blessing was when it came to partying. From back flips to death drops, and between the Hennessey and Dusse, she knew for a fact that it would be a night to remember. After eating and mingling more with her guest, she was pulled out into the hallway by Boss.

"What's wrong? You okay?" she asked the moment he stood in front of her.

"I'm good baby. I love how you always ask me that but just know I'm always good as long as you are," he pulled her in by the waist and replied, placing a kiss on her lips.

"But ummm, I wanted to give you yo birthday gift and..."

"Boss, another gift? I don't need anything else, you've made this the best Christmas and birthday ever. The keys to your crib was enough and..."

"And that was for Christmas, we do birthdays even bigger. Come here," he said, grabbing her by the hand and leading her out the front door.

"Baby it's so cold. My gift out here?" she quizzed, while shivering looking up and down the street.

"You good, we won't be out here long," Boss replied, guiding her to the building next door.

Stopping at the front door, Blessing danced as she tried to stay warm while Boss pulled out a set of keys. Unlocking it, he grabbed her hand tighter, pulling her further into the darkness. Confused more than ever, Boss finally flipped on the lights as all her party guest screamed, "Surprise!"

"Happy birthday Coach B!" All her Angels, including Arianna, appeared from within the crowd and yelled as Ty walked towards her with a two-layer cake.

"Oh my God. What is this, what's going on?" Blessing looked around and asked before noticing the purple and gold graffiti written on the walls.

It read **BLESSING'S STUDIO...**

❧ 40 ☙

"You have a resumé?"

"Nope. I just heard y'all was hiring and walked in. I worked at Family Dollar for a couple years, so I got good experience."

Black sat behind his desk at Affiliated where he had spent the last couple of hours holding interviews to fill Nisha's position. Unable to separate business and Boss, she had walked out and quit in the middle of her shift last week. After asking a series of questions, he was outdone and over the hiring process.

"Thank you. We'll call you."

He ran his hands over his face as the last candidate of twenty stood to her feet. He had never in life seen so many ghetto bitches, especially the one standing in front of him. She chewed gum during the entire interview and had the nerve to flirt with him a few times. Glad to see Boss dart through the door, he dismissed the woman but not before getting a glimpse of the ass she was carrying on her back. She walked past Boss but not before they sized one another up.

"Damn," she said, finally making her way out the door.

"You hired her?" Boss asked, watching her walk out the store.

"Hell naw. You the reason we in this predicament now," Black joked, leaning back in his chair.

"I ain't on that, but it ain't my fault these hoes be turning crazy."

"Definitely your fault."

Boss closed the door before taking a seat across from his brother. Pulling his burner phone from his pocket, he slid it across the desk. Catching the spinning phone before it hit the floor, Black tuned into the recording playing on the screen. With his face frowned, he watched on as his blood cousin, Lil Kenny, bragged about shooting him. After replaying it multiple times, he had seen enough. Slamming his fist down on the desk, he jumped to his feet.

"I'm killing that nigga!" Black spat, throwing a black hoody over his head and snatching his keys up.

"Chill, this video circulating and that nigga hiding. We gone get him when he least expects it."

Everything Boss said went in one ear and out the other. Black had a tunnel vision and all he saw was red. Knowing exactly where to find his cousin, Black walked toward the door.

"That nigga can't hide, only place he can go is to Auntie Mary house. I'm on that."

"Pop gone have a fit, but fuck it, let's slide," Boss said, standing to his feet and following his brother out the door.

The two shared a blunt as they always did when they were together. The weed instantly put Black's mind into overdrive. Crazy how their own blood wanted them dead, and at that moment, that family shit meant nothing to him. Kenneth Bryant had signed his own death certificate.

Pulling over across the street from their aunt's bi-leveled townhouse, they sat there finishing their blunt. Both of their eyes zoomed in on the porch as Kenny helped his mother down the snowy stairs and removed the snow from her car. Really not giving a fuck about how his father or aunt was going to react to the murder that was about to take place, he secured his pistol. Waiting impatiently for his aunt to pull away from the house, Black had his eyes glued to his target as he made his way back inside. Once Aunt Mary was out of their view, both men exited the car and walked across the street.

Getting straight to the point of their visit, Black walked up the steps and rang the bell. Like a fool, Kenny opened the door.

"You forgot yo..." Kenny stopped talking mid-sentence when he locked eyes with his first cousins.

"Get yo bitch ass in the house!" Black grabbed him by his shirt, pushing his way inside as Boss followed closing the door behind him.

"What the fuck is y'all doing?" Kenny asked, playing his role.

"So, you around this bitch bragging about shooting at mufuckas, huh? Like it wasn't gone get back, " Black spat before slamming him to the floor, delivering a blow to his face.

"Man ain't nobody come to fight this nigga, watch out," Boss said as Black moved to the side, giving him a clear shot.

"Bitch!" Black kicked Kenny's limp body one last time for his own pleasure before walking out behind his brother.

Climbing back in the car, the duo pulled away from their aunt's house like it was a normal visit. Putting another blunt in the air, Black felt good. They weren't to be fucked with and had no problem making anyone out of an example.

"You wanna grab something to eat?" Black asked, inhaling a huge cloud of smoke before passing the blunt to his brother.

Boss hit the blunt before speaking. "Nah, since we killing niggas, I got one more stop," he said before turning the radio up.

❦ 41 ❦

Now tell me who want to fuck with us?
Ashes to ashes, dust to dust
I bang - and let your fuckin brains hang, snitches
Fuck all them able bitches with riches
who carry 22's, up in they hosiery
A black teller when my father bust and unloaded me
Think he just finished sniffin a ki, and dippin the D's
Don't hate me, hate Nicky Barnes for hittin my moms
Letting the condom pop, nigga I was born in the drop

BOSS AND BLACK PASSED THE BACKWOOD WHILE SHYNE'S HIT SONG
Bad Boy serenaded their ears. One of their all-time favorites, the
brothers not only enjoyed the song, they also lived by the lyrics.
Turning down the music slightly, Boss directed his little brother
towards Kevin's real estate office. Lighting another blunt and putting it
in rotation, he hit it twice before passing it to Black. Going inside the
glove department, Boss pulled out his gun and twisted the silencer on
before placing it under his hoodie.

"Park in the alley right there," Boss directed as Black followed his instructions.

"There's cameras walking into the building and by the elevator, so we gon take the stairs. Put yo hoodie on," he continued, stepping out of the car first.

"What about the cameras in buddy's office?" Black questioned, following behind his brother with his head low.

"Ain't none. I peeped everything out the first time I slid up here. I hit up the receptionist, Lisa the day after, slid her a few bucks and sent her on a vacation but before she left, she sent me the keycard passwords and Kevin's schedule. There's a temp up front and dude lame ass should be wrapping up a meeting right about now," Boss explained, looking down at his Rollie before crossing the street.

Going inside through a set of revolving doors, the brothers slid by unnoticed, heading to the stairwell where they took it to the fifth floor. Just like before, he followed the arrows towards McCall's Realty Agency. Instead of entering through the glass doors near the receptionist desk, Boss went the opposite direction, through a hallway near the breakroom. Roaming the halls like they belonged there, the Bryant men made it to Kevin's office unseen. Entering without knocking, Boss went first, opening the door slightly, allowing Black to slide through behind him.

"What? What the fuck is this?" Kevin stood from behind the desk and asked, his eyes traveling back and forth between the brothers.

"Nigga you know what the fuck this is," Boss removed the pistol from his hoodie and barked, aiming it at Blessing's ex-husband.

"You—You're not stupid enough to shoot me in front of my co-worker," Kevin stuttered.

"Aw this nigga? I ain't even notice him sitting there." Boss replied, looking down at a black man in a navy-blue suit.

"And nigga I'm stupid enough to kill anybody behind my family. I told you nicely to leave my bitch alone. Now you gotta die behind some pussy," he finished, pulling the trigger and putting a hole in Mr. McCall's head.

Turning to the gentleman sitting in the chair, Boss stared at him for a second before turning the gun in his direction.

"Anthony Crump. Accountant manager," Boss bent down and stated, reading the work ID around his neck.

"How you wanna do this? I got a few stacks for you. Move away, in fact, you called in sick today or I can give it to your family and help them bury you," he explained, ultimately leaving the decision up to him.

"Shid, I ain't like the nigga anyway. I'll be in Philly with my baby moms if you need to wire me my money. Y'all niggas have a nice day. Happy New Year," Anthony sang before gathering his things and running out the door.

Sharing a laugh, Boss and Black left out, closing the door and leaving the same way that they came. Jumping in the car, Batman and Robin headed back to the clothing store where they changed their clothes, getting rid of everything they previously had on. Taking a seat behind his desk, Boss pulled out a stash of weed from the drawer while Black sat across from him on his phone. Sitting in silence for five minutes or so, Boss lit the blunt just as his phone rang.

"Nigga, you got a contact photo of you and shortyyyyyy," Black teased, leaning over the table while Boss connected the call.

"Get yo goofass outta here. She put that shit on there," he replied before directing his attention to Blessing.

"Hey baby. I was just calling you to let you know I cancelled practice today. I still don't feel better, so I'mma stay in bed," she told him before promising to call him back after she took a nap.

Ending the call, Boss reached for the blunt but paused after noticing the look on Black's face.

"What?"

"She pregnant, ain't she?" Black said with a devilish smile.

"Nigga who?" Boss chuckled and asked.

"Beyoncé muthafucker..... Blessing. Who else?"

"Hell nah, she made it clear she ain't fucking with a nigga. Dat girl make me pull out now," Boss confessed as Black choked from the blunt.

"Pull out? I be nutting all in Mel," Black replied just as there was a knock on the door.

"Come in!" Boss called out, sending Arica storming in with the look of death on her face.

"The fuck you doing here?" Black stood up and asked, walking past her and towards the door.

"Mind yo business Black," Arica replied with threatening eyes as he skated past her.

"Mind yo business Black," he mocked before laughing loudly and closing the door behind himself.

"But nah for real, the fuck is you doing here?" Boss asked, trying to control his laughter.

"I got a bone to pick with you about my fucking daughter!" she snapped, placing her hands on her hips.

"Aight, have a seat. We can talk like adults," he suggested, motioning with his head for her to sit down.

"No, I'm good, and I won't be long. I am sick and tired of you and yo bitc—I mean your girl trying to replace me," Arica said, swinging her neck from side to side.

"Man what the fuck is you talking about now?"

"You know what I'm talking about. I found a pad in Ari's bookbag."

"Okay and?" Boss took a seat and asked.

"And....I am her mother. Why is it that I didn't know my daughter got her first period?"

"Oh, cuz Blessing was there, and she took care of it." Boss shrugged, pulling out and opening the MacBook Pro.

"And that's the problem. I am Ari's mother, and I should have been the first to know the second it happened."

"Mannnn, this Ari's second cycle, yo ass late, per usual," Boss advised, his words only making her angrier.

"You know what. Fuck you Boss. Fuck you and that bitch. You not Ari's only parent and if I have to, I'll teach the both of y'all a lesson," Arica threatened before turning on her heels and slamming the door shut.

❧ 42 ☙

"Lord, we thank you for this day. We thank you for this opportunity to dance in your name. Heavenly Father, I ask that you not only watch over my Angels but watch over every team on the floor. It's been a long year, but through your guidance and grace, we've made it to today's final competition. Lord, I ask that no hurt harm or danger come our way and that you give us the strength we need to bring home that trophy this evening. In Jesus name, I pray."

"Amen!" the entire room said along with Coach B before erupting in cheer and dance.

It was definitely a celebratory moment and although Blessing knew her Angels had it in the bag, she always remained humble. There were a little over twelve teams competing in today's competition, which included a stand battle and a creative dance routine in which Arianna had a solo. It was a spot she had to audition for, and everyone including the other Angels, agreed that she'd be best fit for their Beyoncé tribute. Working hard at the studio and home, Blessing knew firsthand how bad Ari wanted the slot.

"Okay, is everyone's hair and makeup done?" she spun around and asked, addressing all twenty Angels in the dressing room.

"Yes Coach B," they said in unison as Melody, Ty, and a few Angel moms assisted in the background with other tasks.

"Y'all look so damn beautiful," Blessing gushed, admiring the yellow crop top hoodies and blue ripped shorts they wore.

Duplicating Beyoncé's 2018 Coachella performance, the girls moved as one, just like a real HBCU marching band. Dressed identical to them, Coach B always did her best to remind the girls that she was more than the coach, but a part of the team as well and she was with them every step of the way. Stepping back and taking one final look at her girls, Blessing then glanced over at the clock on the wall. Pulling numbers earlier to determine the order of performers, Coach B as well as her Angels, were happy to be going on eighth.

"Ty, who up now?" Blessing asked while gathering all the props needed for their dance routine.

"Tigers of Bellwood, they number six and wrapping things up now," he reported.

"Okay Angels, let's line up. I need my captains in the front of the line, and Ari you know you walking on last, so stay behind Heaven."

After getting them in order and making sure everything was in place, Blessing and her Angels made their way into the hallway and near the entrance to the gymnasium. Smiling from ear to ear, Blessing thought of ways to show her girls how much she appreciated them, win or lose. They were her blessings and although she didn't have biological children herself, she still mothered twenty beautiful young black girls.

"Aight, so it looks like they are finishing up. Ty has two minutes to set up the floor with our props and whatnot. Y'all know it's the regular shit for us; give face, watch your space and leave it all on the floor. I love y'all."

"We love you too Coach B!" they all excitedly replied while hitting their own signature dance moves in the narrow hallway.

"Okay ladies and gentlemen, we have an amazing team and a crowd's favorite coming up next. Chicago, give it up for your cities very own, Blessing's Angels!" the announcer said over the microphone just as everyone in the stands went crazy."

"Go! Go! Go!"

"Let me make sure they got y'all music right. I'll be back," Coach B said to everyone, specifically Ty who escorted the girls onto the dance floor.

Looking on from near the judges table, Blessing observed the crowd first and then all her girls who were scattered across the floor. Giving them all a quick stare, Blessing thought she was losing her mind when she didn't see Arianna in her spot. Scanning through them all again just as fast, it was confirmed Arianna was not on the floor.

"What the fuck?" Coach B anxiously looked around and cursed, finally landing her eyes on Ty.

Practically running over to where he was standing on the sideline, Blessing's heart beat rapidly just as the music started. Darting her eyes back onto the floor at her girls, who were only a few seconds into the routine and already affected by Ari's absence. On top of her having a solo, she was still a key part in every move they made as a team on the floor. One girl out of place was bad enough but a missing body was tragic.

"Where's Ari?" Blessing grabbed Ty by the elbow and asked, pulling him off to the side.

"I just noticed that she wasn't out there. She was in line when we was walking out but..."

Rolling her eyes to the back of her head, Coach B pushed passed Ty, storming into the hallway in search of Arianna. Checking the bathrooms and rooms nearby, she came up short and that's when the frustration kicked in.

"Kelly, you seen Arianna? She's not on the floor with the rest of the girls," Blessing asked a parent who headed towards the concession stand.

"Nope, but the girls walking off the floor now," she replied.

Walking away without a response, she made her way back to the gymnasium just in time to see her girls exiting in tears. Blessing knew the reason behind the wet eyes and as hard as she tried to be strong for them, seeing them hurt killed her. Thinking of ways to console them on the way over, she came up empty, but she had a few questions.

"Anybody seen Arianna? Melody, Ari in the stands with the Bryants!" Blessing shout out, her eyes searching all theirs for answers.

"No. I'll check the dressing room though," Mel replied, running off down the hallway just as Boss, Black, and their parents appeared.

"Baby you good? Where Ari? I ain't see her out there," Boss stepped up and stated, noticing immediately something was wrong.

"I – I – I'm looking…"

"She wasn't in there, and I checked the bathrooms too," Mel came back and reported.

"Anybody seen Ari?" Blessing yelled aloud so everyone could hear her.

"Coach B, Ari was standing behind me in line when her mama came and snatched her out and…"

Running down the hallway at top speed, she didn't give Heaven time to finish her sentence. She knew exactly what happened to Ari and where she would be. Arica had been sending threats since Thanksgiving and although Boss told her not to worry, she should have. Pushing through the double doors, Blessing stopped on the steps, looking over the parking lot when she spotted her target.

"Blessing. Blessing. Blessing," everyone caught up to her and called out just as she jumped off the porch running.

Blessing could hear Boss and Melody calling out to her, but she ignored them, and all she could see was red. Not only did Arica pull Arianna out of competition, she also cost the rest of her Angels the win as well. The more Blessing caught up to Boss's baby mother, the more her anger grew and all she could see were the tears in her Angel's eyes. She had tried to be the bigger person and turn the other cheek, but Arica had officially fucked up and whatever penalties came behind whooping her ass, Blessing was ready for it.

"Arianna!" Coach B yelled out, stopping the two before they made it to the car.

"Coach B!" Ari cried out and screamed, snatching away from her mother and running into Blessing's arms.

"It's okay baby. Stop crying," Blessing held her head up by the chin and said, wiping away the tears with her free hand.

"I messed up the competition. I'm so sorry," Ari wept.

"Nah you ain't did shit. You good," she rubbed her back and assured, glancing up, noticing Arica approaching them.

"Go back in the building with your sisters. I gotta take care of some business." Blessing released her to Boss who was now standing on the side of them.

"I'm about to beat yo baby mamma ass," she looked over at him and stated while pulling her hair into a ponytail.

"Do yo shit bae," Boss replied, taking her phone and stepping to the side.

Walking towards Arica, Blessing smiled at the thought of what was coming next. She couldn't believe the lengths she went just to be a bitter bitch. In the beginning, she thought things would work, however, she was sadly mistaken. Arica could have done anything in the world to hurt Blessing, but she chose the one thing that could get her killed, her Angels.

"Bitch, what you gon do? What you gon do?" Arica taunted while getting in a fight stance.

Chuckling aloud and shaking her head from side to side, Blessing walked up calmly, landing the first punch, literally knocking the wind out of Arica. Grabbing her chest and throat, Blessing watched as she gasped for air, eventually tumbling onto the hood of a red Dodge Charger. Continuing a slow strut, Blessing stood in front of Arica and grabbed her by the hair, banging her head into the now dented hood.

"You had one job bitch. Take pictures and shake yo ass on Instagram but noooo, you wanna fuck with me!" Blessing barked, landing a shot to the face, making her nose leak instantly.

"Aight baby, that's enough," Blessing heard Boss say from behind before feeling a pair of arms around her waist.

"Aight. Aight. Aight. I'm good. Let me go." She yanked away but visions of her Angels plagued her mind again, sending her back into a rage.

"Nah fuck that!" Blessing broke away and screamed, charging Arica with a combination of blows.

Completely blacking out, not even Boss's strength could stop her from the damages she was set out to make. With blood on her knuckles and a few of Arica's teeth on the ground, nothing or no one mattered. She had a point to prove. Melody, Black, Boss, Mr. and Mrs.

Bryant tried their best to get through to her, however, it was only Ari's cries that tamed her.

"Coach B, please stop. You gone kill my mommy."

"Wake up bae, we gotta go pick up our shit," Black said, causing Mel to slowly move under the covers.

After sitting around drinking and eating with Black's friends and family the previous night, Mel was exhausted. Finally opening her eyes and adjusting her sight to the sunlight beaming through the window, she stretched and flipped the covers back. She had a long day ahead of her with preparing for Black's birthday/New Year's Eve party taking place that night.

Black hired a designer to customize him and Mel's outfit for the night. Being that Misty turned the ballroom of the Palmer House hotel in the heart of downtown Chicago into an all-black setting, black attire was a requirement. They also rented the entire two top floors of the hotel so that their guests could enjoy the open bar and crash safely without having to drive.

"What time is it?" she asked in a tired, groggy voice.

"Almost three o'clock."

"Damn, that Hennessy took me under last night," Mel said, climbing out of the bed.

"Nah, that dick put you down," Black joked as she flipped him the middle finger.

"Whatever nigga."

"So that's cap?"

"You know what, I ain't gone stunt on you. I'm with you when you right," Mel joked before disappearing into the bathroom to handle her hygiene.

With Black looking down at his at watch, Mel knew she had to put a little pep in her step because they were definitely pressed for time.

"I'm coming bae," Mel said, sliding her foot into her shiny UGG boot.

"Ain't no rush baby, they on our time."

"Ok, I have to grab our shoes for the fitting, and the stuff that's going to the room is by the front door," Mel said, making sure she wasn't forgetting anything since they were going straight to the hotel after running errands.

Walking out the house hand-in-hand, they made their way through the flow of the city traffic. Finally making it to their destination after driving for almost an hour, Mel was starving; all she had been doing was eating lately. She silently prayed that she could fit into her outfit since the last fitting. They were greeted and escorted straight to the fitting room. Insisting that Black went first, Mel stood outside and waited to see her man's complete look for the night. When he stepped out in the black fitted suit, black button-down shirt and the Hermes belt to match, she was ready to ride his dick in the fitting room. Though she had to practically beg him to wear the shiny Christian Louboutin loafer that she copped him, they complimented the hell out of his look. The man was clean.

"Fuck em up then birthday boy!" Mel boasted walking over and dusting the invisible dirt off his shoulder.

"Birthday man; this grown man shit right here baby," he replied, adjusting his jacket in the mirror.

"Talk yo shit then, fine ass."

It was now Mel's turn to go into the fitting room. Walking in on faith, she fit into her outfit with the help of one of the employees. Like she thought, it was slightly tighter than her last fitting because it was now hugging her curves like a glove. She slipped her feet into the thigh high bedazzled Giuseppe six-inch stiletto boots before admiring herself in the mirror. Mel was red carpet ready in the black fitted blazer short set and the bedazzled bustier halter that matched her boots perfectly.

"Girl, you look amazing!" the female that had been helping her said from behind her.

She wasn't lying, Mel was serving all body, and she was ready to share her look with Black. Slightly sucking her stomach in before stepping out, Black licked his lips and sized her up as if he was undressing her with his eyes.

"I got the coldest bitch, no disrespect," he clarified, admiring his lady.

"Facts! You like it, huh?" she asked while turning around, giving him a back view.

"Like it? I love it, we gone fuck em up tonight," he replied, causing her to blush. He had that effect on her.

Once Black dropped the four-thousand dollars to cover their outfits, they were out the door and heading to the hotel. By the time they arrived, Blessing and Ari was already in the room reserved for the girls to get dressed while the guys occupied another. Though Arianna couldn't attend the big party, she was content with the unlimited room service and pool.

"About time you got here. Bathroom, now," Blessing said with a two-pack box of pregnancy tests in her hand.

They were both having thoughts of possible pregnancies, so they agreed to take a test together. Being that Arianna was out of the room, they thought it was the perfect time. Blessing took one while Mel took the other. No sooner than they were done and waiting on the results, Arianna used her key to walk in the room. Grabbing a dry towel, Blessing tossed it over both tests and hurried out the bathroom with Mel in tow.

"Y'all, this hotel is lit!" Ari said, falling back on the bed as someone knocked lightly.

"Stop wandering off by yourself, little girl," Blessing fussed, walking toward the door.

Mel's mind was somewhere else; she was so anxious to see the results on those tests that it was killing her to stand still.

"I was with Maw Maw. She showed me where y'all party gone be, it's a DJ and everything!" Ari said as Boss stepped in carrying a garment back that Mel assumed contained Blessing's dress for the party.

"Thanks baby, we about to start getting dressed now," Blessing took the bag and kissed Boss.

"Daddy, so you and Blessing said I can order whatever I want, right?"

"Go crazy kid. We'll meet y'all in the lobby in a couple hours," Boss said as the two MUAs that the girls had hired to beat their faces for the night arrived.

It was time to get glammed up, but all Mel could think about was the test. As soon as Boss walked out the door, Blessing and Mel walked into the bathroom while Ari kept the ladies company as they set up.

"Bitch, what they say?" Mel anxiously asked as Blessing removed the towel and grabbed both tests.

Fidgeting with both sticks she whispered the results. "This one is negative, but this one is positive!"

"Which is which?" Mel asked, grabbing the tests to see for herself.

Being that they both panicked when Ari came in earlier, they had mixed the sticks up. There was one thing for sure and two things for certain, one of the two was with child. Mel sat the test down and hugged her best friend. They both stood there like some emotional fools, crying tears of joy because someone was becoming a mommy.

"So, it's safe to say neither one of our dumb asses can drink tonight," Blessing said, wiping her eyes.

"Yeah, it looks that way," Mel said before they exited the bathroom and prepared for their night.

Mel had plans of getting fucked up with her man, but those results changed all of that. Once they were both dressed, Ari became their personal photographer as they held a quick photoshoot. Both women looked stunning.

"Best friend, you wearing the hell out of that dress!" Mel complimented Blessing as she walked in front of her in a black sequence mini halter dress with a pair of black Rene Caovilla ankle wrap stilettos that gave off a diamond snake illusion around the leg.

"Thanks baby, but let's not get into the details of your look! Giving me all kinds of Mary J. Blige vibes," Blessing said, returning the love as they made their way toward the door.

"Y'all did snap!" Ari chimed in as she followed closely behind them.

"Thanks baby, remember, we're right downstairs and don't..."

"Go wandering off by myself," she finished Blessing's sentence, insuring her that she knew the rules.

They hugged Ari and headed to the lobby. They spotted the guys along with their entourage as the girls headed in their direction. Though there were plenty other females in the room, the duo walked in and demanded everyone's attention; they couldn't be fucked with.

"Look at my girls!" Sandy said, standing next to Boss and her husband in an ankle length Vera Wang gown.

"You look stunning as well!" Mel replied as they blended in with the family.

"All of you ladies look beautiful tonight," Dino chimed in, tilting the Keith and James fedora hat he was wearing.

"Thaaanks!" they said in unison.

"They aight," Boss joked as Blessing playfully punched him as he blocked it.

"Damn bro, I didn't take you for the hater type," Mel shot back while laughing.

Black was already lit and turned up, handing out bottles of Ace of Spade champagne to everyone in the lobby. Finally making his way over to his family, he complimented his lady and Blessing while opening a bottle.

"What y'all laughing at?" Black asked, motioning a nearby employee to bring glasses.

"Boss tried to clown us, talking bout we look aight," Mel explained the joke as Black flashed a smile.

"Nah, y'all clean up nice," Boss ultimately complimented the ladies.

"Thanks bro," Mel replied as Black passed out glasses.

Once everyone had a glass filled with champagne, every man stood with their significant other as Dino did the honors of making a toast.

"Tonight, we celebrate life and another year on the land of living. To my sons, though we may bump heads often, but I raised you both to have a voice and you've proven to me over and over that you're not afraid to use it, even if I disagree. Mason, tonight we celebrate you with all of these beautiful people. So, happy birthday to you son, and Happy New Year to you all!" he said, sending the lobby into an uproar as they made their way to the ballroom to officially start the party.

Black pulled Mel aside as the crowd headed inside. She looked at him as he stared at her.

"Thank you."

"For what?" she quizzed with a confused look on her face.

"For being you, Ms. Caston, one day Mrs. Bryant."

Mel smiled as her man placed a kiss on her lips; she couldn't wait to spend the rest of her life with Black. He grabbed her hand and walked inside to join the party; the rest of the evening was a blur. Mel and Blessing had the best sober night of their lives, but both of their men were lit and loud as they made their way up to their floor. Ending up in the same room, the couples were greeted by Arianna at the door.

"What are you still doing up?" Blessing asked, stepping out of her heels.

"I waited up for y'all, so tell me about yall night! I need all the details. Coach B, did you kill the dancefloor?" she asked, doing one of her TikTok dances.

Boss shook his head at his daughter; Ari's personality was unmatched.

"Arianna, go to bed," Boss demanded as she folded her arms across her chest and pouted.

"Aw come onnnnn," she whined, throwing her arms in the air.

"Now, Ari."

"Ok Daddy, I have to pee. Can a girl release her bladder?" she replied, disappearing into the bathroom as the adults laughed at her choice of words.

"What we gone do with her?" Blessing asked Boss as he pulled her onto his lap.

Mel looked around at the people she loved; everything in life was finally perfect. Everyone around her was happy, especially Blessing. Everything was everything, thanks to the Bryants. With Arianna being the magnet that brought them all together, she was perfect in their eyes—well almost.

"Ummm somebody left this on the counter. What does two pink lines mean?" she asked, emerging from the bathroom while looking down at the pregnancy test in front of her.

"Shit," Mel and Blessing said in unison, almost whispering as Boss and Black's eyes shot at them like daggers, causing both women to look away.

"So which one of y'all pregnant?" Boss questioned, sending the room into an awkward silence.

EPILOGUE
SIX MONTHS LATER

L ove overboard
My love's in need of help
Love overboard
I sure can't help myself
Love overboard
I don't know what to do
Love overboard
I'm so in love with you.

Mel walked into the kitchen where her mother along with Aunt Vera and Sandy sang along with the melodies of Gladys Knight that played loudly through the Bluetooth speaker. The three women had become thick as thieves over the months and being that Sandy had the biggest home, most of their gatherings were held there. With the Fourth of July being no different, all of their family and friends occupied the huge backyard.

"What you know about Gladys?" Aunt Vera asked Mel, dancing around the kitchen as she sang into the spoon she was holding.

"Nothing," Mel replied, grabbing the pan of ribs that Blessing's dad had sent her inside to get.

Walter and Dino had their aprons on and separate grills going as they agreed to a friendly grill off over Heinekens. Mel scanned the yard for Black as she started getting the tables ready for the food to come out. Things between the two were great. She had finally let go of her condo and moved in with Black and waking up to him every day was everything. Finally spotting him in the crowd along with Boss and some of their friends, she set out in search of Blessing who was supposed to be helping her set the tables.

"Y'all saw Blessing?" Mel asked, rejoining the ladies in the kitchen.

"She's in the theatre hiding from you," Ari walked past and whispered in Mel's ear as she headed in that direction.

Mel walked into the room Ari directed her to and flipped the light on before placing her hands on her hips.

"Really!?"

"What? Shit I'm tired."

"You ain't even did shit yet, gone leave me out there with all them old ass people," Mel fussed, finally taking a seat in one of the reclining chairs.

"My bad, I was coming back," Blessing laughed, shifting in her seat.

The two friends sat back and talked about how their lives had done a total one-eighty for the better.

"You know I thought you was gone be stupid for Corey's ass forever, I didn't see none of this growth coming," Blessing admitted, causing Mel's mouth to drop.

Mel knew at one point she was stupid, but what female hadn't been? Glad she was able to find true love, she hoped the same for Corey.

"Chile, don't remind me."

They both laughed at the old times as Blessing's phone started to ring.

"Speaking of the devil," she shared her screen with Mel as Corey facetimed her, and she slid the bar over to answer.

"Yeah, umma head out," Mel said, leaving Blessing alone to talk to her past.

"Hey big head!" Blessing answered the facetime call with a smile as Corey grinned from the other end.

"Hey whore. You good?" he asked, his choice of words causing her to giggle.

"I'm good. I miss you man. How the fuck you miss yo flight?"

"Mannnn, let me tell you. I hit up Magic City last night, came in drunk, got to arguing with Kim and that bitch cut my phone off, so I ain't hear the alarm," Corey explained.

"Boy, I don't know why you move yo ass to Atlanta with that hoe anyway. I told you," Blessing stood to her feet and stated as she prepared to leave the theater room.

"You ain't told me shit and besides, its yo fault anyway. Had you not drove Melody to Kim's crib last year and..."

"Corey, byeeeee! Cause I ain't trying to hear it!" Blessing yelled, over talking him and joining her family back in the backyard.

"Nah for real man, you bogus for that. It's yo fault I'm here miserable with this fat bitch. Then you hook her up with them Bryant niggas, knocking out all hope I had on getting my girl back," Corey rambled on and on just as her other line beeped.

"Call yo mama phone. I love you, bye," Blessing said to her favorite cousin before ending the call with him and clicking over.

"Hello," she answered, sliding the patio door back and motioning for Arianna to come to her.

"Hey Blessing, is Ari around? I been calling her phone and Boss's phone, neither of them answering," Arica asked.

"Hey girl, here she come now. They back there popping firecrackers so neither of them paying attention to their phones."

"Oh okay. Tell her I'm pulling up and to come out."

Ending the call with Boss's baby mother, Blessing delivered the news to Arianna before helping her gather her things and walking her out front. Since the ass whooping last winter, they had been on good terms, in fact, after realizing that Blessing was there to stay, Arica tried to build her own relationship with Blessing. Although Blessing probably would never forgive Arica for the stunt she pulled at the competition, she could at least be cordial for Ari's sake.

"See you later Blessing," Ari said, running past her and out the door but not before doubling back and giving her a hug,

"I love you baby. Have fun."

"I love y'all too," Ari beamed, rubbing Blessing's stomach and skipping down the stairs.

"You glowing, girl!" Arica rolled down the window and yelled as Blessing waved and smiled back.

Going back inside the house, she headed to the backyard but was stopped by Boss who was coming up the basement stairs. Grabbing her by the tail of her shirt, she playfully tried to run away but was scooped into his arms instead.

"Ari left without even saying bye," Boss said, placing a trail of kisses down her neck.

"Stooopppppp." She squirmed.

"She practically did me the same way, but I'm glad she's enjoying the time she's spending with her mother," Blessing continued, finally breaking free from him.

"Yeah me too, it's just fucked up that it took you to make her be a mother. Shiddd, I would've paid some hoes to whoop her a long time ago," Boss joined her at the kitchen counter and replied, causing her to laugh.

"Well I don't give a fuck what it took, I'm just glad she's more active. Every girl needs her mother," Blessing explained in a sadden tone just as Melody and Black joined them in the kitchen.

"What y'all talking about? Baby names? I told you to gon' head and name the lil nigga Black Jr."

"Boy stop playing with my son," Blessing said, picking up a toothpick and throwing it at him.

"But nah sis, all jokes aside. What happened? I thought you wasn't letting Boss baby mama you…Was those the words she used bro?" Black looked over at Boss and clarified.

"Yup. Straight told my ass…. *Fuck I look like, Arica?*" Boss answered in his best Blessing's impersonation.

"Wait. Wait. Wait. Y'all not finna clown my best friend or godson," Melody chimed in from the refrigerator.

"Man ain't nobody clowning her goofass. She talked all that shit and now look at her, wobbling around six months pregnant and shit," Boss looked over at her and stated before winking his eye.

Blessing felt attacked and her hormones had her wanting to whoop both Boss and Black's ass. Finding out she was pregnant had come to her as a shock more than anybody else. With abortion being out of the question, she was still able to stand on her word, by not being just his child's mother.

"Y'all can joke and laugh all y'all want but I came out the winner.... STILL..."

"Talk yo shit best friend!" Mel screamed across the island.

"Boss got his junior, but I got my ring. Give me four months, and it'll be Mrs. Bryant to you bitches," Blessing beamed, holding up her two-carat oval shaped diamond ring.

From baby mama drama, to kicking ass in the hallway, Blessing was still able to find her **A BOSS FOR THE HOLIDAYS**....

THE END

Happy Holidays!!!

DEDRA B'S CATALOG